Rosa Nouchette Carey

The Old, Old Story

Vol. II

Rosa Nouchette Carey

The Old, Old Story
Vol. II

ISBN/EAN: 9783337044770

Printed in Europe, USA, Canada, Australia, Japan

Cover: Foto ©Andreas Hilbeck / pixelio.de

More available books at **www.hansebooks.com**

The Old, Old Story.

A Novel.

BY

Rosa Nouchette Carey,

Author of
" Nellie's Memories,"
" Not Like Other Girls,"
" Sir Godfrey's Granddaughters,"
etc.

In Three Volumes.

Vol. II.

LONDON :

RICHARD BENTLEY & SON,

PUBLISHERS IN ORDINARY

TO HER MAJESTY THE QUEEN.

1894.

CONTENTS OF VOL. II.

THE OLD, OLD STORY.

CHAPTER I.

THE GATE HOUSE.

" Witch-elms that counterchange the floor
  Of this flat lawn with dusk and bright ;
  And thou, with all thy breadth and height
Of foliage, towering sycamore.

  . . . . .

" Till from the garden and the wild
  A fresh association blow,
  And year by year the landscape grow
Familiar to the stranger's child."

         In Memoriam.

IT was with somewhat mixed feelings that
Gloden set out to keep her appointment
with Miss Winter. She had given her first lesson
to Hilda Parry on the previous afternoon, and it
had been very successful. Mrs. Parry, with much
tact, had left her alone with her pupil ; and, as

Winifred was shut up in the distant schoolroom with the other children, Gloden had no cause for nervousness, and she and Hilda were soon on excellent terms with each other. In teaching, some of Gloden's finer qualities came into play. She was patient and painstaking by nature, and her own enthusiasm and love of music seemed to communicate itself almost magnetically to her pupil; and, as usual, when Gloden forgot herself and her dignity she was charming. When the lesson was over, Rosalie brought a message that her mother would be pleased to see Miss Carrick in the drawing-room, and she found a quarter of an hour's chat with Mrs. Parry quite refreshing. From that day she only looked on her visits to the Red House in the light of a pleasure. The good-hearted doctor and his wife soon got interested in her, and as time went on they mutually liked and respected one another. Dr. Parry's large-hearted benevolence and wide views easily triumphed over mere conventional obstacles, and, as his wife always shared his opinions, they soon agreed that it was their duty to be kind to Miss Carrick.

"She is a thorough gentlewoman, any one can see that," Mrs. Parry observed to her husband; "and then she is Miss Logan's friend, and Hilda has taken such a fancy to her. Really I wonder Miss Logan is not jealous of her. I do not think there can be any objection to our showing her a little attention."

"Certainly not," returned the doctor, briskly; but his eyes twinkled a little, for, as usual, his wife had assimilated his opinions, and was innocently and unconsciously reproducing them as her own. Was it not only the other day that he had re-marked that, in their dealings with Miss Carrick, it would be well to take her on her own merits, and not remember that Reuben Carrick's shop was in the background? "If only our Hilda were as ladylike, I fancy you and I would be satisfied, Cecilia," he had concluded, and now here was Cecilia endorsing his speech with annotations of her own.

It was this harmless habit that made certain malicious folk call her "the doctor's echo." "Mrs. Parry has no opinions of her own; she only reflects her husband's," they would say, which was somewhat of an exaggeration. But the doctor, who never laughed at her, only looked at her now with kindly amused eyes, and suggested that Miss Carrick should be asked to tea.

But Gloden's first visit to the Gate House was far more formidable. In the first place, she and

Miss Winter had never met, and Gloden, shy and reserved by nature, seldom got on well with strangers. Her retired life had seldom brought her into contact with fresh faces, and during her visits to town she had been far too much taken up with her musical studies to mix in society, even if she had had the opportunity of doing so.

To a proud and sensitive nature like Gloden's, the first steps towards achieving independence are thickly sown with thorns. It was not an easy thing for Miss Carrick of Eltringham Vicarage to enter any house except on terms of equality. She was quite willing to work and to do her best for Miss Winter, but, in her present prickly state of mind, it was more than likely that her first impression on Violet would be as unfavourable as possible. "You will find her very shy and distant at first," Winifred had said ; "but she feels herself in an uncomfortable position, poor girl!" And Violet's reply to this had been that she got on with most people, and that she did not expect that Miss Carrick would be an exception.

Gloden's nervousness was increasing as she turned off the Grantham road and entered the shady little lane that led to the Gate House. Already she could see the handsome bronze gates shimmering in the distance. Involuntarily her steps

slackened. The next minute she started with a
slight scream, as a large black retriever suddenly
cleared the low hedge beside her and alighted at
her feet ; but, as the animal only wagged his tail
and looked up in her face in a friendly way as
though to apologize for startling her, she soon
recovered herself. The next moment a young
lady came hurriedly out of the nut-copse. "I am
so sorry Captain frightened you!" she exclaimed
apologetically. "He is always startling people by
jumping over the hedge, but he means no harm.
Look! he wants you to take notice of him ; he is
quite ready to shake a paw with you ;" and, as
though understanding what his mistress said,
Captain held out a black curly paw.

"He is a beautiful creature," observed Gloden,
caressing him, whereupon he circled round her
with excited barks of pleasure.

"Be quiet, Captain, and behave like a gentleman," remonstrated his mistress. Then she looked
at Gloden in a friendly manner. "You are going
up to the Gate House, are you not? You are
Miss Carrick, I know"—with a glance at the violin-
case that Gloden was carrying. "Let me take
you through the copse—it is so shady and pleasant ;
and then we can go in by the garden door."

"I hope I am punctual," observed Gloden, in

rather a professional tone. "Miss Logan told me that I was to be here at three."

"Oh yes, thank you," returned Violet, carelessly. "Is this not a delicious little copse? quite a miniature wood. In the spring it is quite full of oxlips; you can see the pale yellow patches everywhere. Captain and I spend a good deal of our time in the wood. I have my books, and Captain has his own private amusements."

"It is very peaceful and pleasant," returned Gloden. "I do so love the country," she added, in a lower tone; but Violet heard her. She was walking a little in advance, but she turned round.

"And so do I. I should hate to live in a large town. I have always been used to the country. Why, I was born here. Fancy spending twenty-seven years of life in one place, Miss Carrick—that is, with the exception of brief visits abroad. No wonder I feel rooted."

Gloden looked at her without answering for a moment, and her glance was very grave and penetrating. Violet's careless ease and engaging manners had taken her by surprise. She was speaking to her as she would to any ordinary visitor, and with the utmost friendliness. How pretty she was! Gloden was moved to sudden admiration; Violet's warm hazel eyes and soft brown hair and small refined features always made an impression on strangers. In her grey tweed dress and deer-stalker's cap she looked young and piquant, and the worn look that Mr Lorimer had noticed was not so apparent. Violet's looks varied with her moods, but to those who had known her in her fresh young bloom there was a marked change in her.

"When one is rooted, it is very painful to be transplanted," observed Gloden, slowly.

And then it was Violet's turn to look at her curiously. She had heard a great deal about Miss Carrick from Winifred, and was quite disposed to pity and befriend her, though she kept her intentions to herself.

"Of course, you will only be on terms of civility with Miss Carrick," Miss Wentworth had observed during luncheon, laying marked sibilant stress on her words.

"On terms of civility? Oh, of course," she had returned; but it was impossible for Miss Wentworth to deduce anything from this vague answer.

When Gloden made this little speech about transplanting, the sadness of her voice told its own pathetic story.

"Oh, I forgot!" returned Violet, penitently. "I am so sorry I said that; of course, you have just gone through the uprooting process yourself. Miss Logan told me all about it." And then she added, with charming tact, " I once passed through Eltringham on my way to Stylehurst. I thought it such a pretty place."

" You have seen Eltringham? " and now Gloden's professional dignity was quite forgotten, and she was speaking in quite an animated manner. They were crossing the moat by means of a slight rustic bridge, and before them lay a wide lawn, with old shady trees and thick clumps of rhododendrons and other shrubs, with only a low fence dividing it from the green meadows. The afternoon sun was shining on the warm red walls and small-paned windows of the Gate House. " What a dear old place ! It looks like the Moated Grange," she continued, interrupting herself, " only the moat is dry."

" Oh, you are thinking of Tennyson," returned Violet, smiling. " I know what you mean.

> " ' About a stone-cast from the wall
>   A sluice with blacken'd waters slept,
> And o'er it many, round and small,
>   The cluster'd marish-mosses crept.'

The moat has always been dry in my time. Look at the ferns growing in it. In the earlier part of the summer it was quite full of wild flowers.

When I was a little girl I called it my moat garden."

" It is so peaceful here," murmured Gloden ; and, indeed, others beside Gloden fell in love with the quaint old Elizabethan house, with its picturesque setting of green lawn and meadows, the last dotted over by feeding cattle. "When I compared it to the Moated Grange, I meant in its happier times, before Mariana came to it."

"Its happier times! Do I remember them?" observed Violet, in a curious inward voice ; and then she repeated still softly—

" ' But when the moon was very low,
    And wild winds bound within their cell,
    The shadow of the poplar fell
Upon her bed, across her brow.'

There is the very poplar"—pointing to it, laughing, "and, by a curious coincidence, I actually see its shadow as I lie in bed. Now, as there is not the least hurry, let me take you round this path and show you our dahlias."

Violet was acting with her usual impulsiveness. Winifred's description of Miss Carrick had already prepossessed her in her favour, but she was hardly prepared for the extreme refinement and grace of carriage that distinguished Gloden from other girls. She was very fastidious in her likes and dislikes, but there was something about Miss Carrick that attracted her at once. "She is not one of the ordinary everyday people," she said to herself, as they walked down a side path leading to the kitchen garden.

"You said just now that you passed through Eltringham," observed Gloden, unable to refrain from the question. "Did you go into the village?"

"Oh yes," returned Violet; "but it is a little country town, is it not?"

"We have got into the habit of calling the cluster of cottages by the church green the village," explained Gloden.

"Ah! I understand now; but I think we saw everything. We had two hours to wait for the Stylehurst train, so we had luncheon at that funny old inn in the town; it was crowded with farmers that day. And then we looked over the church. There was a low grey house near it, with great yellow roses climbing over the porch, and my friend and I decided that it must be the vicarage."

"You are right," replied Gloden, in a low voice. "I have lived all my life in that house."

"It must be a sad change for you;" and Violet's voice was full of sympathy.

"How sad I will not say. I should not care to live again through the fortnight that I have just passed. One's home seems a part of one. When I first came to Grantham I seemed hardly sure of my own identity. I dare say you have never known that curious feeling, when one seems a stranger to one's self."

"It sounds rather like a paradox, but I think I grasp your meaning. Yes, Miss Logan told me all about it. She seemed to pity you excessively."

"Miss Logan is very nice, is she not?" The painful contraction of Gloden's throat, and the sudden rush of bitter-sweet memories, warned her to change the subject.

"Yes, very nice indeed," returned Violet; but she spoke without enthusiasm. She liked Winifred with a calm, equable liking; she admired her straightforwardness and thorough honesty, and envied her for her cheerful serenity, but there was little in common between them. Violet, who was critical and retrospective, demanded a great deal of her friends, and in consequence she had few intimates. Constance Wyndham was her only close friend, and it would not be too much to say that she loved her dearly; but even Constance at times had failed to satisfy her.

"A thoroughly happy woman cannot understand me," Violet would say to herself. "Constance is very dear, very large-minded and lovable, and she has plenty of imagination ; but she is so brimful of satisfied life, that my yearnings seem to her to border on discontent, though she would never tell me so."

As soon as Violet had opened a little gate that admitted them to the kitchen gate, a blaze of colour met their eyes. A grand phalanx of dahlias stood in stately rows, turning their broad solid faces towards them, and forming a mass of almost dazzling bloom.

Gloden, who was passionately fond of flowers, fairly gloated over the beautiful sight. The wonderfully varied shades of ruby and pink, orange and yellow, creamy white and pale delicious lilac, formed an exquisite foreground, while the delicate tints of the single dahlias made them look like floral ladies against the broad massiveness of the gay knights who flaunted their bravery beside them.

" I wonder what a world without flowers would be ? " murmured Gloden, half to herself. " Fancy the poor old earth without her children ! "

Violet did not immediately answer this speech. She revolved it slowly as they made their way back to the house. It pleased her ; in the dull prose of her daily life, it was like stumbling on a line of poetry that suited her. No, this was no ordinary girl.

"I must introduce you to my mother and Miss Wentworth before I take you up to my private den," she observed, when they had reached the side door. "I have a little growlery of my own on the first floor, which I call my castle. There are plenty of sitting-rooms down below, but they all communicate with each other in a tiresome way, so there is no chance of privacy."

Gloden fully endorsed this remark as she followed Violet through room after room, all quaintly and handsomely furnished, and full of pictures and choice antiquities gathered together by generations of Winters, until they reached a large inner drawing-room, shut in with heavy red silk curtains, where two ladies were sitting, one working, and the other reading aloud, their ordinary afternoon employment. Both of them bowed, and Mrs. Winter half rose from her seat as Violet introduced Miss Carrick; but Miss Wentworth drew her brows together and addressed Violet a little abruptly. As she often said, she never minced matters, but always came to the point at once.

"I thought your lesson was to be at three, Violet? It has just chimed the half-hour." She spoke in a tone of polite inquiry, rather tempered with reproof.

"Yes, I know," returned Violet; "but it is such

a lovely afternoon that Miss Carrick and I were tempted to linger out-of-doors. I suppose you have no objection, Cousin Tess?"—with a slight curl of her lip.

"It is no concern of mine," returned Miss Wentworth, calmly; "only your mother remarked just now that it was a pity to waste Miss Carrick's valuable time."

"I don't think we lost our time. Anyhow, we shall make up for it presently," was the curt answer. "Will you come with me now, Miss Carrick?"

Then Miss Wentworth coughed a little meaningly, and Mrs. Winter called her daughter back.

"I was thinking, Violet," she said languidly, "that Miss Carrick might play to us a little, if she would be so good. Theresa thought—that is"— as Miss Wentworth frowned—"we both thought that it would be as well to judge of her style of teaching. You know what I mean, Miss Carrick" —looking at her pleasantly; "it would be more satisfactory to all parties, and would give us a great deal of pleasure, for we heard you play most beautifully."

"If you wish it," returned Gloden, stiffly, "I can certainly have no objection."

But there was such repressed haughtiness in her manner that Violet took alarm.

"I thought I told you, mother, that there was no need of troubling Miss Carrick," she said impatiently. "I dare say she will play for us by-and-by, but I should prefer taking her to my room now. When we have finished, I will bring her back to have some tea. Come, Miss Carrick; I am determined not to waste your valuable time any longer;" and Violet's tone was decidedly sarcastic.

"You see, my dear Amy, how little Violet respects your wishes," observed Miss Wentworth, taking up her book again. "It was only at luncheon that you told her that you would like to hear Miss Carrick play; that you were anxious to see if Miss Logan's account of her wonderful execution were not a little exaggerated."

"I thought that was your speech, Theresa."

"Was it? I could have declared the words were yours; but we always think so alike, Amy. I remember I did tell Violet that we ought to be allowed to judge of Miss Carrick's style of playing; but, as Violet's sole aim in life seems to thwart every wish I am so unfortunate as to express, no wonder that she carried Miss Carrick off."

Miss Wentworth spoke with real bitterness; she looked warm and angry. She was not a bad-natured woman, but she had a quick temper, and Violet always aggravated her.

"Dear Theresa, I wish you would not talk so," observed Mrs. Winter, plaintively. "It is such a trial to me that you and Violet do not get on better together. I am sure I try to keep the peace, but it seems as though you had always a grievance against the poor child; and she was looking so pretty and bright just now, quite like her old self." For there were times when Mrs. Winter writhed a little under the yoke of her devoted friend, and natural maternal yearnings made her long for fuller intimacy with her daughter.

"I do not know what Violet's good looks have to do with it," returned Miss Wentworth, sharply; "but it is a pity that she shows such self-will to the best of mothers—for you are that, with all your faults, Amy."

Then Mrs. Winter, whose feelings were easily touched, began to cry, and, in spite of herself, to feel injured. It was not kind of Violet to take Miss Carrick off in that abrupt fashion.

"If you were only firmer, and put your foot down; but where Violet is concerned, you are as weak as water. If Violet were my daughter—

which Heaven forbid," she added piously to herself
—" do you think that I should allow her to master
me on every occasion ? Why did you not say,
' Violet, I must insist upon having my wishes
carried out. I particularly desire to hear Miss
Winter play ' ? "

" I do hate a contest of wills between Violet and
myself," sighed Mrs. Winter. " She is masterful,
as you say, and perhaps I am a little weak."

" Weak as water," interpolated her friend, with
more truth than politeness.

" There is no need for you to say such hard
things, Theresa. We are not all alike, and I
suppose I was born so."

" That is a mischievous fallacy, Amy. I have
often argued this with you before. We can correct
and overcome our faults of nature. There is a
sermon on that subject that I will read you next
Sunday ; it puts all this so lucidly before one.
Weakness can be strengthened. I used to tell you
so when Violet was a child, and you refused to
punish her for her wilfulness."

" I do so hate giving pain to any one, even for
their good," lamented Mrs. Winter. " I like
people to be comfortable, and I like to be comfortable myself. You may smile, Tessie, but you do
not know a mother's feelings."

This was Mrs. Winter's reserve arrow. She had more than once seen Theresa wince, as though it struck her. The most strong-minded woman has her weak point, some undefended part, where the enemy's javelin may enter with deadly thrust. And there had been a time in Theresa Wentworth's life when she had hoped to be a wife and mother like other women, and the disappointment had been felt keenly. Even now she did not love to be told that she could not enter into a mother's feelings; it seemed to hurt her pride and her heart, and it invested Amy with some sacred and mysterious dignity.

"Perhaps not. But I may as well go on with our reading; it will be using our time more profitably than in fruitless discussion."

And, without waiting for her friend's permission, she began to read in a clear, resonant tone; and poor Mrs. Winter, who never ventured to contradict her when she was in this lofty and virtuous mood, sighed wearily as she went on with her work, and wished with all her heart that she were more like Theresa, and that she were not such a poor weak creature.

CHAPTER II.

THE YOUNG VIOLIN-PLAYER.

"There is a pleasure that is born of pain."
OWEN MEREDITH.

AS soon as they were out of hearing, Gloden said gratefully, "Thank you so much for coming to my relief; but I am afraid I have been cowardly. I ought to have played to your mother just now."

"I saw how much you disliked the idea."

"Yes; but all the same I was wrong. I must try to conquer this tiresome shyness, and to take everything that comes in the day's work; but I have never been asked to play just in that way;" and her lip quivered.

"Mother meant well, but she expressed herself a little awkwardly. Miss Logan has given us such glowing accounts of your execution, that I hope you will let us hear you some day, when you are more accustomed to us ;" and Violet spoke so winningly that Gloden's wounded pride was insensibly healed.

"I will play for you whenever you wish it," was her answer. "I know I was wrong; but I felt, if I played just then, that I should not have done myself justice. My poor violin has to suffer for my moods. With a sympathetic audience, I can forget everything and lose myself in the music; but under those circumstances this would have been impossible."

"Never mind," returned Violet, gently; "you will know us better soon. Now, this is my den, sanctum, or whatever you like to call it."

Gloden looked round it with interested curiosity. It was rather an oddly shaped room. One of the corners had been cut off, and the only window, a deep, low bay, formed an angle of the room; a low padded seat occupied the entire recess. The view was restricted, but charming; it looked over the moat and rustic bridge to the nut copse and the lane.

The room was low, and a heavy beam ran across the window; but all available space had been utilized. Bookcases lined the lower part of the walls, and the upper part was wholly covered by choice engravings and photographs. An old oak bureau, a curiously carved table, and two or three easy-chairs composed the furniture.

"How delightfully quaint!" exclaimed Gloden; "that window recess is charming. I am afraid, in your place, I should spend most of my time there."

"I am very fond of my dear old gable-room," returned Violet.

And then they established themselves cosily in the recess, and for the next hour worked busily. Now and then Violet would have strayed off into desultory conversation, but Gloden refused to be seduced into idleness.

"We must not waste our time," she said firmly.

And, though Violet pretended to grumble, she respected her young teacher's conscientiousness. At the end of the hour she suddenly interrupted herself.

"There! I have had a splendid lesson, and am entirely convinced that I know nothing at all, which is a wholesome frame of mind for a beginner."

"I cannot endorse that," returned Gloden, seriously; "but you have been badly taught, and your style is faulty. You have a good deal to unlearn before you can make progress, but you have a good touch."

"You are trying to encourage me, but I am quite flattened out. You are a capital teacher, Miss Carrick; you seemed as though you enjoyed the lesson as much as I did." And Gloden did not deny this.

"I always liked the idea of giving violin-lessons," she replied. "Dear father and I used to talk about it. We planned, if anything should go wrong, that I should turn my talent to account. Teaching is no hardship to me."

"So I see. Now I propose that we go down and have some tea, and then we will read some Italian afterwards. We are a little erratic to-day, but it does not matter. I hope that Miss Logan gave you my message."

"I am not sure that she brought me any special message."

"Well, I will refresh your memory. I particularly requested that there should be no hard-and-fast rules; that the two hours' study should not be too rigidly enforced. I believe I need companionship and occupation, so, if you are not otherwise engaged, I hope you will sometimes extend your stay."

"Thank you; I see what you mean, and will willingly oblige you until the evenings get shorter and darker. If we are going downstairs, I think I will take my violin. My conscience is still uneasy, you see, and I want to get the better of my cowardice."

"That is plucky of you, and I will not combat so good a resolution. You shall leave it outside in the lobby, and then it will be handy if you want it. This is the quickest way to the red-room;" and she preceded Gloden down a narrow passage lighted from the staircase window, and opened the door.

Gloden followed her closely; and then a sudden wave of shyness assailed her. The room seemed full. A lady in a long grey cloak was sitting by Mrs. Winter, and a dark, slight man was talking to Miss Wentworth.

"Constance, my dear Constance!" exclaimed Violet, in a delighted tone, as she almost flew across the room; and the next moment a voice that sounded strangely familiar addressed Gloden. Mr. Lorimer was just coming out of the Japanese-room; he stopped short as he saw her.

"Miss Carrick, this is a surprise. I had no idea you knew the Gate House people. Let me find you a seat, and then I must speak to Miss Winter."

"Thank you; any seat will do. Please do not let me detain you." She spoke with the cold sedateness that always veiled extreme nervousness.

Mr. Lorimer glanced at her, then he went across the room and talked a little to Violet ; while Gloden sat holding her head high, and looking very dignified and unapproachable, but trembling inwardly in agonies of trepidation. What was she to do ? Miss Winter ought not to have exposed her to this ordeal. She was in a false position among all these people. Mrs. Winter would think her in the way. If it were not for the Italian lesson, she would slip away unobserved. She could easily do it ; she was close to the curtained recess. She would find her way back to the gable-room, and await Miss Winter's convenience ; she had no right to intrude on the family in this manner. At this point she half rose, but Mr. Lorimer was making his way back to her.

" Miss Winter has asked me to bring you some tea," he said pleasantly. " I wish you would not exclude yourself in that corner, as though you disliked the present company." Then, sitting down beside her, he continued in the same friendly voice, " Have you known the Winters long ? They are very old friends of mine."

" I have never seen them before "—and now Gloden's cheeks began to burn—" I am giving Miss Winter violin-lessons ; we had the first lesson this afternoon."

" Indeed "—in a tone of great interest—" and in the gable-room, I suppose. So you teach the fiddle, Miss Carrick ? You are quite in the fashion, every one writes a novel or plays the fiddle nowadays."

" I am afraid necessity has more to do with it than fashion."

"Oh, I dare say," returned Mr. Lorimer, carelessly ; but of course he knew what she meant. She had to earn her livelihood, poor girl, and very likely she did not take to it kindly. "I used to play the fiddle myself once, but my people seemed to have an objection. My sister was almost abject in her entreaties, she said it was the most painful hobby that I had ever indulged in, and so I gave it up. One does not like to be a nuisance."

" If you had persevered you would have ceased to be a nuisance," returned Gloden, quietly.

" By Jove ! should I ? I never thought of that. But I am an easy-going fellow, and like to please people, so I just chucked it up. I don't mind telling you," he continued, in a confiding way, " that there was no chance of my doing much, and when Hamerton—that's Hamerton over there— called it beastly caterwauling, I thought I had had almost enough of it."

Gloden smiled ; she could not help it. The

frank boyishness of Mr. Lorimer's manner seemed
to drive away her nervousness and to put her more
at her ease. She began to like him, and to feel
some pleasure in his society ; and then a sudden
recollection put her on her guard again.

That quick, wavering smile gave Reginald a
feeling of triumph. The very difficulty of making
way with her and of disarming her cold reserve
gave a piquancy to his intercourse with her. He
had sought her out in her distant corner with the
good-natured intention of making her more
comfortable, but he became interested and
remained.

He was quite aware that she snubbed him in a
ladylike way, and kept him at a distance, and the
experience was a new one ; he never remembered
having been snubbed before. The discipline was
wholesome ; besides, it showed a great mind to forgive injuries. So he began talking to her about
Harvey, until he saw his sister looking at him, and
then a sudden idea came into his head. He excused himself to Gloden, and waited for an opportunity of drawing his sister aside.

"Con, I want to speak to you a moment. The
young lady over there to whom I was talking just
now is Miss Carrick."

"Yes, I know. Miss Wentworth has just told

me so;" and Constance's voice was a little in-different. "She looks rather out of it, Reggie."

"No wonder, when no one takes any notice of her. That is why I talked to her myself."

"There was no need for you to absent yourself so long. Miss Wentworth was a little sarcastic about it. She said you were such a stranger that they did not like losing a minute of your company; and, you know, Reg——"

"What do I know?"—quite ignoring her meaning.

"Well, it is not quite easy to explain; and you always take me up so. You are so dreadfully democratic."

"Oh, I know now at what you are aiming. We will drop all that, if you please. I want you to talk to Miss Carrick, Constance, and befriend her a little. I think it would be only kind. There! Violet and Hamerton are with her now, but you can watch your opportunity."

Constance threw back her head and smiled amiably in her brother's face. She had not the slightest intention of walking across the room and talking to Miss Carrick; it was just one of Reg's ridiculous, lax ideas which Car had always so disliked. He would associate on terms of equality with any one. She had thought it a mistake of

his to single out Miss Carrick and to talk to her
so long. There were positively no limits to Reg's
good nature ; but she was determined not to be
drawn into it.

"Thank you, dear. I will see about it," she
said calmly. "But Mrs. Winter is looking at us ;
go and talk to her now ;" and Reginald was just
making his way to his hostess, when Violet's clear
voice arrested him.

"Mother dear, Miss Carrick will play for us
now, if you still wish it. Mr. Hamerton has been
asking her."

"I shall be delighted, Vi."

"A gentleman can often prevail when we poor
ladies meet with refusal," observed Miss Wentworth, so audibly that Gloden heard her and
coloured with annoyance.

"Miss Carrick brought down her violin on
purpose to play to mother," returned Violet, firing
up in a moment. "Neither of us knew any one
was here, so your speech goes for nothing, Cousin
Tess. Perhaps you would rather not play now,
Miss Carrick"—in a low voice.

"I don't think I need be so foolish as that,"
replied Gloden, very properly. "Miss Wentworth
is only punishing me for my backwardness. Next
time I will do as I am asked at once."

"Hear, hear!" exclaimed Mr. Hamerton, clapping his hands softly. "I applaud your good resolution. Where is the violin-case? May I fetch it?"

But Gloden thanked him, and declined; she would rather fetch it herself.

"Miss Carrick seems a very peculiar young person," observed Miss Wentworth confidentially to Constance. "I never saw a young woman in her position give herself so many airs. She crossed the room just now like a tragedy queen, and as though every one were looking at her; and you know that she is just a mere nobody, and has to work for her living."

"I know all about her," returned Constance, quietly. But this sort of talk was not to her taste. "Dear Mrs. Winter"—leaning forward a little—"I do hope you will spare Vi to me as much as possible. We want her to-morrow for a long day, and if she could stay the night——" But while this little matter was being argued, Gloden returned with her violin and took up her position against the curtains.

Gloden was in a curious mood, bordering upon recklessness. She had informed Violet, only an hour and a half ago, that it was impossible for her to play to an unsympathetic audience, and yet here she was, crossing the room in sleep-walker's

fashion, hardly alive to her surroundings, and with
her violin in her hand.

But all the time the proud spirit within her was
saying, "They all patronize and keep me at a
distance. Not Mr. Lorimer, perhaps, but the
others. I will show them that I can play; that I
have something in me that they cannot touch. I
will not allow this foolish nervousness to get the
mastery over me. An hour ago I could not
have played, now I can. I feel it." And it was
under the irritant of some unknown pain, for which
she could find no name, that Gloden began to
play.

Mr. Hamerton, who was close to the girl, was
struck with the strange proud look in her eyes
as she passed him. His profession had given him
a good deal of insight into character, and the few
words he had exchanged with her had excited his
interest. He now watched her closely. It was not
that he admired her, for he thought her rather
plain than otherwise; but she somehow attracted
him.

Reginald had sunk down on a settee beside
Violet, with his arms lightly crossed over the arm
of his sister's chair; but, as Gloden played on, he
straightened himself, and his look became more
intent. Except at St. James's Hall, or in other

concert-rooms, he had seldom heard such playing as this.

For the first moment the music had dragged a little harshly, as though the player's mood affected the instrument. Then there was a change. Gloden's brow cleared as though by magic. She drew her bow delicately and lightly across the strings in a sort of tender prelude. Then came warmth, colour, and melody. A passionate protest of sound seemed to flood the room. By-and-by it trembled and wavered into plaintive, pathetic chords. Was it a miserere, a dirge? It grew slower and more solemn.

Good-bye to the hopes of youth, to the glorious anticipations of manhood, of womanhood, to all things human. "Ma chère Gabrielle, jamais, jamais." Why should those words have risen suddenly to Reginald's memory, when he saw Felix Hamerton's fixed dark face? Yet it came again and again, "Jamais, jamais, ma chère Gabrielle." But in another minute he had forgotten Felix. Those sweet, long-drawn chords seemed playing on his own heart-strings. Why had this sadness returned? What was the meaning of this sudden feeling of strange vacuum—this divine discontent? What did he want? Was it Car, his painstaking and affectionate helpmate, whose strong white hand had helped him over the rough places of life—was he pining for her? But he knew that the grief at her loss had settled into calmness. This pain was more subtle and penetrating; it stretched into unknown depths. He sighed as though the vagueness troubled him, and then he looked at the young violinist.

Gloden had no idea, as she took up her position against the red silk curtains that divided the two drawing-rooms, what a striking background it would make to the straightness of her black dress. As she manipulated her bow, he could see the delicate white wrist and thin hand. What had become of her paleness and her proud melancholy? Her eyes were bright; there was warm colour in her face; her lips were parted; she looked transformed—almost beautiful. " Good heavens!" he said to himself, " the girl is a genius, and she knows it. She is a disguised princess of art." But what more he would have told himself in his dreamy soliloquy was checked by the sudden silence. Gloden had struck the last chord.

The next minute Constance had started from her chair and was halfway across the room, and her beautiful face was flushed, and there were tears in her eyes.

" Thank you—thank you so much," she said

very earnestly, and holding out her hand. "It was exquisite; it was simply perfect! How have you ever learnt to play like that? Miss Carrick is a wonderful performer, is she not, Felix?"

"Miss Carrick would not allow us to remember her existence," replied Mr. Hamerton, quietly.

Then Gloden turned to him with a radiant smile. "That is the greatest compliment you could have paid me," she said gratefully. "So few people understand that it is only the music, not the performer. Until I can forget myself I can enjoy nothing."

"I am delighted to have secured such a teacher for dear Violet," murmured Mrs. Winter aside to her confidante. "She is a remarkable player, is she not, Theresa? She reminds me of Mademoiselle de Mersac."

"Mademoiselle de Mersac's playing was far more brilliant," returned Miss Wentworth, grudgingly. "I am not fond of these funeral dirges; but Miss Carrick plays well, though there was affectation in her style. She poses too much for my taste, but I suppose we must ask her to play again."

"Thank you, you must excuse me," returned Gloden, as Miss Wentworth, with much volubility, besought her to give them another treat. "I must really go now; it is getting so late."

The fire was fast dying out. She looked wan and exhausted ; whenever she played in this passion of self-forgetfulness, whenever she suffered herself to be carried away and possessed by the music, there was always this exhaustion for a time.

"Of course you shall go if you wish it," observed Violet, kindly ; but when, a minute afterwards, she and Gloden walked through the rooms, Mr. Hamerton followed them.

"One day I hope you will let me hear you play again," he said, with kindly seriousness. "I never pay compliments, do I, Miss Winter? so you must believe me when I tell you that you have given me intense pleasure."

"One cannot help believing you when you speak in that way," returned Gloden, simply, and there was no trace of coldness and haughtiness in her manner as she shook hands with him.

She knew nothing about Felix Hamerton. She had never heard of him ; he was a stranger among strangers. He had just crossed her path, and she might never see him again ; but his look and manner inspired her with confidence, and she felt that she should not forget him. "He is a true man, and there are not too many in the world," she thought, as she walked down the little lane, with red hips and haws shining in the hedgerows. "But something tells

me that he is unhappy, or my violin would not
have said so much to him. I wonder if I am too
imaginative about people when I form these hasty
conclusions? Sometimes they are wrong, and I
find out my mistake ; but I am often right. It is
interesting to make up stories about people, and it
does no harm. Some men have no secrets in their
life ; Mr. Lorimer is one of these. To look at him,
one would say his life was perfectly simple. He
has known trouble. Yes, indeed, we are born to
trouble ; but there is no background, no hidden
mystery. I hardly know what I mean ; I am just
guessing about strangers in the dark ; but there is
a worn look about Mr. Hamerton's face, as though
he has suffered."

Gloden was amusing herself with these fanciful
speculations. It was a favourite habit of hers ;
but by-and-by a question obtruded itself. Why
had Mr. Lorimer not thanked her as he bade her
good-bye ? Every one else in the room had paid
her some compliment, but he had been perfectly
silent. " Good-bye, Miss Carrick ;" those had
been his sole words, and he had scarcely looked
at her as he had given her his hand. Was it her
fancy that then there was a slight coolness in his
manner? Strange to say, this question troubled
her during the remainder of her walk.

"Reggie," observed Constance, as they drove home in the twilight—they were in Reginald's dogcart, and Mr. Hamerton sat behind them—"I am very much struck with Miss Carrick; she looks quite a gentlewoman, and then she plays so beautifully. It is such a pity that she has not been trained as a professional; she could play at concerts."

"How do we know that she would like that, Constance?"

"Why not, dear? People would think ever so much more of her, and then she would make money; even now she is good enough to play at 'At homes,' and that sort of thing. I really feel very much interested in her. Miss Wentworth told me just now that she was dreadfully poor, and that she was quite dependent on Mr. Carrick. It does seem such a poor sort of life, living in a back parlour, and giving violin-lessons in Grantham. She ought to come to town and study, and then make her *début*. I wish I could talk to her, and put the thing properly before her."

"There is no reason on earth why you should not talk to her." But Reginald spoke in rather an irritable tone. For almost the first time in their lives, he and Constance were not quite hitting it off; she was not in touch with him, somehow.

She had at first refused, or as good as refused, to make Miss Carrick's acquaintance, and now she was taking upon herself to direct the course of her life. Why should she play at concerts, and be turned into a professional hack? A delicate, shy girl, a girl with plenty of pride in her, too, was not the best sort to come out in public; and he wondered at Constance for making such a proposition.

"But, Reg dear, how could it be managed?" went on his sister, quite innocent of the fact that her remarks were making Reginald cross. "I could not call on her; it would look too patronizing, and she would not like it. Perhaps"—reflectively—"Violet might think of something; or—— I have it—they have their lesson in the gable-room. You remember the gable room, Reg. I will drive over one afternoon, and run up there as I used in the old days. We are much too formal at the Gate House now; it is that tiresome Miss Wentworth, I believe. But I shall tell Mrs. Winter that I must have one of my old chats in the gable-room, and then I shall get my way."

"As you women always do," returned Reginald, dryly; but he refused to be drawn into any further discussion about Miss Carrick's fitness to make her *début.* He drove on, touching up the mare

rather smartly, and talking incessantly about the
boys and Tottie.

"What are you and Harcourt going to make of
Rex?" he asked. "As his godfather I have a
right to be consulted, but Harcourt is so con-
foundedly close about the boys."

But all the time he talked, and Constance
answered, Felix sat silent, looking down the dark
road and at the faint moonlight stealing over the
tops of the trees, and his lips were firmly closed;
but within himself he was saying over and over
again, "Not my Gabrielle now, or ever will be.
All that was finished long ago."

CHAPTER III.

A FIRESIDE CIRCLE.

"I love everything that is old—old friends, old times, old manners, old books, old wine."—GOLDSMITH'S *She Stoops to Conquer.*

"Tell me the tales that to me were so dear,
Long, long ago—long, long ago."
THOMAS HAYNES BAYLEY.

CONSTANCE WYNDHAM had been quite in earnest when she declared her intention of giving Miss Carrick advice about her future. She was one of those large-minded, liberal women who delight in playing the part of Lady Bountiful to their less fortunate neighbours, and who do not object to be regarded in the light of a minor providence. Natures of this calibre are bound to be rash, and at times to act impulsively; the full tide of their sympathy and benevolence is apt to overflow its marginal boundaries, and to fertilize alien pastures. Sheer warmth of heart, and a desire to see those she loved as happy as herself, had made her an unblushing matchmaker. "Do as you would be done by, and a little more," was Constance's motto, and the mere urgency of need was a sure passport to the inner citadel of her tenderness.

She had already several cases of shy poverty, as she termed them—needy sempstresses, broken-down governesses, and even a bankrupt coster-monger, who looked upon her as a sort of wingless angel. A struggling artiste, a genius whose light was obscured in a remote country town, appealed at once to her imagination and heart. Here was another human being who needed help and guidance ; for, with the zeal of hasty conversion, Constance had already repented of her momentary lukewarmness. She remembered now that Reginald had appealed to her, and asked her to befriend Miss Carrick, and that her response had been hardly satisfactory. Since then she had changed her mind. She would do what Reginald had wished her to do. She would extend the ægis of her beneficence over the young violin-player ; she would interest Harcourt in her ; their house should be thrown open for her *début*. Constance, who held charming little receptions in the season, was not at all unwilling to furnish some novelty for her guests. The more she reflected the deeper grew her enthusiasm, and when Violet arrived the next morning, she was half amused and half provoked to find that Constance could talk about nothing but Miss Carrick and her wonderful playing.

" She is a natural genius; she only wants good training," she remarked, almost with solemnity. " She almost made me cry. I thought about poor Car, and the tears were absolutely running down my cheeks. And did you see Felix's face?"

" No ; he had his hand over his eyes."

"Ah ! but I saw him ; he looked as though some vision had come to him. I never saw such an expression in his eyes before. Then he got up and shook himself; he did not think that I noticed him, but it was a revelation."

" Of what?"

" How is one to explain ? "—rather thoughtfully. " Felix is an enigma. But I do not want to talk about him. Was your mother pleased with Miss Carrick?"

Then Violet frowned impatiently. "She was quite enthusiastic until Cousin Tess damped her. You know her tiresome way when she does not take to people ; a little bit of praise, and then a half-sneer and a good deal of fault-finding. She calls Miss Carrick's style of playing affected and exaggerated, and she will have it that she poses for effect."

"Miss Wentworth is a Philistine. You may tell her so if you like."

"Yes; but she has the thews and sinews of war, and is terribly strong. And now mother has quite changed her opinion. Miss Carrick has too many mannerisms, she is rather conceited, she gives herself airs, and so on. Don't you know exactly how mother would echo every word that Cousin Tess has said. It put me in such a rage that I went out of the room."

"You ought to have stood up for poor Miss Carrick. She is not in the least affected; she is a little stiff and reserved, perhaps, but she is really very nice in her manners."

"What is the use of saying the same thing over a hundred times?" returned Violet, wearily. "If I get mother's ear for a moment, I can make her believe anything; but if Cousin Tess chooses to contradict me, she veers round like a weathercock. 'If dear Theresa be right—and she always is right—then I must be wrong'"—with a sad mimicry of Mrs. Winter's tone.

"You poor darling! how trying it must be for you!"—kissing her. "Well, never mind, we will circumvent the Empress"—one of their old names for Miss Wentworth; and thereupon she retailed her little plan for Miss Carrick.

Violet listened with somewhat mixed feelings. Constance was right, and Miss Carrick's talent was far too good to be wasted on Grantham; but she would be sorry to lose her. She was already interested in her, and was looking forward with pleasurable anticipation to her next lesson. But if it were for Miss Carrick's good—and then she accused herself of selfishness, and threw herself heart and soul into Constance's scheme.

"You know, Violet," Constance was saying at this point, "Harcourt is so dear and kind that he will do anything to please me. I dare say that he would advance money for the training if I have not enough in my private purse; you see, it would only be a loan, an investment, as I should tell him, and Miss Carrick would repay it. He did it once with Caroline Morgan; you remember, Vi, when we set her up in her school at Brighton. It was rather a pull on us at first, and Harcourt grumbled a little; but she has paid us back every penny. Her school is doing splendidly, and she has two of her sisters to help her. Harcourt was so pleased when I took him the money and read him Caroline's letter."

" I dare say Mr. Lorimer would help you."

" Oh, I should not ask Reggie," returned Constance, hastily. " It is no business of his ; it would not do for him to mix himself up in Miss Carrick's affairs."

" I suppose not "—a little doubtfully.

" Reg is the last person in the world to be consulted," was the decided answer ; "he is far too soft-hearted and unpractical. He would not see any reason why he should not put himself forward to help Miss Carrick, and in his position it would be so damaging."

Violet felt inclined to ask why, but some inward doubt made her abstain from putting the question. Of course, Constance knew best about such things ; she had her brother's welfare so much at heart, that she was not likely to make mistakes. And now that he was a widower, and the best match in the county, as Miss Wentworth had once delicately put it in her hearing, it certainly behoved him to be careful.

Violet grew a little weary of the discussion at last ; her bumps of benevolence were not so largely developed as Constance's. She endeavoured to wind it up to a conclusion by cordially inviting her to pay an early visit to the gable room, to open negociations with Miss Carrick.

" I think it will be best to talk things over with her before we make plans that may come to nothing," she said quietly.

And at this strong hint Constance reluctantly changed the subject. Like other enthusiastic people, she rode her hobbies a little long and heavily.

After all, Violet's visit was a great success. In the afternoon they drove out with the boys in search of the sportsmen, and brought them back in triumph to tea ; then followed one of those delicious twilight hours which the quartette had often enjoyed in old days, when they gathered round the fire in the library ; but on this occasion it was a quintette, as Reginald significantly informed his brother-in-law.

" Could you not take yourself off somewhere, Harcourt, and have a smoke ? " he asked, with a persuasive pat on the back. " Order him off, Con ; you have him well in hand. He is an interloper ; we want to be just the old quartette again, don't we, Violet ? I beg your pardon, I mean Miss Winter."

But Mr. Wyndham refused to be turned out ; he said he meant to stay and keep them all in order.

" What makes you and Violet so ceremonious ? " asked Constance, innocently. " Why, you were actually apologizing to her just now for calling her Violet; it is so odd to hear you."

"I have no wish to be ceremonious with an old friend and playmate," returned Reginald ; "but Miss Winter always calls me Mr. Lorimer."

"Yes, of course," returned Violet, hastily ; "but there is no formality in my feelings. One grows out of such things, and we have seen so very little of each other for the last few years."

"You began it," he half whispered. "I was so surprised when you first mistered me ; it made me feel quite small."

Violet coloured a little ; the subject embarrassed her. It was foolish of Constance to make such a personal remark. How well she remembered the occasion, and the somewhat scornful surprise in Lady Car's eyes, when Mr. Lorimer had addressed her carelessly by her name ! From that moment she had decided to put things on a different footing.

"She does not recognize old friendships. She will not approve of our intimacy," she had said to herself, with a swelling heart.

She found it a little difficult to respond to Mr. Lorimer's jesting remark. He was in a mischievous mood—she could see that clearly; but Mr. Hamerton came to her relief.

"Upon my word, Reg, I think Miss Winter is right, and one does grow out of these things; and in my opinion the change is for the better. I remember the time—before Wyndham put in his claim—when I took the liberty of calling his wife by her Christian name, but I stopped it on her wedding-day. You will bear me out in that, will you not, Mrs. Wyndham?"

"I thought you dreadfully punctilious, and told Harcourt so. I quite cried about it; did I not, dear? And he only laughed at me. But I shall always call you Felix; you may be sure of that."

"And I am infinitely obliged to you," he returned, with a grave smile. "I have only you and Reg in England to call me by my Christian name. By-the-by, I must read you a letter of Laura's about her son and heir; I know it will interest you."

"Yes, of course. And you must tell me about Sophy too, and your brother Charlton. There are a hundred things I want to ask you when I get you to myself; but you and Reg are so inseparable just now."

"You see, we have a community of interest; we are just now full of fire and fury, and bent on shooting partridges. Even the charm of your conversation, Mrs. Wyndham, could not tempt me to forsake Reginald."

"Ah, I know!" she returned contemptuously. "You are all the same, you men. Even Harcourt, good as he is to me at other times, cannot be induced to give me a moment of his society now. Well, I will bide my opportunity"—significantly.

"Is it not time to dress?" suggested her husband, who had been all this time trying to read his paper by a distant lamp; but it took a good deal of argument to induce Constance to move. She liked the play of the firelight and the desultory talk and small vague sentences, alternating with silence. During dinner the gentlemen always talked politics or argued with Felix, but here in the gloaming the womankind held the sway. Of course they were wasting their time, as Harcourt said, and talking infinite rubbish. Not altogether, though. For example, Reginald was recalling a squirrel-hunt they had had one autumn afternoon, and how he and Felix had climbed the tree, while Constance stood below weeping and wringing her hands for fear Reggie would be killed. Certainly the branch had broken, and he might have had an awkward tumble if it had not been for Felix's presence of mind and ready help. And did Miss Winter remember, pray, how she had scolded them all round, like the veriest termagant, instead of rejoicing over his escape?

"You deserved to be scolded," returned Violet. "It was cruel of you to frighten Constance in that way; and you know Mr. Hamerton said himself that if you had fallen you must have been killed, and if he had not caught you—— Well, we will draw a veil over that."

"I shall not forget it, Felix," observed Constance, "and how grateful I was to you. Well, dear, what is it? Must we really go? and we are all so comfortable." But Mr. Wyndham's sole answer to this appeal was to hold up his watch before her eyes, and then she yielded and went off meekly enough.

But that evening there were no politics discussed —perhaps Violet's presence restrained them; but at dinner and afterwards it was still of the old days that they talked, and Reginald and Felix capped stories which Mr. Wyndham criticized and annotated in his shrewd clever way. Only now and then his eyes softened as they rested on his wife's bright face. He had not been there. How strange that sounded to him! Had there really been a time in his life when the beautiful woman beside him had not been the very heart of his heart?

And as though she guessed his thought, Constance's hand stole into his under the cover of the table-cloth. Married though they were, they were still lovers, and could understand each other without a word.

"You shall not feel yourself out in the cold while we are telling our foolish stories"—that is what her warm pressure told him.

"Harcourt is laughing at us. But it was before your time, old man. We could not have got such a rise out of Con if she had had you to back her. There was not much fun when you began prowling about the place; even Miss Winter turned sober." And then Reginald turned to Violet and asked her if she had no special little reminiscence which they had forgotten; whereupon Violet exchanged an amused look with Constance, and they both laughed.

But it was in vain that the gentlemen pressed her for an explanation; she only shook her head and laughed again.

"We must get to the bottom of this, Felix," observed Reginald. "You are up in cross-examination, and all that kind of dodge; I think I shall leave you to settle the business."

"There is not the slightest need for me to cross-examine Miss Winter," returned Felix, looking at the girl meaningly. "I recollect the occasion perfectly. Wyndham was expected that evening; it was Christmas Eve. You had been in an insane mood all the afternoon, and had teased your sister until she was almost beside herself. Miss Winter had been singing 'The Mistletoe Bough' to us, and very likely that gave them the idea, but Mrs. Wyndham suddenly electrified us with the suggestion that she and Miss Winter should hide. 'You will never find us, if you search from now until midnight,' she said, 'and the exercise will do Reggie good.'"

"To be sure; I remember now," interposed Reginald. "Don't cut it short, Felix; let Wyndham have it;" and then Violet began to blush.

"Oh, I always finish a story that I have begun," returned Felix, coolly. "You had only been engaged about a week, Wyndham, and were coming down to the hall for Christmas. It was your first visit, and your *fiancée* was particularly anxious that Reginald should be on his best behaviour, and that you should be received with fitting honours."

"And I came by an earlier train than I had said."

"Yes; you arrived full two hours before you were expected, and we were still searching for

Miss Winter.   I believe Mrs. Wyndham had come
out of her hiding-place directly she heard the
door-bell, for she passed us looking very flushed,
and went into the drawing-room.   Will you
continue the story, Mrs. Wyndham ? ”

“ Oh dear ! I was quite shaking with nervousness,” returned Constance, unable to keep silence
at this opportunity.   “ It was so dreadful meeting
Harcourt like that, and I did not dare tell him
that Violet was within hearing.   I was too much in
awe of you then, dear, and I was afraid you would
think our game childish.   I only felt I must get
you out of the room somehow.   You were standing
just by the grandfather’s clock, Harcourt, and I
could not induce you to move.   I kept begging
you to come into the library and see Reg, but you
would not take my hints.”

“ Of course not.   I wanted you all to myself,
and I only thought you were a little bit shy of
me.”

“ Yes ; but it was most embarrassing for Violet
as well as myself, and there she was listening to all
your foolish talk.”

“ Indeed I was not ! ” interposed Violet, indignantly.   “ I had my fingers in my ears, and I
never heard a word.”

“ Well, I thought you did, and I was ready to

sink into the ground ; and then I heard, or pretended to hear, Reg calling me, and I ran away,
and Harcourt followed me, just as Felix entered
by the other door."

"I am to be allowed to finish, then," observed
Mr. Hamerton, as Constance ceased to speak. "I
had given up the search in disgust. I had beaten
over the whole area of the ground-floor, cupboards
and all, and Miss Winter was still invisible ; so I
threw myself down on a couch and took up my
paper, and then it was well I had no nerves, but
I certainly did jump when a voice from the grandfather's clock addressed me, 'Do please unlock the
door, Mr. Hamerton, and help me out,' and there
was Miss Winter. To this moment I don't know
how you managed it."

"In the grandfather's clock !" exclaimed Mr.
Wyndham, almost unable to believe his ears ; and
then he threw back his head and laughed. "Why
have you never told me, Constance ? Ah ! I understand now why you seemed so embarrassed. But
how on earth could Miss Winter find room."

"Well, you see, it was under repair ; there were
no works, and even the face was removed. It was
a mere skeleton case, so she had plenty of air."

"Yes, but I was horribly cramped. I could not
have borne it five minutes longer. I thought once

of putting my head through the hole and begging to be released, but I was ashamed to appear in such a guise before Mr. Wyndham; besides, I should have had to unstop my ears and open my eyes."

Violet said this with such droll naïveté that all three gentlemen burst into peals of laughter, and the merriment was still at its height when Constance gave the signal to rise from table.

"I never thought we should have such an amusing evening," she observed, as she and Violet drew their low chairs to the fire. "Dear Reg is quite himself to-night, and Harcourt does love to hear those old stories. Felix put it very nicely and delicately, but it was no laughing matter; Harcourt was not to be kept in order at all, and I was so afraid you would hear his silly compliments. Ah! you think he is quiet; he was never a great talker, but when we are alone he is so different."

"I always said you were the happiest woman I know. I told Mr. Hamerton so this evening."

"And what did he say?"

"That you and Mr. Wyndham exactly suited each other, and that a more satisfactory marriage had never taken place. He spoke with so much feeling; you would have liked to have heard him."

" Poor dear Felix ! " And then she said thoughtfully, " One ought to make large returns for so
many blessings. Sometimes when I am happiest
I feel as though I must go out and do good to
somebody ; as though it would be a safety-valve,
and would let off my surplus happiness. I have
more than my share," she added ; and now her
eyes were shining with feeling. " What do you
think, Violet? Have I robbed any other woman
of her share? I hope not. But when I look
round on Harcourt and my boys and Reggie, not
forgetting dear old Felix and you and all my
friends, I almost tremble to think that I am
beginning my heaven on earth."

" You deserve it all, Constance ; you are the
most generous-hearted woman I know."

" Oh, don't praise me ! "—putting up her hands
imploringly. " Would you commend a traveller
who is walking well on a smooth road, with beautiful prospects round him ? Harcourt and Reggie
praise me far too much for my soul's welfare, but
all this cannot last ; I must grow grey and old like
my fellows, and the troubles will come."

" Yes, dearest "—touched by the sadness on her
lovely face. " But when they come you will be
strengthened to meet them. I do not think I ever
heard you make such a foreboding speech before,

but perhaps I have forgotten ; no one was ever less morbid."

" Is it morbid to talk seriously ? You should hear my conversations sometimes with Harcourt, —on Sunday nights, for example, when we have been to the Abbey service and have heard a grand sermon. Indeed, we have always been like sisters, and I don't mind telling you that the only trouble I could not bear would be to lose Harcourt."

" You would bear that too, Constance, for your children's sake."

" Should I ? You speak very decidedly, but I am not sure ; but it is the one thought that will intrude even at my happiest moments—my very happiness breeds it. But it is foolish to talk in this strain, and they are all coming in. Go and sing something, only for heaven's sake let it be lively."

" What makes you so pale, love ? " whispered Mr. Wyndham, a little anxiously, as he made his way to his wife's corner, while Mr. Hamerton and Reginald joined Violet at the piano."

" We were only groping a little in the dark, Violet and I," she returned softly. " Sit down by me, Harcourt. Violet is going to sing to us, and I like to have you near me. When the boys are grown up and have gone out into the world, we shall be a regular Darby and Joan, shall we not ? "

He assented to this with a smile ; but her answer
had not satisfied him, and before he slept that
night' he made her tell him what she and Violet
had said, and when she had finished, he rebuked
her with grave tenderness.

" What faithlessness, my darling ! "

" But it is there—always the fear.   Why does it
come, Harcourt ?   You are so much stronger than
I ; you ought to teach me how to repel it."

"And what if the same fear assail me ? "   And
as she looked at him wonderingly, he half smiled.
" It must always come to those who love intensely.
The fear is an integral part of love.   Do not
disquiet yourself about it, my sweet wife.   I shall
not be taken from you an hour sooner because
you have it ; neither shall I lose you a moment
before your allotted time.   Now do you feel more
satisfied ? "

" I am always satisfied when I have you to talk
to me," she answered simply ; and before another
half-hour had passed she was sleeping as calmly
as a child.

" I shall not tell her Dr. Littleton's opinion," he
said to himself, as he went back to his dressing-
room to finish his letters.   " It would be a shame
to cloud such perfect happiness ; besides, there is
no need to tell her."

"Take care of yourself, do not overwork your-self, and you may outlive me." Those were Little-ton's words, and he meant them too. "A weak heart. What does that signify? Hundreds of men have weak hearts. Moderate exercise, plenty of work, and a quiet conscience, and I may make an old man yet. God grant it for my wife's sake!" For it was of her he had thought when he went to the clever specialist to ask him the reason of some troublesome symptoms that had lately troubled him; of her, and not of the brilliant future that his friends had prophesied for him.

Two years before he had made his maiden speech in the House of Commons, and since then he had been regarded as a rising man, and one who would be invaluable to the members of his party.

CHAPTER IV.

"I AM NOT FREE."

"Duties are ours, events are God's."
CECIL.

WITH all her good intentions, Mrs. Wyndham found it somewhat difficult to carry out her little scheme. Numerous engagements obliged her to defer her visit to the Gate House. There were shooting breakfasts, luncheons, and a dinner to which she and her husband had been invited, and it was ten days before she could secure a leisure afternoon.

In the mean time Gloden had again accidentally encountered the young master of Silcote Hall.

It happened in this wise.

Gloden had left the Gate House, and had just turned out of the little lane into the Grantham road, when she saw a young man in shooting-dress walking down the middle of the road, with

his gun on his shoulder and two dogs following
him closely. At the sound of footsteps behind
him he turned, and to her surprise she saw it was
Mr. Lorimer. He pulled off his cap with a look
of unmistakable pleasure when he saw her, and
joined her at once.

"I am in luck to-day," he said genially, as
Gloden, perhaps to hide her shyness, stooped down
and caressed the dogs. " I have had capital sport
at the Gate Farm, and now I have the pleasure of
meeting you. We are going as far as Grantham
together, are we not?"—as she seemed to hesitate
what to do next. But Mr. Lorimer seemed to
think it the most natural thing in the world that
they should walk on together, and as it did not
seem possible to get rid of him, Gloden resigned
herself to her fate.

" Don't you find that thing heavy ?" he inquired,
with a glance at her violin-case.

But Gloden only shook her head with a dissent-
ing smile; and, indeed, as he noticed her light
springy step and upright carriage, and the alert-
ness of her movements, there seemed no need to
offer his help.

"You have been to the Gate House, of course?"

"Yes ; I am always there two afternoons in the
week."

" I suppose you keep regular days?" he observed carelessly.

"Tuesdays and Fridays." Then Gloden felt as though she had been a little indiscreet. "I give Hilda Parry violin-lessons on Mondays and Thursdays," she said hurriedly. "The Parrys are so kind ; they have promised to find me some more pupils. I hope soon to be fully occupied."

"The work seems to agree with you," he returned, looking at her a little keenly. "You seem as fit as possible ; ever so much better than when I found you in the plantation. I never saw any one so done up as you were that afternoon."

" I believe I was very tired."

" I should think so. Grantham seems to agree with you, after all."

" Oh no ; please do not say so!" for this was more than Gloden could swallow. "If you only knew how I hate it!" Then, as he looked rather surprised and disconcerted at the energy of her tone, she went on apologetically, " Perhaps it is horrid of me to say that when people are so kind in finding me work, but if you only knew what *heimweh*—real home-sickness meant, you would understand how I long for Eltringham."

" Should you care to go back to it now?" he asked in a sympathetic tone. He was not sorry to hear her speaking in this way. It showed that under her coldness there was plenty of heart. She had quite lost her prim manner, and was talking to him as naturally as possible.

"You mean, should I care to go back with strangers at the vicarage? It would be painful, of course, but I think I should choose the pain. I would be willing to live in a cottage—a little white-washed cottage on the green—if I could only wake up every morning and find myself at Eltringham."

"By Jove! you are fond of the place." And then he stopped, and asked a little curiously, "Were you thinking of Eltringham when you played to us on Tuesday?"

But as he put this question, the blood rushed to Gloden's face.

"No," she said, rather shortly; and then she turned her head away and bit her lip. Why had he asked her such a question? If he could only have read the proud, ambitious thoughts that had surged through her mind when she had commenced playing! Those wild yearnings that had infused such pathos into the notes, those passionate appeals and regrets, seemed to stretch and widen into infinity. Could she give them a name? How was one to brand or label the immeasurable cravings of the human soul?

Reginald felt somehow as though he had said the wrong thing.

"I could not tell you that afternoon what I felt about your playing. I believe"—with a laugh, as though to hide deeper feeling—"that the music fairly bowled me over. I had a fit of the blues afterwards, for which I have to thank you, Miss Carrick."

"Oh, I am so sorry ! "

"There is no occasion for you to be sorry. I rather liked it myself, only it has filled me with the desire to hear you play again. If I were to drop in at the Gate House on Tuesday afternoon by accident—the Winters are such old friends, and are always glad to see me—would you play to us again ? "

"You must not do that," she returned decidedly. "My time is pledged to Miss Winter, and it is no part of our programme that I should entertain her visitors." She spoke with considerable firmness ; and then her manner changed. "Please do not expect me to do that, Mr. Lorimer. I think, I am almost sure, that Mrs. Winter does not care for my playing, and it would create awkwardness. If there be any other opportunity, I shall be very happy to play to you."

"Thanks awfully. I am quite sure lots of opportunities will turn up, and then I will keep you to your promise."

But he thought it safer policy to change the subject. He supposed Miss Wentworth had been ungracious; he knew of old that it was not always easy to gain her favour. Very likely she had made up her mind to keep Miss Carrick in her place, and not to encourage Violet in any intimacy with her young music-teacher. Perhaps she did not come into the drawing-room at all, and he could hardly ask for admission to the gable-room unless Constance were with him. He must just wait and see what turned up; but on one thing he had fully made up his mind—that Miss Carrick should play to him again.

He was astonished himself at the persistency with which her playing haunted him. He had wakened up one or two mornings with those wild melancholy strains sounding in his ears; and not only that, but her striking personality that day had been a revelation to him.

Was she always transformed in the same way? When she played he wanted to hear her again, and to answer his own question. He had not thought her at all pretty, hardly good-looking, when he had first seen her—only a pale, unhappy-looking

girl with a proud, chilling manner. Not insignificant, certainly—Miss Carrick could never be that ;
but, compared to other women that he knew, to
Constance, to his own poor Car, to Violet Winter,
she was almost plain.

He looked at her now as these thoughts passed
through his mind, and he acknowledged that he
had been wrong in his first hasty criticism, and
that she was certainly not without her good points.
She was wonderfully graceful, and her face was
full of expression ; but she did not look as she had
looked that afternoon at the Gate House, with the
background of red silk curtains behind her, and the
glow of some strange beauty in her face. Then,
by an odd transition of thought, he wondered
what Car would have thought of her. He imagined
her sitting in his place, looking fair, calm, and
stately. "Good execution, but too many mannerisms for my taste, Reginald ; " he could almost
hear her say that.

"How is Harvey?" he asked, rather abruptly ;
for they were nearly in sight of Market Street
now, and Miss Carrick had become rather silent.
" By-the-by, I shall expect him to look me up next
Saturday."

" But you are engaged ; you have visitors," she
objected.

"What of that?" he returned airily; "the more the merrier—that is the motto at Silcote Hall. If I had my own way, I would cram the house from now to Christmas. Well, perhaps not this year"—checking himself as he remembered this was hardly a speech for a disconsolate widower to make—"but most years. I am a very sociable person, Miss Carrick; I am fond of my fellow-creatures, and I am especially fond of giving them a good feed."

"Yes; but about Harvey, Mr. Lorimer," she said, colouring, but keeping to her point, for she was glad of having this opportunity of speaking to him. "You are very kind to my dear boy, and you made him so happy in giving him those rabbits, but you must not encourage him too much. Harvey is so young, he does not quite understand. If you are too kind to him you will win his affection, and then he will be always wanting to go to Silcote, and you will find him terribly in the way."

"Not a bit of it; he and I understand each other perfectly," was the blunt answer.

"Yes; but you must not be so kind," she persisted, though her task was making her a little nervous, and she was stumbling over her words. "It is putting Harvey in a false position. You must see that, under his present circumstances—in our present situation "—correcting herself—"he must not expect to be on terms of equality with people. In the old days it was different, and people were glad to know us ; but now—— Surely you understand what I mean, Mr. Lorimer "—a little resentfully, for he did not show the least intention of helping her.

"I know you have been talking awful rubbish, begging your pardon, Miss Carrick. Oh, I understand what you mean well enough, but I am not going to put it into words. You may just make your mind easy about Harvey ; he is a fine little chap, and I am going to see a good deal of him. He is coming up to Silcote on Saturday, and I will send him back in the dogcart. You are not afraid to trust him with me ? "

"Oh no, of course not."

"All right. I was half afraid you were going to say that next. What an awfully scrupulous person you are, Miss Carrick ! Harvey and I are easy-going, happy-go-lucky people, not your sort at all. On second thoughts," continued Reginald, reflectively, "your kind of conscience would not suit me ; it is too prickly. It would give me moral indigestion. Ah ! here we are at Market Street, and I am sorry to see you intend to leave me. Will you let me step in and give Mrs. Carrick this brace of partridges? I meant to have offered them to you, but, on my honour, I dare not after this amazing display of scrupulosity. I see plainly that you intend to have nothing at all to do with me."

Then Gloden, for once in her life, acted on a curious impulse, for she put out her hand palm uppermost in a most suggestive way.

"If you really meant those partridges for me, I will take them, and thank you very much, Mr Lorimer; but you must not be so extravagantly generous. Harvey brought back some beautiful game from Silcote ten days ago."

"Did he? I forgot that. Well, you are making handsome amends for all the rubbish you talked;" and Mr. Lorimer's face brightened. It brightened still more as Gloden thanked him with one of her radiant smiles.

"Aunt Clemency," she said, a little breathlessly, "I met Mr. Lorimer just now, and he has given me these partridges; he has just shot them. Uncle Reuben will enjoy them; he is so fond of game."

"Yes, but he rarely tastes it; beef and mutton are more in our line. I don't call to mind that the squire has ever sent us even a rabbit before; but it must be all along of Harvey."

"Of course it is Harvey, Aunt Clemency," re-

turned Gloden, a little sharply ; and then she went
up to her room.

"Was I wrong to take them ? Was it forward of
me ?" she asked, tormenting herself in her usual
fashion. "But when he said that, that I meant to
have nothing to do with him, I could not help putting
out my hand for the birds. He is so kind that it
quite pains me to be so stiff and disagreeable ; but
I do it for the best." And she sighed ; for Gloden
was young, far too young to lead this self-
dependent, repressive life, and the youth within
her was beginning to clamour and rebel against
such unnatural conditions.

Another week passed. Harvey had paid a third
visit to the hall. There had been no further
present of game ; but Gloden was beginning to be
afraid that Harvey intended to spend all his
weekly holidays there, and that he regarded
Silcote as his private hunting-ground. The
Wyndham boys, young as they were, were ad-
ditional attractions to him, and when Mr. Lorimer
invited him to bring Bernard Trevor with him on
the following Saturday, Harvey's cup of bliss was
filled to the brim.

"Isn't it awfully jolly of him, Glow?" he exclaimed that evening, as they walked up and
down the best room in the twilight. This was an

old habit. Harvey called it "prowling a bit." They would walk up and down with arms interlaced, keeping step and talking hard, until Gloden declared she was tired. "Bernard wants to go dreadfully, only he says his mother does not know Mr. Lorimer, because she never goes out. Won't he be fine and pleased, as Aunt Clem is so fond of saying? He will be ready to jump out of his skin when I give him Mr. Lorimer's invitation."

"Will his mother let him go?"

"Of course she will, like a shot. Bless you! everybody ¡in Grantham thinks no end of Mr. Lorimer. The boys are as envious as possible when they hear I am going to Silcote. Bob Stourton—his father keeps the grocery stores, Stourton Brothers, in High Street—he is a mean, carneying sort of chap, and I can scarcely keep my hands off him. Well, what do you suppose Bob had the check to say yesterday? Wouldn't I take him to Silcote just to see the rabbits? Catch me. Stourton Brothers, indeed!" and Harvey gave a short derisive laugh.

"But, Harvey dear, our position is not much better. Uncle Reuben says that Stourton Brothers are so rich that they mean to retire. They have a private house now near the Parrys', and there's

some talk of my giving violin-lessons to the two
girls."

"Yes ; but they are awful cads. Do you think
Mr. Lorimer does not see the difference ?"

"Ah! but think of Uncle Reuben, Harvey."
She ought not to have said it, but the words
escaped from her involuntarily.

"Come now, I call that too bad, Glow," replied
Harvey, in an injured tone. "You are always
spoiling things for a fellow, and it is not fair, either.
Why, Stourton Brothers wear white aprons, and
you can see Stourton junior any day in the
butter department, slicing fat bacon for the old
women, and dropping his *h*'s all over the shop.
And to compare them with poor old Uncle Reuben !
It is not nice of you a bit, Antelope; and as
for Aunt Clem, though she does talk about being
fine and proud, well, that is only her way, and
I am as fond of her as possible !" cried the lad
bravely, only his cheeks were burning in the
darkness. "And if she isn't a lady like our own
mother, she is a lady in her way, and it is a grand
way, too." And Gloden had nothing to answer to
this tirade.

But, after all, it was Harvey who was nearer the
truth than Gloden, for Clemency's innate gentleness and sweet old-fashioned notions made her at

least a lady of the new kingdom, where reality, and
not its shadow, shall be the only coinage ; where
all disguises of mere rank or circumstance shall be
torn away, and in that goodly company of heaven's
aristocracy the first shall be last and the last
first.

By-and-by Mrs. Wyndham found her opportunity, and one afternoon, just as the violin-lesson
was over, and Gloden had opened Dante, there
was a knock at the door that Violet evidently
recognized, for she jumped up, exclaiming, "That
is dear old Constance!" and brought her in
triumphantly.

She greeted Gloden with much cordiality, and
then settled herself cosily in the window-recess,
talking all the while.

"Is this not like old times, Vi? only Miss
Carrick is an interloper.   Now, pray do not look
alarmed, Miss Carrick, for my visit is to you as
well as to Miss Winter, so, you see, you are not a
bit in the way.   Were you going to read Dante ?
Never mind ; the gruesome old Florentine will
keep, and I want to talk to you instead, and this is
my first visit to the gable-room for a year and a
half at least.   Do you remember that Reg always
would call it the "gabble-room," because he said
we did nothing but chatter in it ? "

"One does not forget that sort of thing, Constance."

"No indeed ; and you and Reg were such great allies. Now, I am going to make a daring proposition. Do let us have tea up here instead of in the drawing-room."

"By all means," returned Violet, easily. "Cousin Tess will be in a nice temper. She always is when I order tea up here, but I often do it. I have arranged a code of signals with Dawson. There !"—as she manipulated the bell—"he will know now that I want tea for three, and he will send Dorcas up with it."

And Violet was right. Ten minutes had barely elapsed before a neat-looking housemaid appeared with the teatray. A low table was drawn to the window-recess, and Constance examined the cups with childish interest, gloating over their quaint shape.

"The same dear old cups !" she said enthusiastically.

Constance was a clever strategist. She did not at once open her mission. She waited until Gloden seemed at her ease with her, and then she approached the subject by judicious praises of her playing.

"You have real genius, Miss Carrick," she said

seriously; "you carried us all away the other
day. We were an appreciative audience, I can
assure you.   Mr. Hamerton, who is no mean
judge, agreed with me that it was a sin and shame
to hide such a talent."

"Do you call this hiding it?" returned Gloden,
in surprise, but she was not a little gratified by
this warm commendation.   "I think I am getting
on famously.   I have two pupils already, and I
expect I shall soon have more."

"Pupils! Ah, I dare say!" exclaimed Constance,
contemptuously; "but fancy wasting such execution on a few Grantham young ladies! You
must come to town, Miss Carrick, and go in for
regular training under Boski. You have heard him
play, of course. He is what my brother would
call the boss of violinists, and then he is so strict.
He never takes a pupil whom he thinks will not do
him credit, and the mere fact that Boski has given
you lessons will be a brilliant recommendation in
itself."

"I have no doubt you are right, Mrs. Wyndham, and I am a devout admirer of Boski; but his
lessons are among the good things that are not
for me."

"But that is nonsense," returned Constance,
speaking so exactly like her brother that Gloden

quite started; she seemed to hear him say again,
"You have been talking awful rubbish." "You
may have your good things too if you will only
open your hands widely enough. Let me finish
what I was saying, and we will discuss details
afterwards. I am quite sure that a year under
Boski would enable you to play at concerts, but
of course he would settle all that. You would
have to take lodgings in town. I know of some
nice rooms near Regent's Park, not at all dear,
kept by an old servant of mine. Mrs. Drake is
such a nice woman. She has a permanent lodger,
an old lady who pays her well, and then she has
these two other little rooms. You would not be
too far from Boski's there—he lives in Connaught
Square. It would be just a nice little walk, and
I would come and look after you and introduce
you to some nice people; so you would not be
dull. Besides, Boski would insist on six hours'
practice a day, so you would really have no time
to mope."

"May I say a word now, Mrs. Wyndham?"
asked Gloden, humbly, but there was a contu-
macious sparkle in her eyes.

"No, not yet; you shall have your turn presently, and I have not quite finished. Of course,
you are going to tell me that Signor Boski's terms

are exorbitant. So they are for rich people, but he is very generous with his poorer pupils, and is always willing to lower his price for them ; he is far more anxious for his pupils to do him credit than to make money out of them. He is a great friend of mine, and I know what a generous-minded man he is."

"I have always heard so "—in a low voice.

"Then you have heard the truth ; and I have only to introduce you in my own way, and I will guarantee that he takes an interest in you. The want of means, my dear Miss Carrick—you see, I am speaking very frankly—need not deter you in the least ; my husband and I would arrange that. It would be a safe investment. You would make your *début* at Princes' Hall, and then at our house ; engagements would flow in, and you would very soon repay us. Come, is this not a grand programme for your future ? "

"It is indeed," returned Gloden, but she spoke in a dreamy manner. Mrs. Wyndham's glowing description had roused a tumult within her. Why, this was one of her old air-castles that she had built so long ago, and it was impregnated with the scent of lilies and the sweet spicy breath of the pine-woods. How often she had closed her eyes and seen herself standing, violin in hand, on the platform of some crowded concert-room—at St. James's Hall, for example, or at the Crystal Palace, with Manns' baton in hand below her—she could hear the applause, the bravos, and the clapping of hands. "The celebrated young violinist, Gloden Carrick"—that is what they called her. Perhaps there would be a bouquet or a wreath flung at her feet, but that would be in the evening. "Oh, I beg your pardon!"—waking up to the fact that there was dead silence, and that both Mrs. Wyndham and Violet were looking at her curiously. "I did not mean to be rude, but your words made me think about so many things."

"That is what I want you to say—that you will think about it very seriously. I hope you do not think me interfering, Miss Carrick, but I am so used to help people; and they never mind me—they know it makes me so happy."

"You are very kind—you are more than kind, and I am ever so much obliged to you." And then Gloden stopped, and there was a great softness in her eyes. It seemed to her at that moment that in all her life she had never seen such a lovely face as the one before her, and surely she was as good as she was beautiful.

"Then you will let me help you?"—with graceful entreaty.

" I would let you help me if I could accept help from any one, but there are other hindrances beside my pride. You tempt me very strongly, Mrs. Wyndham. The life you describe is one that I should love, and, though perhaps I ought not to say it, I do not think that I should have disappointed your expectations ; but I am not free to choose my life."

" Not free, my dear Miss Carrick ? "

" No. I have my young brother to consider. I have promised my father—I promised it when he lay in his coffin—that I would never leave Harvey; on his death-bed he committed him to me as a sacred charge. I said then that I would keep near him, that I would find some way for our being together as long as he needed me ; but I said more than that afterwards. This is why I am living at Grantham, though I hate my life here, because I am too poor to make any sort of home for him ; because it is better for him that I live in this way. But perhaps by-and-by, when he is older and I have formed a connection, we may still have a home of our own."

" Could it not be arranged for Harvey to come to town too ? " asked Mrs. Wyndham, but she spoke with some hesitation. " Perhaps Mr. Carrick would be chargeable for his nephew's maintenance ? "

"Impossible! Not for worlds would I ask him; he and Aunt Clemency would be shocked at the mere idea. They are old-fashioned people, and have such limited ideas; and then they are so fond of Harvey—it would be so cruel to propose to take him away; besides—oh, there are so many besides! —Harvey would be miserable in London. He is a country boy; he likes plenty of space and freedom, and though he looks so well he is not strong; more than once we have been anxious about him. No, no; if everything else were arranged—Signor Boski's lessons, Harvey's maintenance, and my own—I could not doom my poor boy to London lodgings."

"I did not expect all these difficulties," sighed Mrs. Wyndham. She was grievously disappointed, but even she could not say that Gloden was wrong; on the contrary, she admired the girl for her resolution and devotion to her brother. "We could not have the boy on our hands too," she said afterwards to Violet. "Harcourt would have put down his foot at once, and rightly too. We might have got him into Merchant Taylors', perhaps. Dr. Morton would have helped us, but he is a delicate-looking boy, and I am afraid the underground railway and small lodgings would not have suited him; but it does seem such a grievous pity that Miss Carrick should be sacrificed."

"Perhaps she will not always be sacrificed," returned Violet; "and after all she is doing the right thing."

"Have you really made up your mind to the impossibility of my scheme? Is there no loophole left, no glimmer of hope?" asked Constance, when Gloden rose as though to close the conversation.

"There is no loophole that I can see," she returned; but she was very pale now, and there were tears in her eyes. "But, all the same, I shall always feel grateful to you for your generous proposal; so few people would have interested themselves in a stranger."

"Ah, but all people are not Constance," observed Violet, with an affectionate glance at her friend. "You will know what she is one day, Miss Carrick." And then they both accompanied Gloden to the top of the staircase.

"I don't wonder she interested him," said Constance half to herself, as Gloden looked back at them with one of her brilliant smiles. "There is something very unusual about her; she somehow takes hold of one."

"Of whom are you speaking?" asked Violet a

little inquisitively, as she bent over the balus-trades.

But Mrs. Wyndham was prudent, and did not explain herself; for " Speech is silvern, and silence is golden," thought Constance.

CHAPTER V.

GABRIELLE DE BRIENNE.

"I have a room wherein no one enters
    Save I myself alone ;
There sits a blessed memory on a throne,
    There my life centres."

CHRISTINA ROSETTI.

"FELIX, I want to ask you a question."

"Excuse me for one moment, Mrs. Wyndham. If you will allow me to ring the bell and despatch these letters, I shall be ready to answer a score of questions."

"Ah, very well," returned Constance, carelessly ; "finish your business first. There is not the least hurry, but, as I have been as quiet as the traditional mouse for the last hour and a half, I thought I might break the silence."

"You have been as good as gold," returned Mr.

Hamerton, as he addressed his last envelope, "and you shall have your innings presently. I have been dull company for you this afternoon, but I will make up for it by-and-by;" and he gathered up his letters and business documents, with a word or two to the servants, while Constance laid aside her knitting and looked thoughtfully into the fire.

It was a damp, cheerless afternoon in October. There had been rain earlier in the day, nevertheless the squire and Mr. Wyndham had driven out some miles to join a shooting-party at Combe Lea; but the morning post had brought Mr. Hamerton such a budget of business letters, that he had been compelled to remain at home.

With the exception of a brisk constitutional with Rex and Ninian as his companions, he had been writing most of the day, and, as he came forward to the fire, he stretched out his arms with a gesture of mingled weariness and relief, and sank in the easy-chair with the air of a man who had earned repose.

"How tired you look, Felix! and yes, I think—I am sure—that you are thinner. Harcourt says you work far too hard."

"Does he?"—rather indifferently. "I will get myself weighed when I go back to town. I wonder what sort of a bag he and Reginald are making? Fancy losing a day at Combe Lea because of that confounded Brabazan case! It is hard lines, isn't it, Mrs. Wyndham?"

"I suppose I ought to sympathize with you, but, you see, I am the gainer. I have never got you alone for a single minute, Felix, and I do so want to talk to you. We never have one of our cosy chats now."

Then he smiled at her, but made no answer. He was quite content to sit there in the yellow firelight, watching the branches of the elms sway to and fro, while the damp leaves pattered down on the grass. He loved October, dry or wet, crisp or humid; he loved the mellowness and the softness, and the full flavour of the late autumn days with their suggestive melancholy, and perhaps the touch of frosts toward night that warns of the coming winter; and he loved, too, the companionship of the fair-faced woman who sat opposite to him, and he was quite willing that she should discourse to him in her cheerful, bright way. Perhaps she wanted to talk to him about Rex. He and Reginald were fellow-sponsors, and he took a great deal of interest in the boy; indeed, both the little lads were dear to him. But Constance's next speech gave him a shock; it might have been a hand-grenade, it routed him so effectually.

" Felix, we are old friends—chums, as you men call it, and I want to ask you a question. Have you ever been in love ? "

He was so astonished that he sat up erect in his chair and stared at her ; but Constance, who was watching him closely, saw that he had turned a little pale and caught his breath.

" Dear friend," she said very softly—and nothing could be more caressing than her manner—" don't think me horrid for asking the question so bluntly ; but you know how much I have your interest at heart. I do not think Laura and Sophy could be more anxious for your welfare. And I have so often wondered why you are so averse to matrimony."

" All men do not marry," he returned, defending himself somewhat lamely ; but the firm lips twitched a little nervously, and he did not look at her as he spoke. " You know I think you almost perfect, Mrs. Wyndham, and you have full liberty to speak to me as you choose ; but if I could bring myself to accuse you of a fault, it is that you are too anxious about your friends."

" You are putting it very kindly, Felix. You mean I am an interfering, match-making woman, and in a way you are right. I must meddle in my friends' affairs, and try and put them right. If I love people, their interests are mine. I cannot separate myself from them. Harcourt often lectures me about it. He calls it abandoned self-indulgence, an over-exuberant sympathy ;" and then she stopped, and looked in his eyes, as he slowly raised them to her. " Tell me all about it, Felix ; our old friendship gives me the right to ask. Who is she, and where did you meet her ? "

" Mrs. Wyndham "—and then he tried to laugh, but it was a failure—" are you a witch ? Who has put such a suspicion into your head ? Have I ever dropped a word that could lead you or any one to imagine that I am not a whole-hearted bachelor ? "

" Never," was the frank answer. " You have always been cheerful and even-tempered, and your thoughtful moods are as much a part of your nature as Reggie's light-heartedness belongs to his. No word or look has betrayed you until this moment, when my abrupt question took you by surprise, and you were not quite ready with your answer."

" Then why——" he began, but she interrupted him.

" It is not easy to say how the surmise has

arisen. I think it was a chance word of Reggie's; he looked rather solemn one day when I was talking about you."

"I can assure you, Mrs. Wyndham, that, in spite of our close friendship, Reginald and I have never spoken on this subject. He has often chaffed me on my supposed hard-heartedness; lots of my friends have done that. A bachelor is a fair target for married men's jokes."

"Nevertheless, I am sure Reggie guesses something," returned Constance, gravely, "though he would be angry with me for hinting at such a thing. But why are we wasting time like this, Felix? You will tell me, will you not, about this old trouble. For trouble there is, and must be; I am certain of that now."

And thus hardly pressed, Felix yielded up his secret. To no one else would he have told it, except to this woman, who had taken a sister's place to him; and, strange to say, as the seal of silence was removed, and his lips spoke the beloved name, the heaviness of that hidden burden that he had carried so many years seemed to lighten strangely.

And this was the substance of what Felix Hamerton told that October afternoon, while twilight faded into dusk, and then into darkness.

And Constance listened in that moved sympathetic silence that is more eloquent than words.

It was during that long summer wandering seven years ago that he had encountered his fate; when the fair face of Gabrielle de Brienne had first flashed on him, for whose dear sake he was indifferent to all other women.

He was staying in the little village of L——, tired out with alpine climbing, and in the mood for a few days' perfect rest and idleness in one of the most delicious of Swiss valleys.

The tiny hotel where he put up was full of guests, but he managed to secure a small room, and, having unpacked his portmanteau and refreshed himself, he sauntered idly through the gardens and across a rustic bridge leading to some overhanging woods, which clothed part of a ravine; beyond these were glorious peaks, clad in eternal snows. The whole scene was superb, idyllic, permeated—nay, saturated with beauty, and as he crossed the little bridge, a curious thought came into his mind. "If I ever marry," he said to himself, "I will bring my bride here; it is just the spot for honeymooning." And then he laughed at his own thoughts, for the busy young barrister was fancy-free, and the woman who was to be his helpmate had not yet entered the Eden of his youth.

A little path led upward through the wood, and here and there rustic seats had been placed for the use of the climbers ; but the irony of fate led him aside from the beaten track to explore a little glade, that looked to him wonderfully inviting.

A sort of archway of tangled branches admitted him to the dell, which was a mere clearing ; but nature, with lavish hands, had embellished it with a thousand flowers, and there, standing under a ladder of sunbeams filtered through the tree-tops, like some glorified youthful angel crowned with yellow sunshine, was a slim girl in white, who looked at him with grave dark eyes, as he stood there for a moment almost petrified with surprise, for he had thought himself alone in the woods.

And afterwards, he told Constance, that picture haunted him, and became to him like a waking dream. It would flash upon him suddenly as he talked and jested with other women. The tiny glade, with its flower-spangled grass, and the sunbeams playing on the girlish, uncovered head ; he could see every fold of her white gown, and even the bright clasp at her waist. Her hands were full of flowers ; but what struck him more than the unconscious grace of her attitude, was the grave, quiet penetration of those dark eyes. And yet how momentary it had been! Surely he had not lingered more than a few seconds before raising his cap. With a muttered apology he had turned away and begun climbing the ravine, but after a while he had desisted. He was breathless, and some feeling of curiosity made him pause and descend the ravine again. He would return to the hotel; he had had enough fatigue for one day. He would loiter in the gardens until it was time for *table d'hôte.*

If he expected to see the white-robed nymph cross the little bridge to the châlet, he was disappointed; he had the gardens to himself. But as he seated himself at table beside an acquaintance, a lively American widow, he saw her a little lower down. She was sitting between a good-looking young man, evidently a Frenchman, and a fragile, pretty woman in gay attire. They were all talking and laughing together. Once their eyes met, and she blushed slightly, as though she recognized him; but she did not look his way again. Now and then a low sweet laugh reached his ear, but he could hear that their conversation was carried on in French.

"Who are those people, Mrs. Brandon?" he asked of his neighbour, as they went out into the garden to enjoy the sight of the mountain peaks bathed in the moonlight, and he looked significantly after the three retreating figures. "Garde tu, ma petite," he heard the gentleman say tenderly, as the young girl stumbled slightly over a fragment of rock in the path; "pas si vite, Gabrielle."

"Oh, that is the Comte de Brienne and his wife and sister. She is an American. I knew her slightly before she was married, when she was Valeria Grant; she calls herself Valerie now. She was a pretty creature, and the New Yorkers went mad about her. They were mad after another fashion when she took up with a French count; but they are pretty devoted to each other."

"And that young lady is his sister?"

"His step-sister. Yes; she is Mademoiselle Gabrielle de Brienne. She has just finished her education, and they have taken her out of the convent. I dare say he intends to find her a husband as soon as possible. She is really a charming girl—spirituelle, but rather gentle and dreamy; the nuns are to blame for that. Valerie is another sort; she has *chic*—you know what I mean. I guess she makes her husband pretty mad at times;" and Mrs. Brandon nodded her head knowingly.

"I wish you would introduce me," he said a little eagerly.

And Mrs. Brandon promised with ready good nature to do so; but either she forgot her promise or she lacked opportunity, for she left the next day without giving Felix the introduction he desired. The whole of that day he saw nothing of the comte and his party—they were absent on some excursion, and did not return until late—but just as he was dropping off to sleep, he was roused by voices that sounded as though they proceeded from the balcony outside his window. "Good night, Valerie; sleep well, ma pauvre, if thou canst. Take the best of care of her, Etienne. Good rest to you both, my dear ones." Those low sweet tones belonged to Mademoiselle de Brienne; he would have sworn to them anywhere.

The next morning they were invisible, and, alas! he had no Mrs. Brandon to question. He ate his *déjeuner* discontentedly, and strolled about somewhat aimlessly. He had his book with him, but he did not read. The mountain air, the dazzling snow-peaks, seemed to intoxicate him, and dispose him for mere idle dreaming; he was in that dangerous state of bodily indolence and mental activity when any excitement would be welcome.

Later in the day he was returning from a walk down a steep little road, which he had discovered would bring him by a short cut to the châlet, when he caught sight of a slender figure in grey standing beside a wayside cross, and looking up at the rude painted figure of the Christ with tender, reverent eyes. Under the straw hat he saw the gleam of golden brown hair. It was Mademoiselle de Brienne. He raised his hat and would have passed her, but she turned round and looked at him almost appealingly, and he involuntarily stopped.

"Is it possible that you need my assistance, mademoiselle?" He addressed her in French, and her face at once brightened.

"That is kind, monsieur," she returned, with childlike naïveté and frankness. "You are English, and I speak the language so badly. Will you have the kindness, the infinite kindness, to direct me to the châlet? I have missed my path and am lost." As she spoke the last word she threw out her hand with an eloquent little gesture.

"With all the pleasure in life, mademoiselle. I am going back myself, and will conduct you. This is a short cut to the châlet. If we take that path, we shall be in the ravine where I saw you yesterday. But"—an after-thought occurring to him—"the path is too steep and difficult; we had better take the lower road;" for, with masculine cunning, he was determined to prolong the walk as much as possible.

But the convent had not taught Gabrielle to comprehend mannish wiles, so she answered with the utmost faith and credulity, "If monsieur be good enough to be my guide, I must leave the route to him." At which Felix did feel momentarily ashamed of himself; but the temptation was too strong, the pleasure of looking into those lovely eyes too great, and after an instant's hesitation he determined on taking the lower road.

Mademoiselle de Brienne accompanied him willingly. She was not at all shy, and answered his questions with perfect frankness; the word "spirituelle" that his American friend had used was exactly suited to her. There was a gentleness and a freshness about this young girl that was almost indescribable. The purity and gravity of the cloister still lingered about her, but every now and then the natural joyousness of her young life seemed to break in upon her sedateness; at such moments she was charming. To Felix Hamerton she was a revelation. He had never imagined this delicate and unique type of girlhood; the dark eyes and pure oval of her face, and her pale olive complexion, appeared to him his ideal of feminine beauty. She was evidently very young and undeveloped, but the years and life would soon ripen her, the slender figure would round and fill out; but as he looked at her he thought that no change could improve her.

Before long he knew all that there was to know about her. She was eighteen, so Etienne had taken her away from the convent. Etienne was her brother, the Comte de Brienne. He was the best and dearest brother in the world. Had monsieur spoken to him? Valerie was not French, or Catholique; she was an American, and Etienne had fallen in love with her beauty. Ah! she was droll at times, this dear Valerie, but one could not help loving her.

How was it she had strayed away so far from the châlet? Would not the comte be annoyed? This was Felix's next question; but Gabrielle only shook her head with a sigh.

Doubtless monsieur was right. Etienne was careful with her—he had always a view to the proprieties; but Valerie was by no means strict. But Etienne would not know of her escapades—he was miles away; a sudden business had called him to Paris.

"To Paris! Is it possible? Do you mean, mademoiselle, that he has left you behind?"

But yes. How could it be otherwise? Had not

monsieur heard what had happened yesterday—
how Valerie had slipped in the ravine over a loose
rock, and had hurt her foot? It was all black
and swollen, and Lisette, her maid, had informed
them that madame had not closed her eyes all
night for the pain. Could monsieur conceive such
tristesse? The poor Etienne had gone off so
unhappy; when anything ailed Valerie he was
miserable.

"But he will return, mademoiselle."

Ah, yes, he would return—in a week or ten days
at the most, and then they must go back to
Brittany, where they had their home. Etienne
would have liked to live in Paris, but he always
said he was not rich enough. "That is because of
me, monsieur," she continued simply, "and because
of the two little sisters, Foinette and Marie, who
are still at the convent."

"Are you not glad to see the world, mademoiselle?" he asked gently.

"Yes, truly, monsieur; but all the same I cried
when I left, and the good sisters cried too. I was
their child, do you see, and I had been there so
long—ever since mamma died; for what could
Etienne do with three little sisters when he was
fighting for his country? It is startling at first to
have one's freedom, and to see people; but when I

go to sleep at night I am always back in the old convent garden, among the tall white lilies, that are the flowers of our lady, and always I seem to hear the tinkling of the bell calling us to the chapel. But, monsieur, will not the châlet be in sight? You must be fatigued with all this foolish talk."

"Is it too far? Have I tired you?" he exclaimed anxiously, for this idea had not occurred to him before, and he fancied that she looked a little weary. "Will you sit down, mademoiselle, on that fallen log, and rest a while?"

But she shook her head. "You must not tempt me, monsieur; Valerie will be so anxious. She charged me not to go too far. When Valerie gets anxious about any one she cries, and then Etienne is angry; he does not like her to shed a tear."

"But if I have tired you, mademoiselle, I shall never forgive myself," returned Hamerton, in such a remorseful voice that Gabrielle smiled.

"Why should you speak in that way?" she said. "It is not your fault or mine that the road is so long; but indeed I did not know it was so far. At the convents our walks were not long, and there were no hills to climb and to put one out of breath."

"Courage, mademoiselle; I see the roof of the

châlet between the trees," he observed in a
relieved tone. "Shall we take this by-path? it will
bring us to the little glade where I saw you first."

"Ah, ciel! how you startled me that day!" she
exclaimed, with her low laugh. "I was in a dream.
I was back in the convent garden among the bee-
hives, and Sister Thérèse was droning—droning
out of her big book; and then something crackled,
and there you stood, monsieur, framed in green
leaves, as though it were your fête day, and you
looked as though you had seen a ghost or a pixie."

"Or a woodland nymph—one of Diana's
maidens," he replied gravely. "Now give me
your hand, mademoiselle; this is a difficult bit of
the path "—and as she laid her warm soft palm
in his, Felix felt a singular throb at his heart.

At the bridge he left her, and went back to the
little glade and threw himself upon the grass.
"Gabrielle," he murmured to himself—"Gabrielle.
So that is her name, and it fits her to a nicety;"
and then he recalled every look and every word
she had spoken. "I have never seen any one like
her," he finished, as he pulled himself together
and returned to the châlet; "she is so grave and
sweet and innocent, so childlike and impulsive,
and yet she is womanly, too."

At *table d'hôte* he watched anxiously for her, but

she did not appear, and he heard afterwards that
she had taken her meal with the comtesse, whose
accident confined her to her room. The next
morning he lingered in the gardens and ravine,
but Mademoiselle de Brienne was invisible; but
after the late *déjeuner* he encountered her in the
corridor leading to the salon. She wore her white
gown and a little black lace fichu, with a knot of
crimson flowers, the whole toilette appeared
charming to him. A blush came to her face when
she saw him, but she evidently expected to be
addressed.

"Good morning, mademoiselle. I trust you
have recovered from your fatigue yesterday, and
that Madame la Comtesse is progressing well."

"Thank Heaven, yes, monsieur; the poor foot
is less swollen and inflamed. Lisette, and that
kind Madame Carruthers—how should one pro-
nounce a name so difficult?—had improvised a
couch in the salon, and Pierre had carried the poor
Valerie in his strong arms. It was better for the
dear sufferer to be in the salon; it was so airy, and
she could talk to people and forget her foot.
Valerie wishes to thank you, monsieur, for your
goodness to me yesterday," finished Gabrielle;
"she saw you in the garden before *déjeuner*. Is
it your pleasure that I make the introduction?"

"Certainly, mademoiselle; it would gratify me much to be presented to madame."

And then Gabrielle gravely and with much dignity introduced the infatuated young man to the salon, where the fragile, bright-eyed countess lay in a nest of Indian shawls on a couch.

She held out her hand to him with a brilliant smile.

"I am pleased to make your acquaintance, Mr. Hamerton. You are a friend of Mrs. Brandon, are you not? I saw you talking to her at *table d'hôte.* You were very good to bring my runaway home yesterday; she was a naughty child, and strayed too far. Yes, Gabrielle chèrie, you were as méchante as possible. I was in a terrible fright. My husband has put her in my charge, and she has only left her convent three weeks, and is like a child learning to walk alone. Ah, what an absurd education for a woman! Do you not agree with me? But I suppose it is treason to say so. There, Gabrielle, Mrs. Carruthers is waiting for you, and Mr. Hamerton is going to amuse me a little. We are compatriots, or at least nearly so;" and, dismissing her with a light kiss on either cheek, the voluble little countess went on with the conversation.

CHAPTER VI.

"YOU HAVE MY BEST WISHES, MONSIEUR."

"Stay, stay at home, my heart, and rest—
Home-keeping hearts are happiest ;
For those that wander they know not where
Are full of trouble and full of care :
To stay at home is best."

LONGFELLOW.

VALERIE COMTESSE DE BRIENNE was certainly a fascinating little person. Under other circumstances Mr. Hamerton would have found his *tête-à-tête* decidedly amusing, but her abrupt dismissal of Gabrielle somewhat disconcerted him, and it cost him some effort to conceal his chagrin.

Perfectly oblivious of his slight constraint, Madame de Brienne chatted on in her free American way. She was a clever little person, and had considerable humour—*esprit*, as her

Parisian friends called it; there was something naïve in her thorough satisfaction with herself and her surroundings.

"I guess that I have made a lucky hit," she had said, when she informed her immediate circle in New York that she had accepted the handsome French count. "Etienne is just mad about me, and I calculate that I shall make it last." And Valerie kept her word, for the Comte de Brienne literally idolized his sprightly but fragile wife.

She adapted herself with wonderful ease to her change of circumstances, and took intense pride and pleasure in beautifying the old Brittany chateau. She delighted in hearing herself addressed as Madame la Comtesse, and secretly adored her husband. She showed a great deal of kindness to his step-sisters, and refused to understand the ill-natured hints of Mademoiselle Stephanie de Brienne, that it was a pity that her nephew should be saddled with the maintenance of three step-sisters. "You will find out the inconvenience for yourself, Valerie," she added grimly, "when Gabrielle is old enough to leave the convent, and Etienne has to provide her trousseau and dot with your money." But if Valerie winced at this plain speaking, she put a good face on it.

"She is terrible—this old Aunt Stephanie of

yours, Etienne," she said, with a grimace, when
mademoiselle had left the chateau; "she puts
my teeth on edge with her sour speeches."

"Pauvre petite!" observed the comte, tenderly;
"but we must have patience. Mademoiselle has a
high spirit; she is a great lady; she never forgets
that she is a de Brienne."

"I am de Brienne too," returned the little
comtesse, stoutly, on which the comte kissed her
hand; "but she shall not set me against those
poor dear girls just because they are poor, and we
have to maintain them. What if it be my money?"
continued Valerie, recklessly; "it is yours too;
we have nothing separate, have we, Etienne?"

"Mon ange! Your generosity is admirable, and
I—I am the happiest of men. What do we care
for Mademoiselle ma Tante? She is Catholique,
but you, my Valerie, are the better Christian, and
the saints will bless your goodness to those poor
children."

"Chut! You will turn my head, my friend, with
all these compliments." But Valerie's bright eyes
were slightly moist. Ah! well, she loved power;
her *rôle* pleased her. She had no children of her
own—not yet, but perhaps one day that happiness
might be given to her. It was not a difficult part to
carry bon-bons and cadeaux to the convent, and to

be almost smothered in kisses in return. " See how Madame la Comtesse loves these poor little ones " —that was what the good nuns said to each other.

Madame la Comtesse, with her sprained, bandaged foot, was in need of amusement. The hotel was emptying fast, and a clever young English barrister was not to be despised. Valerie loved society, and, though she no longer flirted, Etienne did not like it ; her cleverness and vivacity made her very attractive to men, and she accepted their homage as her right.

To his delight, Mr. Hamerton soon found himself on intimate terms with Madame de Brienne. Her helpless condition made his assistance indispensable. He could fetch and carry ; offer his arm when, with the aid of a gold-headed stick, she managed to hobble to the *salle à manger* or to a garden-seat ; and, as Gabrielle was always with her, he could enjoy her society without stint or limit.

Madame de Brienne's free American notions were very far removed from the traditional Parisian etiquette. Mademoiselle's scanty grey hairs would have stood on end if she could have watched the trio ; that Gabrielle should be conversing with an unmarried man ; that she should saunter about the garden and even in the ravine under his guardianship would have seemed inconceivable to her.

" ' When the cat is away ; ' " how runs the good
old proverb? Perhaps her husband's absence
made Valerie a little reckless. "What is the poor
child to do," she said to herself; "I cannot chain
her to my couch. These French notions are
absurd—antiquated. Mr. Hamerton is a gentleman, his people are good, he is quiet and gentle,
one can trust him. When Etienne returns he can
take Gabrielle about with him, and then there will
be no need for Mr. Hamerton. Why should she
lose her holiday for an idea, a bubble, a paltry
French sentiment?" And it was in this way that
madame washed her pretty little hands of all
possible mischief.

The count was detained in Paris, and more than
a fortnight passed—an enchanted fortnight to Mr.
Hamerton ; while to Gabrielle? Alas for her, that
a sweet new light had begun to dawn in those
lovely eyes ; while the mere sight of the quiet
young Englishman would bring a vivid blush to
her cheek. They were always together at *déjeuner*,
at dinner, and even when they drank their coffee
on the balcony. In the fresh dewy mornings he
knew where to find her—in the little chapel halfway up the road, above the châlet. Sometimes he
would saunter up the hill to meet her, as she came
down, looking pure and sweet in her white gown,

with her missal in her hand. At other times he
would steal into the dim scented chapel, and watch
her kneeling at her devotions. It did him good
only to look at her. They were not of the same
church, and yet he longed to kneel beside her, and
join those pure petitions.

"Of what sins could she accuse herself?" he
thought, when he saw her approaching the con-
fessional. The sight made him angry, and drove
him away ; and then his brow cleared as he softly
quoted Tennyson's words—

> " I know her : the worst thought that she has
> Is whiter even than her pretty hand ;"

for he felt, with a lover's unreasoning instinct, that
he could have staked his all on the purity and
goodness of this young girl, of whose existence
three weeks ago he had not been conscious. Yes,
he loved her—he knew it now—with the whole
strength of his nature ; and, if possible, he meant
to win her for his wife. And why should it not
be possible? As far as Gabrielle herself were concerned, he would have no difficulty. He could not
be blind to the fact that already there was strong
sympathy between them ; they talked less, and
the silence between them was often unbroken.
She grew shyer with him, and sometimes her voice

trembled. Yes, he could make her love him—he
was sure of that.

Would the Comte de Brienne countenance such
a marriage for his step-sister? True, the difference
in their religion was an obstacle; but he thought
it might be got over. He was not a religious man
himself, he owned with compunction; possibly the
comte might be equally worldly, as he had allied
himself with a Protestant. He need not consider
this point. If Gabrielle married him, she should
be free to worship as she liked.

Then as regarded other matters. She was poor
and dependent on her brother; her dot would be
small. She could not expect to make a great
match. He had some private fortune of his own,
and his prospects were good. He could offer his
wife every comfort, and an entrance into the best
society; he thought even the Comte de Brienne
need not look down on him. On the whole, he
was far from hopeless.

That day, as they strolled together through the
ravine, he talked much about himself and his
earlier life. He drew a vivid portraiture of his
sisters Laura and Sophy, and of his only brother
Charlton; and he explained to her, smiling a little
to himself at the naïve ignorance she displayed on
all practical matters, the nature of his profession,
and his plans for the future.

"I shall marry. It is always best for a man to marry," he said rather hurriedly; "and I am domestic, and should like a fireside of my own."

"Monsieur should please himself, certainly;" but she turned aside as she spoke to break off a flowering branch beside her, and he could not see her face.

"You think I am wise, that my circumstances would warrant such an intention?" he persisted, somewhat foolishly it must be owned, for what could this convent-bred child know of such things?

"Monsieur is the best judge of his own circumstances," she said shyly; "to me," she continued, laughing a little over the wonder of being consulted, "monsieur seems rich, fabulously rich— n'est ce pas."

"No, mademoiselle; but I have enough for comfort, and it seems to me"—looking at her downcast face—"that we are alike in not caring about money."

"I have never had money, monsieur, in the convent. We did not need it; and now Valerie is so kind she gives me all I want. If I ask for anything it is mais oui certainement, as though it were the most natural thing. Such generosity makes one ashamed."

"I should love to give you things, mademoiselle." He said it almost under his breath ; but she heard it, and a blush overspread her face, but she made no answer. "Perhaps I ought not to have said that," he continued, and there was softness in his tones ; "but sometimes you seem such a child to me."

" But I am not a child, monsieur," she whispered.

" I know that. Please forgive me. If you knew how I reverence you, Mademoiselle Gabrielle "—her name escaping him in his excitement. " I want you to do something for me."

" For you ? "—lifting her dark eyes to his face.

" Yes, for me. We are friends, are we not? great friends, so I trust. Will you take my hand and say that you wish me success—that you hope my dearest wish on earth may be fulfilled? I think it will be a good omen for my future if you could tell me that."

She stood for a moment hesitating, as though she were doubtful of his meaning. " Is that all ? " she asked at last, in a low voice.

" It is all that you can do for me at present."

" But it is such a bagatelle," she returned, trying to laugh. But his repressed agitation communicated itself to her, and he could see that she was trembling; her very fingers were fluttering as she placed her hand in his.

"You have my best wishes, monsieur. May le bon Dieu give you your heart's desire. Have I said that rightly?"

"You have said it perfectly; thanks a thousand times. Now we must go back to madame;" for he was afraid of himself—afraid that if he remained longer with her, he might be tempted to speak more openly of his hopes. His heart's desire; did she guess what that was? He had no means of knowing, for Gabrielle did not open her lips again; and the moment they entered the garden she left Felix to make his way alone to the seat where madame was reclining, and took refuge in the house.

"What have you done with Gabrielle?" asked madame, a little inquisitively, as she looked up at him. "She has sped across the grass like a frightened fawn."

But Mr. Hamerton returned an evasive answer; he had an idea that Madame de Brienne guessed at his infatuation for her young sister-in-law, and did not discourage it. He wondered if it would be well to make her his confidante, and get her to plead his cause with her husband; but before he could make up his mind on this point, she began another subject.

" I wanted to speak to Gabrielle ; she would be
so pleased. My husband is returning to-night ;
he will arrive late, and perhaps he may bring a
friend with him, the Comte D'Arcy. They are
old friends, and have fought in the same regiment.
He was Etienne's colonel—— "

"And the comte returns to-night ? " He felt a
sudden pang as he said this. Their time of freedom,
of happy wanderings, of careless surveillance was
over. Gabrielle would now be always under her
brother's wing. The Comte D'Arcy would be a
bore ; he almost felt vexed at madame's radiant
good-humour. She was delighted at the prospect
of seeing her husband again, and had made a
brilliant toilette in honour of the occasion.

" My husband seems in high spirits," she continued. "He speaks of having something very
pleasant to communicate to me, to enliven my
fête day. He is mysterious ; perhaps he has some
wonderful cadeau. I have never met Count D'Arcy.
La comtesse died last year, and he was in retire-
ment. He has a fine estate in Normandy. Etienne
has often spoken of it."

She talked incessantly in this strain, until Felix
made an excuse to leave her. In the corridor he
came upon Gabrielle ; she was standing at a
window, looking at the snow-peaks with the last

pink glow lingering on them. She wore a jewelled cross at her neck that had belonged to her mother, and the rubies shone redly on her white dress as he stepped up to her. She started and would have moved away, but he detained her. He must keep her by him a moment. After this evening they would not be alone together.

" Mademoiselle—Gabrielle "—he separated the words involuntarily—" there is something I must tell you. Madam has just informed me that the comte is to arrive this evening."

" Etienne! but that is good news. Why do you look so solemn, monsieur? I shall be charmed to see that dearest of brothers. Oh, how enchanted Valerie will be! "

" Madame certainly seems in wonderful spirits. Your brother is to bring a friend with him, the Comte D'Arcy."

Then Gabrielle's eyes began to sparkle.

" The brave colonel, who is Etienne's hero? But it will be adorable to see and perhaps speak with him. He is so brave; once he saved Etienne's life. Valerie must tell you that story, but it always makes her cry. In the convent chapel Marie and I have often prayed for him—for the brave man who carried our dear wounded one out of the battle. Once I gave him my intention. When one is grateful, monsieur, and has nothing else to offer, one can always give one's prayers—'the dews of charity,' as Sister Nathalie used to say, 'which are drawn up to heaven, and return again in showers of blessings.' Was she not right, monsieur?"

"How can I tell?" he replied a little hoarsely, and his eyes fell under that pure glance; "but doubtless you are right. I am glad my news has pleased you; for myself, I shall regret our pleasant walks and talks. With your brother and the Comte D'Arcy, I am afraid my society will be no longer needed."

He tried to speak coldly, nay, indifferently, but his eyes told another tale, and a deep glow spread over the girl's face.

"One must always need one's friends. Why do you speak as though you would be de trop, monsieur? Etienne will be charmed to make your acquaintance."

She spoke quickly, almost nervously, moving away all the time. But he followed her closely, and they reached the head of the stairs together.

"One moment before you descend, mademoiselle —only one moment, Gabrielle."

And then, as she turned to him, steadying herself by laying a hand on the balustrade, he put his

over it with a firm detaining grasp. " Tell me one
thing for my comfort—that you do not want to
get rid of me ; that you will always keep me for
your friend ? "

It was a declaration of love, said in those tones,
and her head drooped until her face was hidden.

" Speak, Gabrielle—just that word."

"I never want monsieur to leave us," she
whispered ; and then at the sound of footsteps
she almost tore her hand away.

"I am not wrong—she loves me," he muttered
to himself. " I will speak to the comte to-morrow."

When he entered the *salle à manger* half an
hour later, he saw at once that the travellers had
arrived. Madame was seated beside her husband
looking positively radiant, and on the other side
of Gabrielle was an elderly, weather-beaten man
with a grey moustache, who looked every inch a
soldier.

Madame la Comtesse made the necessary intro-
ductions, and both the gentlemen accosted Mr.
Hamerton with perfect civility and good breeding.
The Comte de Brienne thanked him for his polite
attentions to his wife.

" Madame tells me how much she is indebted to
you for your kindness, monsieur. She would have
been terribly ennuyée in this strange place without

your friendly services. I am heavily in your debt, Monsieur Hamerton."

" I am afraid the debt is all on the other side," returned Felix, trying to appear at his ease ; and then he glanced at Gabrielle. She was listening attentively to something the Comte D'Arcy was telling her. Her cheeks were flushed, her eyes downcast, but she looked unmistakably happy. But throughout the meal Felix never once heard her voice. She was evidently too shy to venture on any conversation with the hero. As soon as dinner was over they all disappeared, and he saw them no more that night.

The next morning he half made up his mind to walk to the little chapel as usual, but a moment later he saw Gabrielle pass under his window. Her brother was with her. They seemed talking rather earnestly, and she did not look up. Felix took his walk in another direction, lost his way, and came back heated and tired to find *déjeuner* nearly over. Madame de Brienne, who was rising from her place with her husband's assistance, nodded to him with a smile. Gabrielle had perhaps just quitted the table, and he sat down in no pleasant mood to appease his hunger. Things were not going well this morning ; as he had predicted, the arrival of the stranger had spoiled

everything. He had letters to write, which kept
him in his own room for a couple of hours. When
he had finished he went down into the garden.
After strolling about aimlessly for a little, he
questioned one of the servants, and learnt from
him that the Comte de Brienne and his friend had
driven out ; he believed madame was with them.

"But not mademoiselle ? "

No ; Pierre believed that la jeune demoiselle was
in her room. Would monsieur like to question
Lisette ?

But Felix could not take such a liberty. He
would only place himself where Gabrielle could
see him from the window. He had already discovered that her room was near his. He would
read, or pretend to read, and perhaps by-and-by
there would be a shadow on the grass, and he
would see her standing before him in her white
gown, and some flowers in her hand—always some
flowers. "Monsieur, what are you reading ? " for
ever she would have some such question to put
to him. Oh, he could hear her voice so plainly !
But he waited hour after hour, but she did not
come, and his heart began to feel like lead in his
breast. Was she ill ? Had anything happened to
vex her ? Why was she shutting herself up in her
room, and driving him to despair, instead of

basking in the sunshine and the sweet air as usual ?

When he heard the sound of wheels, he dragged himself up moodily and went up to his room to prepare for dinner. Thank Heaven! they must meet in half an hour, and even if he could not speak to her, he would be able to see from her face if anything troubled her, and afterwards, before he slept, he would demand an audience from the count.

What was his disappointment, then, when he entered the *salle à manger*, to see her empty chair. He looked so pale and apprehensive that Madame de Brienne, who was watching him, leant forward and, under the cover of her husband's talk, said in a low voice in English—

"My little sister has a bad headache, and we have recommended her to rest. Come to me in the garden presently. I have much to tell you while the gentlemen take their walk;" and then she unfurled her fan and motioned away the soup. "It is too hot to eat, my friend," she said, addressing her husband. "It seems to me that we shall have a storm presently, and the fear of it has taken away my appetite."

"Is she not a coward, count?" returned her husband. "Fear of a thunderstorm is thy last fancy, my Valerie. Shall I remain with you in the garden, or will you take refuge with Gabrielle?"

"Now you are laughing at me, Etienne," observed madame, with a pout; "and I hate any one to laugh at me. No, no; go—go with your friend and finish your business. Mr. Hamerton will take care of me; is it not so, monsieur?" and she looked across at him with her brilliant smile.

But Felix only responded with a bow. He was not in the humour to indulge in harmless badinage with the fascinating Valerie. His thoughts were with the dark-eyed girl who was suffering in her chamber above, or with Lizette's kindly ministration. "May le bon Dieu give you your heart's desire;" he could hear her say that over and over again.

CHAPTER VII.

A LOST PARADISE.

"That loss is common would not make
My own less bitter, rather more :
Too common ! Never morning wore
To evening, but some heart did break."

TENNYSON.

"MR. HAMERTON, why are you so triste and bored this evening? Have your English letters brought bad news ? "

Madame de Brienne put these questions in her usual airy fashion, as she disposed of herself and her laces comfortably on the balcony seat. Lizette had just brought her out some light wraps ; but, in spite of her gay *insouciance*, an unprejudiced observer would have detected a slight uneasiness in Valerie's manner.

"My domestic budget has been perfectly satisfactory," returned Felix, striving to appear at his ease, but failing signally. "How have you passed the day, madame?"

"To tell you the truth, Mr. Hamerton, it has seemed like three days rolled into one, so much has happened in it. What do you suppose is the wonderful piece of news that my husband has brought? It has almost taken my breath away. Etienne is so impetuous; if he thinks of a thing, it is already done. He was like that in his court-ing—'Take me or leave me; but if you leave me, I shall blow my brains out.' That is the sort of wooing that makes a woman sure of her own mind. Oh, these De Briennes are terrible! Their yea is yea with a vengeance."

"And the news?"

"Oh, the news"—and Valerie's voice was a little shrill, as though it were not quite under her command—"is nothing more or less than the betrothal of Mademoiselle de Brienne to the Comte D'Arcy; voilà tout, monsieur."

For one moment, one insupportable moment, there was dead silence; the solid ground beneath Felix's feet seemed to rock; and then, in a voice that sounded strange to himself—

"Are you jesting with me, madame?"

"Mon Dieu, should I jest on such a subject? Etienne's sister, too. Alas, no; it is a fact accomplished, it was arranged in Paris. They were all there—Mademoiselle Stephanié and the Marquise de Beauvilliers. She is Count D'Arcy's sister. It is a brilliant match; my husband is enchanted. Think of a man like Comte D'Arcy wishing to ally himself with our little one, who has no special beauty, at least at present, and whose dot will be so insignificant! No wonder my poor little sister is overwhelmed."

"Good heavens, madame!" exclaimed Felix, in a tone that betrayed inward torture. "Is this what you call a marriage? That child who has but just left her convent, and a man old enough to be her grandfather."

"Fie, Mr. Hamerton; you are exaggerating. The comte is not sixty yet; and he is a fine-looking man. True, he is a widower, but he has no children; he is a kind-hearted gentleman, and a brave man. He will treat Gabrielle with the utmost tenderness. Do you think Etienne would give his cherished little one to a monster? The comte is his friend. In old days they were in the same regiment. Comte D'Arcy saved my husband's life; he carried him out of the battle under fire. Etienne is devoted to him; he says nothing has ever pleased him so much as this marriage."

"One moment, madame. Has Mademoiselle de

Brienne consented to this monstrous arrangement ? "

"You talk strangely, Mr. Hamerton ;" and Valerie
drew herself up a little stiffly. " But perhaps your
English notions make it difficult for you to understand. Gabrielle is a good, obedient child. She
adores Etienne ; his will is law to her. She re-
verences the Comte D'Arcy ; it is part of her
family creed. To me she confided that she had no
wish to marry ; so many girls say that. The
subject agitated her, but she knew better than to
remonstrate. And the comte was very gentle with
her ; his manners are perfect. In spite of his grey
hairs, any woman could lose her heart to him."

" Am I to understand, madame, that mademoiselle is not permitted a choice in her own destiny ? "
Felix's words came thickly through his dry lips.

" Gabrielle is quite resigned to her brilliant lot,"
returned madame, rather pettishly.

She was a kind-hearted little person, and hated
to inflict pain ; and this sombre young Englishman,
with his pale face and fierce eyes, seemed to
reproach her as though she were the author of
his unhappiness. Why had she not been more
strict in her surveillance ? He has lost his heart
to Gabrielle. It was a pity, certainly, but he would
get over it. Etienne would not have entertained

his suit for a moment; he was ambitious for his sister. Gabrielle was not striking at present, but she held the prospect of future beauty.

"I have been talking to her for more than an hour," she went on; "until she told me that I made her head ache. The comte is adorably generous; he will make magnificent settlements. He has a fine estate in Normandy, and a suite of apartments in Paris that are truly superb; and he intends to refurnish her rooms in the chateau. He already regards her with true affection."

"Madame, why have you permitted us to be so much together? Could you not see?" and then he stopped, almost choked with his emotion.

Then Valerie started, and two burning spots came into her cheek.

"Mr. Hamerton, for Heaven's sake be careful, or you will get me into trouble with my husband. I was careless; I meant no harm. How could I guess what was in Etienne's mind? We had not discussed Gabrielle's marriage. She is so good; she is a little angel of patience and resignation; she would not grieve us for worlds. If you value my peace—her peace—ah, what am I saying?— the peace of a happy united family, go away, and leave us together. I am selfish; I ask too much, perhaps; but you do not know the De Briennes.

Etienne is proud; he has a high spirit. He would
not permit an Englishman to love his sister, or to
talk to her; he would regard it as an insult. The
De Brienne women hear of love first from their
husbands."

In her misery she laid her small feverish hands
on his arm. It was evident that Valerie was in
grim earnest for once in her life. Her reckless
disregard of family traditions might cost her and
Gabrielle dear. Perhaps she was selfish in her
fear, but she was nevertheless very sorry for the
young man.

"Very well, I will go; but I must see her first,"
he began; but Valerie gave him a little push.

"Hush! they are returning, my husband and
the comte. Go into the house. I want Lisette;
she must bring more wraps—anything—everything.
They must not find us talking like this. Another
shawl; yes—go—go!"

She stamped her tiny foot in her impatience,
and Mr. Hamerton reluctantly went on her
bidding. He found Lizette, gave her the order,
and went up to his room. He was still numb and
dizzy with the blow he had received, and which
the irony of fate had dealt him; the walls of the
châlet seemed to suffocate him; but he must be
near her this one night more!

As the thought passed through his mind, the faint gleam of something white at the far end of the corridor attracted his attention. The end where he stood was dark, but the moonlight illumined the upper part. Could it be Gabrielle? It moved, and then stood still. His heart began to beat more quickly ; the painful stricture of the throat relaxed, and he drew his breath more freely ; then he walked noiselessly up the corridor.

It was Gabrielle, but she was absorbed in her thoughts and did not hear him. Was she at her devotions? Her hands were crossed over her bosom, and her lips were moving. She looked paler—etherealized in the white light, and there was a great sadness in her beautiful eyes.

"Jamais—jamais. Oh, mon Dieu, must it be so?" he heard her murmur. But at his softly uttered "Gabrielle" she turned and extended her hands to him.

"It is you, monsieur. I saw you with Valerie ; she has been telling you. Oh !" for his grasp hurt her, and she was looking in his face as though she saw something there that pained her.

"Yes, I have heard. Gabrielle, for God's sake tell me if you are happy ; if your brother's arrangement pleases you. You have been weeping ; your eyes are swollen. Gabrielle, my dearest, will you not refuse to marry this man, who is old enough to be your father?"

"Oh, hush, monsieur!" and she strove to disengage herself, casting a frightened glance behind her, but he held her hands too tightly. "You are kind; you mean well; but you do not understand our customs. How can I refuse to marry the husband my brother has chosen for me?"

"But it makes you unhappy?" he asked tenaciously.

"Unhappy? Oh no. I have to obey Etienne, and I reverence the good man who is to do me so much honour. It is true that I wept a little, because I did not want to be married, and I begged that Etienne would send me back to the convent, where I was so happy; but they laughed at me and called me a silly child, and Valerie talked about my corbeille. Perhaps I am foolish," she continued; "but life is so solemn, and the future frightens me; and I must bid you good-bye, monsieur, and that troubles me too; but I shall never forget your kindness."

"Gabrielle, I cannot let you go. How am I to live without you?"

Then she looked at him with a smile of divine tenderness. "I shall pray for monsieur, that le bon Dieu may give him his heart's desire."

"My heart's desire? Oh, Gabrielle, when you know!"

"It is not for me to know monsieur's private affairs," she said quickly, and there was a new dignity about her that recalled to his mind that she was a De Brienne. "Monsieur has been good to tell me so much already. It is well to pray for one's friends—that the saints and the Holy Virgin may have them in their keeping, and in my new home"—she sighed, and then recovered herself—"I shall still remember my friends. Will you suffer me to go now, monsieur?"

"One word. Is there to be no hope at all for me? Have you indeed given your word to marry the Comte D'Arcy?"

"Most certainly my word is given. We are affianced! Is that not the term?"

"And you mean to be happy, Gabrielle?"

"I mean to do my duty; happiness is a gift of le bon Dieu, n'est-ce pas, monsieur? It is for Him to give or withhold; that is what the good sisters taught me. But I will pray always for monsieur's happiness."

"I am not worthy of your prayers," he replied, kneeling down beside her and covering the thin young hands with his kisses.

These were his last words to her, and only a

deep sigh answered him. Then he left her, and
stole down the gallery. He paused for an instant
on the threshold of his room, and looked back.
Her hands were crossed on her bosom again, and
she was looking up at the clouds scudding across
the moon.

The next day Felix left the châlet. When he
took leave of the Comte de Brienne and his wife,
Gabrielle was with them. She looked very grave
and pale, and when he took her hand it was cold
as ice.

" I wish mademoiselle every happiness," was all
he said.

" Monsieur has my good wishes also," she returned, almost inaudibly.

But Valerie, who was watching them both very
closely, shivered as though she were cold.

" I always honour a brave man, Mr. Hamerton,"
she said, in the lowest possible voice, as he bowed
over her hand.

But to this no response was possible ; and then
as he went out the gate of his paradise closed
behind him.

Such was the substance of the story that Felix
Hamerton related to Constance, but he told it
very briefly. It was not until years afterwards,
when the circumstances of his life were changed,

that he ever told it in its entirety. Nevertheless, Constance wept freely as she listened.

"Felix, my poor Felix, do forgive me!"

"Forgive you, Constance!" he repeated, in his surprise. He had expected sympathy, and even her tears did not astonish him; but this was the last speech he was prepared to hear.

"Yes, forgive me for having teased you so unmercifully. When I think of all the nonsense I talked, I am ready to sink into the ground with shame. But how was I to guess that your life had held such trouble? You have been so patient and so long-suffering. Well, it has taught me one lesson—never to judge any one again."

"Then in that case I am content to be a finger-post."

"Oh, do not laugh; I cannot bear it. What a story—how pathetic! That sweet Gabrielle! And it is seven years ago. Let me think a moment. Was it not the time when you came back looking so ill, as though you had had a fever?"

"I had had a touch of fever in Paris."

"Yes, I remember. We were all so shocked at your appearance; but we never guessed;" and her eyes were full of tears again.

Then he took her hand and pressed it in his brotherly fashion.

"You are very good to give me so much sympathy. Your kindness makes me feel as though I ought to have told you before; but it is not easy to speak of such things."

"I understand what you mean, but it is safe with me. I should not speak of such a thing even to my husband. Felix, this is not all, surely. In all these years have you heard nothing, have you never seen her again?" But she was almost sorry that she asked the question when she saw his face.

"I have seen her once," he returned; "it was in the opera-house in Paris two years ago. I recognized her at once. She looked much older—ten years older, but very beautiful. I always knew how beautiful she would be some day. She was blazing with diamonds, but her grandeur had not changed her. I could read that in her eyes; she was still Gabrielle."

"Do you think she is happy, Felix?"

"How can I tell? Did she not say herself that happiness was a gift of le bon Dieu? Her eyes were sad, but then she had just lost her child."

"Her child?"

"Her only one—a boy. Madame de Brienne told me; I met her accidentally at Cannes. She was very friendly and pleasant. She was talking about her two children, when she told me that suddenly. 'He was two years old, and as beautiful as an angel,' were her words. 'The count idolized him ; he will never get over it ; the sorrow has aged him. Gabrielle is as unselfish as ever. She hides her own grief that she may not add to his, but her boy was everything to her. I tell Etienne that she is more a saint than a woman. I never knew any one so good. The poor people round the château D'Arcy quite worship her.'"

"Do you think she saw you, Felix?"

"I do not know—I am not sure, but I almost think not. Until I spoke to Madame de Brienne the sad look in her eyes troubled me, but of course it was the loss of her child." He sighed a little wearily. "Let us change the subject ; it is not good to dwell on the past."

"Let me say something more, and then you shall be left in peace. Does not the mere fact of her being married make things easier to bear? Do not think me unsympathetic, Felix ; I could not be that, but seven years is a long time, and—— " She hesitated.

"You want to ask me if I have not got over it, but you lack courage. In a way I suppose I have, but while Gabrielle lives I feel as though no woman could ever take her place. Do I shock you?"

"No, for I understand you too well. You have

a faithful nature, Felix. Perhaps I ought not to say it; but if the count be old——" Then she saw at once that the remark displeased him.

"We must be very careful not to formulate such a thought, even to ourselves," he returned slowly. "The count is hale and hearty, and I trust has many years of life before him." Then he paused a moment, and went on as though he were pursuing an old and familiar line of thought. "The mere fact of your hinting that, shows that you have not grasped the salient point of Gabrielle's character. She is utterly unselfish; she would not rest until she had taught herself to love her husband. There would be first gratitude and veneration for the hero, and then affection for the father of her boy." He spoke as though he were thinking aloud, and Constance felt rebuked—as though she were treading uninvited in some holy place. Gabrielle de Brienne was only a sacred memory to Felix; but none the less, so she felt, had she spoilt his life. But for that brief romance of his, he might be making some other woman happy. "Oh, the pity of it!" thought Constance, speaking out of the fulness of her satisfied life. "If any man deserves a good wife, it is Felix; he is so strong and so gentle, and I think he is less selfish than other people."

"I have talked you into the blues," observed

Felix, regretfully. "Let me ring for the lights;" and he put his hand on the bell.

He had scarcely done so before they heard carriage wheels, and the next moment Mr. Lorimer and his brother-in-law entered the room. They looked fagged and muddy, but seemed in high spirits, and condoled with Felix on losing the day's sport.

"Do go and change your things; you are both as wet as possible," remonstrated Mrs. Wyndham.

"Well, it was a trifle muddy," remarked Reginald, "especially in the spinney; in fact, it was a perfect swamp. Well, come along, Wyndham; I am as hungry as a hunter. I feel like Esau before he had his lentils. By-the-by, Felix, Sir William sent you his compliments, and would be glad to see you on Friday."

"Thanks awfully, but I have made up my mind to go up to town to-morrow; honour bright, Reg, I cannot spare another day. If you like to invite me to eat my Christmas dinner with you, I will not refuse; and perhaps I might stay over the New Year."

"But we wanted Reg to come to us, didn't we, Harcourt?" and Constance looked appealingly at her husband.

"No, no," responded Reginald, eagerly; "Hamerton is booked, and I mean to keep him to his engagement. You and Harcourt and the boys must come too. I hate Christmas in London, and it will be a less dreary affair if I can see you all round me here." And as Reginald seemed in earnest, the thing was definitely arranged, though Mr. Wyndham pretended to grumble as soon as he reached the privacy of his own dressing-room.

"Reginald makes us awfully comfortable, and I believe he likes to have us, but we must not tire out our welcome; a fellow does not always want to be saddled with his own belongings."

"We should never tire out Reggie," returned Constance, confidently. "He does love to talk to you, Harcourt—he often tells me so; and the change is so good for you."

"When Reginald marries again, he will not want us quite so often," observed Mr. Wyndham.

But to this Constance made no reply. Felix Hamerton's sad story had struck deep; for the present at least she was cured of her love of matchmaking.

CHAPTER VIII.

THE LETTER WITH THE BLACK SEAL.

"God keeps a niche
In heaven to hold our idols ; and albeit
He brake them to our faces, and denied
That our close kisses should impair their white,
I know we shall behold them raised, complete,
Their dust shook off, their beauty glorified,
New memnons singing in the great God-light."

E. B. BROWNING.

THERE are curious coincidences in life. Ever afterwards Felix Hamerton thought it one of the strangest experiences that had ever befallen him, that he should have told that story to Constance on that evening. If he had guessed what was in store for him, would he ever have brought himself to break the silence ? But not then or afterwards did he answer this question.

Human life is full of these mysterious surprises.

Our friend has gone away, perhaps to the other end of the world ; he has passed out of our daily existence ; we have ceased to think of him ; the hand of Time, the inexorable, has blotted out the familiar lineaments from the canvas of the present. One day we remember him ; something he has said or done occurs to us with peculiar vividness ; his face, his very tricks of voice and manner, are fresh in our memory. Suddenly we look up ; there is our friend coming round the corner and smiling at us. A sort of shock goes through us. What does it mean ?

Or, again, we have heard nothing for so many years ; but no news is good news, so all must be well. All is well, indeed, but not in our way. That black-edged envelope with the foreign stamp bears a sombre message to us.

Such a letter lay beside Felix Hamerton's plate the next morning. He glanced at it curiously once or twice as he went on with his breakfast. Such letters were no novelty to him ; his business brought him a host of strange correspondents. Had he ever seen that small pointed handwriting before ? A sort of conviction that it was not quite unknown to him made him at last break the heavy black seal and read the signature. Constance, who was that moment glancing in his direction, saw a quick startled look spring to his eyes. Then he laid down the letter again, and made some attempt to finish his meal.

A little time afterwards she encountered her brother in the hall. He had been interviewing his housekeeper.

"Where is Felix ?" she asked.

"He has gone for a walk," was the reply. "He said he had some business to think over, and he wanted to be alone; something vexatious, I expect, for he looked awfully glum. He has made up his mind to take the 5.40 train from Grantham. I shall drive him in, and be back in time for dinner."

"I suppose Harcourt is writing his letters in the library. By-the-by, Reggie, he has quite decided that we must go back on Monday. He wanted to leave me behind for a few days, but I would not hear of that; he does not give himself proper time for his meals unless I am there to look after him."

"I must not press you to stay," returned Reginald, discontentedly, "but it is a pretty clean sweep—Hamerton this evening, and you and Harcourt and the boys on Monday. I shall be fit to hang myself on Monday evening."

"Dear Reggie, if you knew how I hate to leave

you!"—pressing his arm caressingly. "But you must go out more. Go over to the Gate House— Mrs. Winter is always so pleased to see you; and then you must run up to us for a week or so at the end of next month."

"Oh, I shall get on all right," was his reply to this; "don't bother your head about me. Harcourt is very good to spare you so much as he does. Would you like me to drive you over to the Gate House to-morrow, to say good-bye? We could bring Miss Winter back if you like."

And Constance joyfully consented to this. If Reginald chose to suggest Violet of his own account, she would not throw cold water on his plan; on the contrary, she would go at once to the library and write the most persuasive little note to Violet, bidding her be ready for them on the following afternoon.

Felix did not come in to luncheon, but Reginald did not seem at all surprised.

"I suppose he has gone for a good long stretch, and will get some bread and cheese at an inn; that is generally his way. He has left orders to have his things packed up. Harcourt and I are going for a stroll by-and-by, but we shall be back long before it is time to start for Grantham. Will you come with us, Constance?"

But Mrs. Wyndham excused herself. She could not quite divest herself of an uneasy fancy that Felix had received some bad news. It was hardly like him to absent himself so long on this last day. As she needed exercise, she put on some wraps—for the day was damp and chilly—and walked briskly up and down the avenue. Felix would see her on his return, and would join her. But she had walked for more than half an hour before she saw him coming through the copse. He was walking slowly as though he were tired, but he quickened his steps as soon as he caught sight of her.

"You have come out to meet me," he said at once.

"Yes. What a time you have been! It is past three, and—oh, Felix, what is the matter?"

She had not intended to put the question so abruptly, but she was almost startled by the change in him. He had a grey, worn look on his face, and yet his eyes were strangely bright. Perhaps it was a little odd of her, but at that moment she realized how Felix would look when he was old. His features seemed pinched and dwindled, but as he spoke the impression disappeared.

"Shall you be afraid to sit down?" was his reply.

"My walk has taken it out of me, and I want to show you something."

Then she looked at him in speechless dread, as he took the foreign envelope from his pocket. He had a small book in his hand, which he put carefully in his pocket.

"You have taken a sister's place to me," he said quietly, "and I am going to let you read this. Do not hurry with it. I must go to the house for a few minutes to speak to Norton, but I will be back directly."

But she laid her hand on his arm. "Let me go back with you and ask Norton to give you some wine ; you look dreadful."

"There is no need ; I will ask for it myself, and a crust of bread as well. I have forgotten all about luncheon. Let me find you here when I return ;" and then he left her.

Constance watched him until he was out of sight. She was afraid to read the letter, she was so sure that it contained bad news. Nevertheless, his confidence gratified her ; she liked to feel that he trusted her.

The letter was as follows :—

"DEAR MR. HAMERTON,
    "We have met so recently that I shall not need to recall myself to your memory. Ah ! how little we thought, that day

at Cannes, when I was telling you about my darlings, that this terrible thing would happen. My husband is in great trouble— what do I say?—we are all in trouble. That dear angel whom we loved so tenderly has passed to her rest; our beloved Gabrielle is gone, and the count is broken-hearted.

"In the old days your heart was broken too. I saw it in your face, though you said so little. Can you forgive me my careless surveillance, my gross negligence? Ah! it was all my fault. Etienne knows it now, and he has permitted me to write. 'It is long ago,' he says, 'and young men's hearts are soon healed;' but I tell him not always, for you have never married.

"This is one reason why I am writing this letter—to ask you to pardon my frivolity and carelessness; but there is also another reason—that our dear one has sent you a message. Do you start, dear Mr. Hamerton? Did you believe yourself forgotten? No, a thousand times, no!

"Let me tell you how it happened.

"It seems to me, on looking back, that my poor Gabrielle has slowly faded from the hour they laid Gaston in his little grave. Maternity was a passion with her, and he was her only one, and so lovely; to see him was to think of the angels. And then her husband was old. Perhaps she hid her grief too much, that she might not pain the count, and her health suffered. But at first no one noticed it. When the physician's verdict came, it was a shock to us all. No hope—not a vestige of hope; and we all loved her so.

"I was with her when she died, and never was death more peaceful or more welcome. '"I shall go to him;" those are good words, Valerie.' I think that was almost her last speech.

"Two days before her death, I was sitting beside her. She was propped up with pillows, that she might see the sunset. Those sunsets from the chateau D'Arcy are superb. It seems sometimes as though the gate of heaven were open, and one had a glimpse of the jasper throne.

"All at once she began speaking of you, and of those days at the châlet. If I ever see you I will tell you everything, and perhaps such words may console you for a past pain. How beautiful she looked as she spoke them! In spite of her weakness there was such radiance in her eyes, as though the fight were over, and she had gained her rest. But I will tell you a few words she said.

"'Monsieur was very good; he saw it all. He knew what he was to me; but he went away, and left me to do my duty. He was so generous, that he spared me suffering. Mon Dieu, what it was to see him go! But it is all over now.'

"And by-and-by—

"'I have seen monsieur again, Valerie. That night at the opera-house. He was changed and older, but I knew him; I should know him anywhere. He does not look happy; I fear that he has not yet forgotten.'

"And then, a little while afterwards, she drew the missal I am sending you from under her pillow, and looked at it. 'I used it at my first communion, and every day since; my old name, Gabrielle de Brienne, is in it. When I am dead, will you send it to Monsieur Hamerton? Tell him it is a token that I have not forgotten my friend, that never have I ceased to pray that le bon Dieu may now and in eternity grant him his heart's desire. Perhaps'—and then with such a smile; ah, if you could have seen it!—'perhaps our hearts' desires will meet us there for the first time.'

"There! my hand is weary, I can write no more; my husband tells me I have written too much already.

"I remain, dear Mr. Hamerton,

"Yours most sorrowfully,

"VALERIE DE BRIENNE."

When Felix returned, Constance was weeping, but she checked her tears as he sat down beside her and put out his hand silently for the letter. All her life long Constance remembered that moment, and the heap of moist yellow leaves that lay at her feet or were swirled slowly down the avenue. Some of the trees were almost bare now, and through the stript branches she could see the dull October sky. There was something sombre and solemn in the prospect; summer and

youth, and the brightness of life, seemed over—
that was what it seemed to say—and there only
remained decay and death and human sorrow.

"Ah, Felix, it is better so;" that was all she
could find to say.

"Much better," he returned gently. "Thank
you in Gabrielle's name for those tears, Constance;
but there is no need for you to shed them." And
then he murmured half to himself, but she heard
and understood him, "Perhaps our hearts' desires
will meet us there for the first time."

They sat a little longer in silence. Constance's
tact told her that no speech was needed to convey
her sympathy—the tears she had shed for the
unknown Gabrielle had told him all he wished to
know. Presently he rose and held out his hand.

"There, it is over; but I will not say the world
is a poorer place to me while I have such true
friends remaining. We will not speak of this
again, you and I. Now I am going to wish you
good-bye. When Reginald comes in, tell him I
have gone to my room. God bless you! and
thanks a thousand times for your sympathy."

And before she could answer him he was gone.

"It is as dull as ditch water without Hamerton,"
observed Reginald, later on that evening. "You
have hardly opened your lips all dinner-time,

Constance, and now you have buried yourself in a book."

Constance coloured a little at her brother's reproach, but her husband answered for her.

"Constance looks tired; I vote we have a game of billiards, Reginald. I think she will be glad to get rid of us to-night."

And Constance was too honest to contradict this. Reginald's talk wearied her this evening. She was haunted by the remembrance of the solemn look in Felix's eyes as he quoted Gabrielle's words. Oh, it was better far that she should be taken from a world that had never suited her—better that he should think of her blissful and reunited to her child, than remember her in her imperial beauty. By-and-by the pain would fade, and only a sacred memory remain; and he was too young to lose all the good of his life for a memory. "Time heals everything; by-and-by he will be consoled," thought Constance, with a touch of philosophy.

When Violet Winter opened Mrs. Wyndham's note, a flush of pleasure came to her face.

"Constance and her brother propose calling on us to-morrow afternoon," she said, in a tone that betrayed her satisfaction. "She is leaving on Monday, and wishes to bid us good-bye. I am to go back with them, she says, and stay over Sunday."

A dubious "Humph!" fell from Miss Wentworth's lips; but Mrs. Winter, who was counting a troublesome bit of cross-stitch embroidery, made no observation.

"Did you hear me, mother?" asked Violet, a little impatiently.

Then Miss Wentworth gave a little sniff of displeasure.

"It was only the other day that you were staying at the Hall," she remarked, in a judicial manner. "I don't know what you think about it, Amy, but it strikes me that Mrs. Wyndham is not showing her accustomed good taste. In her brother's peculiar position, she ought to be a little more careful."

"Of what, Cousin Tess?" and Violet looked dangerous.

"I was speaking to your mother, my dear," returned Miss Wentworth, who in her provoking moods was wont to set aside Violet as though she were a child, "and I know she will agree with me. People are talking already about Mr. Lorimer. When I was calling at Combe Lea the other day, Lady Martin asked me, in rather a peculiar tone, if Mr. Lorimer were not a great deal at the Gate

House. It was not so much the question as the way she looked that put me at once on my guard."

"I wonder you care to repeat gossip," Cousin Tess," returned Violet, disdainfully. "I hope you told Lady Martin that Mr. Lorimer has always been a great deal with us;" then she carried off her letter, and shut herself up in the gable room. "If I had stopped downstairs a moment longer, I should have lost my temper," she said to herself, and her cheeks were burning. "How dare she insinuate that it is bad taste for me to go so much to the Hall? as though he would ever think of such a thing now, if he did not then!" But Violet did not fill up the gaps in her sentence. Could not even her friendship be sacred from desecration?

"I wish you had not said that, Theresa," observed Mrs. Winter, with mild reproach. "Violet is so very sensitive, and so soon takes alarm. You know what a disappointment it is to me that the dear child does not settle; and if only she and Reginald Lorimer would come together I am sure I should be delighted. She is seven and twenty now," she added, in the tone of regret which matrons are wont to use with regard to their unmarried daughters.

But Miss Wentworth chose to feel aggrieved at this remonstrance.

"I was not talking against Reginald Lorimer," she said stiffly. "He would do well enough for Violet, and I for one would be thankful to see her married, for certainly her temper does not improve. But I must maintain my opinion, that nothing could be in worst taste than the way Constance Wyndham tries to make a match between them. If he came over here of his own accord I should say nothing, but she brings him with her, and then they take Violet back with them."

"Dear—dear! I wish you would not put such uncomfortable ideas into my head, Theresa. Lady Martin, too, seems to suspect something. It puts us all into such a delicate position ; and then poor Lady Car has not been dead more than nine or ten months, so it is dreadful to have all this talk. What are we to do about Violet? She will be so disappointed if I beg her to refuse ; and after all Constance is leaving on Monday, so there can be no harm for this once."

"That is how you always compromise matters," returned her friend, in her harsh sibilant voice. "You have no backbone, Amy ; I always tell you so. In your heart you agree with me, do you not?"—pausing for an instant, and fixing the poor lady with one of her dominating looks.

"I would much rather that Violet should stay

at home after what you say," returned Mrs. Winter, in a hesitating voice.

"Just so; I was sure that your good sense would triumph, but you lack courage to disappoint Violet, though it is for her own good. That is what I call false kindness."

"Yes; but, Theresa, Violet is no longer a child."

"You mean that she will take her own way? She has done that ever since she could run alone; but even a grown-up woman will consent to be guided sometimes. Let me go and talk this matter over with her. It will make no difference to me if she lose her temper, and I shall insist on her hearing my view of the case. Violet is not wanting in delicacy, and I shall be very much surprised if she persist in going back with them."

But this bracing treatment alarmed Mrs. Winter, and she refused to allow Theresa to go up to the gable room. A scene with Violet always agitated her nerves. She would talk to her herself, and see what was to be done, but she could not have dear Constance's feelings hurt. And she and Violet were so fond of each other, and after all there might be nothing in it. How did they know that Reginald Lorimer had a thought of Violet?

Miss Wentworth raged inwardly. She was a woman who always grasped an idea quickly, and acted on it. Lady Martin's significant looks had really troubled her. She would have been the first to rejoice at the prospect of Violet's marriage, but she thought these frequent visits to the Hall under the present circumstances were in the worst possible taste.

" If he wants her he knows where to find her," she argued shrewdly ; " and it is never well to make things too easy for men—a little difficulty enhances the pleasure. I know enough of human nature to lay any amount of odds that Mr. Lorimer will take another wife before next year is over. He is too sociable to enjoy loneliness, and he will marry all the quicker that Lady Car made him so comfortable." And in the main Miss Wentworth was right, though she might have expressed her meaning more pleasantly.

When Violet re-entered the red drawing-room, two or three hours later, she found her mother alone. The moment was propitious, and she could not let it pass.

"Mother dear," she said, kneeling down on the rug, and speaking in her softest voice, for there was a worried look on Mrs. Winter's face, " what am I to do about Constance's invitation ? Do you think you could spare me until Monday ? "

" Do you really want to go, Violet ? "

"Of course I want to go. I think I am happier at Silcote than at any other place; but then, Constance and I are such close friends."

"You don't think that it would be better to decline just this once?" Then, as Violet drew herself up and looked hurt, she continued apologetically, "I do not wish to interfere with your pleasures, my love, and I think it was a mistake Theresa saying what she did; so if you have set your heart on going—— "

Then Violet smiled and kissed her. "Thanks, mother dear; then I will go in spite of Cousin Tess's shocked sense of propriety. It is a comfort that one's mother is married, and not an old maid"—which was a little spiteful on Violet's part, seeing that she was victorious.

Miss Wentworth looked very glum when she saw Violet's trunk carried down to the carriage the next afternoon, but she made no remark.

Violet greatly enjoyed her visit. Constance was not quite in her usual spirits, but she was more affectionate than ever; Violet rather missed Mr. Hamerton—she had seen so much of him lately; but Reginald took care that she should not find herself dull. He was full of animation, and seemed to find a good deal of pleasure in her society. On Sunday afternoon they were in the park together. Constance had gone back to the house to give some order, and while waiting for her they paced slowly up and down the avenue.

Reginald had been silent for a few minutes, and then he said casually, "I suppose you are still having violin-lessons with Miss Carrick?"

"Yes, indeed; and I am making good progress. Miss Carrick is such a splendid teacher. I quite look forward to my lessons."

"You find her interesting?" Reginald put the question carelessly as he kicked some red and yellow leaves that lay in his path.

"Most interesting. She is so thoroughly in earnest. She so evidently believes in herself and in all she does, and then any one can see she is a gentlewoman. If it were not for Cousin Tess, I should make a friend of her; as it is, we suit each other perfectly."

"Your friendship would be a grand thing for her," observed Reginald, with unusual seriousness. "I pity Miss Carrick. Her position is so uncomfortable, and no wonder she finds it galling. Why should you mind Miss Wentworth? She has nothing to do with your friends." Then Violet looked up in surprise; she had not imagined that Mr. Lorimer felt any interest in Miss Carrick.

"I should like to hear her play again," he went on.

"Should you?" and then Violet checked herself and began to smile mysteriously. "After all, I think I will take you into confidence, Mr. Lorimer. Cousin Tess and I have been concocting a charming scheme. We are going to give some musical At Homes next month. You know how dull November is. Well, we think a few social gatherings will be a boon to the neighbourhood. We must have them in the afternoon, because of people coming from a distance. Just tea and coffee, and then Miss Carrick will perform. Cousin Tess said it was an excellent idea. Miss Carrick would be a novelty, and everything else is so stale; so if you like to reserve your Thursday afternoons, you shall have a card."

"Oh, you may count on me," returned Reginald; with admirable promptitude. "I call it a capital notion. You will be a benefactor to the neighbourhood. It seems a pity we can't utilize the music-room for the same purpose. Perhaps when Constance comes down at Christmas——"

"What are you saying about Constance?" asked his sister, who joined them this moment; but when they had enlightened her she became enthusiastic at once, though she gently but decidedly negatived the idea of the music-room. "It would not do at all, dear—not at present, I mean," she said, in a tone that at once conveyed to Reginald's ear that he had been indiscreet. "After February you might entertain, but not before. Are you sure, Violet, that Miss Carrick will play at your *réunions?*"

"Certainly she will play. She was quite excited at the idea; she said that it would be such a splendid advertisement for her, and would help her to get pupils. I think her great desire is to make herself independent of her relations. I dare say, in her place, I should feel the same. There cannot be much sympathy between them."

"It is a grievous pity that that boy stands so much in her light," observed Constance, regretfully; "but for him she might achieve a brilliant success. Don't you agree with me, Reggie?"

"No, I don't," he answered a little shortly. "I hate brilliant successes for women; and it is far better for her to stick to her lessons and look after the boy;" and then he sent the dry crackling leaves flying again.

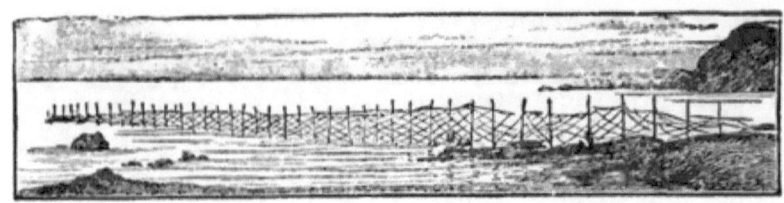

CHAPTER IX.

MR. LORIMER HAS HIS OPINIONS.

"Labour is life ! 'tis the still water faileth ;
    Idleness ever despaireth, bewaileth ;
    Keep the watch wound, or the dark rust assaileth."
                                    FRANCES S. ASGOOD.

"THE dark hollow of the year," as Carlyle
        phrased it, was before Gloden. Every
roadside, every patch of woodland, every plantation breathed the same story of gradual decay.
The dry leaves that fluttered from the trees
collected and lay in rotting heaps under the
feet of the passers-by. The bracken in Silcote
Park looked yellow and shrunken. At night and
in the early morning there was a suspicion of
frost in the air ; the grey skies and sombre melancholy of November were approaching. Nevertheless,
any clear-eyed observer of human nature would

have detected an added cheerfulness in Gloden's manner.

There is a surprising elasticity in youth. The old well-worn comparison between life and the shipwrecked mariner is profoundly and pathetically true. The billows of human trouble roll on perpetually, now submerging and now being gallantly surmounted by the brave swimmer; at one moment the huge crested wave has rushed over him, beating the strength out of him, and the next has carried him on a few more paces, until finally he finds himself on the shore, looking out over the tangle of seaweed and broken spars of his wrecked hopes. "All Thy waves and Thy billows have gone over me," wrote the minstrel king of Israel. How many a quivering, palpitating heart has re-echoed those words!

"Good-bye to Eltringham, good-bye to my dear old life and to happiness," had been Gloden's moan, as she looked back despairingly at the grey walls of the home that had sheltered her youth; and in the bitterness of that farewell she really believed that she was bidding farewell to all joy. Nevertheless, the sap of her youth was still mounting, and in due season the fresh young buds must inevitably appear. Happiness entombed in the rocky cave of grief is for ever awaiting its resurrection. When the angry billows have spent their force, they recede, there is calm and stillness, and the white sails gleam in the sunshine, while under the ripples and the dancing waves the drowned mariner has sunk fathoms deep. "There is a time for everything," wrote the wise man—a time for grief, and a time for healing ; a time for regret, and a time for budding hopes, and for spreading out young wings in the sunshine ; and such a time would come by-and-by to Gloden.

Since Mrs. Wyndham's visit to the gable room, there had been a marked change in Gloden's manner. She was still sad, but she no longer drooped so persistently. Recognition and the delicate breath of flattery were expanding her perceptibly ; her work braced and interested her ; contact with congenial minds such as Winifred Logan and Violet Winter refreshed her mentally. When she woke in the morning the day looked no longer like a stretch of barrenness that must be traversed before night ; not an hour was unoccupied.

Clemency, waiting on her customers, or busying herself with her homely tasks, marvelled secretly at the girl's patience and perseverance as the opening door brought her the sound of the violin hour after hour. When she was not giving lessons, or helping Harvey with his, she was practising beside the window in the old room looking over Market Street ; and more than once Reginald Lorimer, riding past with his dogs, caught sight of the small brown head against the curtain, and the quick motion of a white hand drawing the bow across the strings. But, though he checked his mare to a foot pace, there was no sign of recognition on Gloden's part ; if her hand shook slightly, there was no one near enough to notice it.

Harvey's visits to Silcote were becoming constant; his half-holidays were all spent in the squire's company, and very often Bernard Trevor accompanied him. Mr. Lorimer, who abhorred solitude, found the lads excellent company ; but Harvey remained his prime favourite, and he was always contriving new pleasures for him.

One Saturday evening Harvey came home almost breathless with excitement. The squire had been teaching him to ride ; they had gone ever so far. He had ridden Robin ; he was as steady as old time. Scrivener had told him that he went a good pace, too, and Mr. Lorimer had praised his pluck. They had had a gallop, and he had stuck on all right. And as Gloden uttered a startled protest at this—"Oh, you need not look so scared," he went on ; " Mr. Lorimer knows what he is about. He was quite close all the time, and once when I dropped the reins, he put out his hand and caught hold of them. I lost my hat, but we went back and picked it up. Oh, it was glorious —glorious! and I am to have another ride next Saturday."

Well, it was no use remonstrating; the squire and Harvey were sworn friends, and meant to remain so; and, as Uncle Reuben took Harvey's part, Gloden and Clemency were obliged to content themselves with a head-shake or two and a few whispered entreaties in the lad's ear to do nothing rash.

Robin's beauty, his gentleness, and his wonderful speed were frequent topics of conversation with Harvey. Once he coaxed Mr. Lorimer to ride in the direction of Grantham, and Gloden, trudging along the road, suddenly saw them coming towards her, the squire on his bay mare Lady Alice, and Harvey mounted proudly upon Robin. Griff found him out at once, and flew at Robin's heels, barking with joy, which made that paragon of gentleness dance on three legs immediately.

"Pray don't be nervous, Miss Carrick!" exclaimed Reginald, reassuringly, as he noticed how pale Gloden turned; "Robin is all right, and so is

Harvey. Be quiet, old man!" and he patted
Robin's neck caressingly.

"Come here directly, Griff. Oh, you bad dog!
how could you behave so?"

But Harvey, with boyish impertinence, broke
into a fit of laughter. "What a duffer you are,
Glow! Why, Robin has been dancing on three
legs most of the way, hasn't he, Mr. Lorimer?
He is in fine spirits, aren't you, old boy? Isn't
he a beauty, Gloden? I wanted you to see
him, that is why I asked Mr. Lorimer to come
this way; I knew you would be prowling about.
Don't you wish you could ride too, Antelope?"

"Don't I wish for many things?" returned
Gloden, smiling, as she stroked Robin; and then
she looked up and encountered the squire's
glance.

"It is no use asking you not to spoil Harvey,"
she said softly.

"I am glad you have made up your mind to
that," he returned lightly. "I am helping on
Harvey's education. I have taught him how to
hold a gun, and now I am giving him riding-
lessons. Don't you think you owe me some
gratitude, Miss Carrick, for bringing him on like
this?" He spoke in his usual careless, good-
humoured way, but he was a little taken aback

when she raised her dark eyes and looked at him wistfully.

"I do, indeed; but I can never hope to repay your kindness," she said, with an emphasis that left no doubt of her meaning; and then she drew back with a grave smile and bow, and walked on.

"What on earth did you call your sister just now?" asked Reginald, as they rode on.

"Eh, what?" exclaimed Harvey, absently. "Oh, I know—Antelope. Dad often called her that; she is rather like a deer, you know."

"Ah, I see;" but, though he said nothing more, the name pleased him; it was so appropriate to the large startled eyes and small head, and the graceful carriage and the light tread. That shy look of gratitude she had given him haunted him all the way home.

In the first week in November the Winters gave their first At Home—"Tea and chrysanthemums," Violet called it, for there was a fine show of chrysanthemums in the big conservatory. But the young violin-player was the chief attraction. There was a goodly gathering at the Gate House. Gloden came early with Winifred Logan, and kept modestly in the background, though Mr. Lorimer and one or two others sought her out.

"You do not look a bit nervous," were his first

words, as he greeted her; "not half so much as when Robin pranced the other day."

"No, indeed;" and then, as she looked round at the crowded room, her eyes seemed to brighten. "All these strangers do not trouble me in the least. When I begin playing I shall see no one—the music and I will be alone."

"I call that selfish, Miss Carrick. What have we done that you should shut us out like that? Music ought to widen your sympathies and make you love your fellow-creatures better. When I listen to playing I like, I always seem to grow philanthropic."

"Ah, you do not understand," she said, a little impatiently. "One cannot limit one's self to one's audience—the feeling is too vast; one is carried away. How is one to interpret the thoughts of a great master if the human countenances before one are appealing to one's consciousness? No; when I play let me forget every one—even my friends."

"You are beyond me there," returned Reginald, vaguely discontented at this; and then, as Dr. Parry came up to them, he went back to the red drawing-room.

By some curious coincidence, he sat in the same place that he had occupied when he first

heard Gloden perform; but Winifred Logan, not
Constance, was in the seat before him. When
Gloden came modestly forward and took up her
station in the shadow of the curtains, he quietly
crossed his arms on the back of Winifred's chair.
He could look at her as long as he liked; she and
her music were alone together—he would not
forget that.

There was no doubt of Gloden's success that
afternoon. Dr. Parry's benevolent face was
beaming; he was in luck to have secured such
a finished mistress for his little Hilda, so he told
himself, as he heard the whispered encomiums
that passed through the room. But Gloden's face
did not brighten as the compliments flowed in
upon her; she looked a little absent and distrait.

"I expect you find all this a bore," observed
Mr. Lorimer in his casual manner; and Gloden,
who had not perceived his approach, started
slightly. "Let me take you out to see the
chrysanthemums; they will do you good;" and
after a moment's hesitation she consented.

There was no longer that barrier of unyielding
stiffness in Gloden's manner to the young squire.
He was Harvey's friend, and as such entitled to
her courtesy and gratitude; they were on neutral
ground, and she could accept his attentions as

she would from any other gentleman. "He knows all about us now," she said to herself, "and if he chooses to be pleasant and friendly to Harvey's sister, there is no necessity for me to point out his mistake to him."

Mr. Lorimer took no advantage of this slight concession. He was beginning to score a little, he told himself modestly; Miss Carrick was not nearly so standoffish as she was.

"What a mass of bloom!" observed Gloden, as they entered the conservatory, which was just at this moment empty. "How beautifully those golden and brown and dull red tints blend and harmonize! It is a perfect feast of colour."

"I am glad you like it," returned Reginald. "We were thinking of building a new con- servatory to open out of the music-room at Silcote; it was a pet scheme of my poor wife's, but it was never carried out. She had a passion for chrysanthemums." He checked a sigh, and then went on, "Do you care for compliments, Miss Carrick? I have never told you yet how much I have enjoyed the music you gave us."

"I did not play as well as usual," she returned quickly; "and it was all your fault, Mr. Lorimer."

"My dear Miss Carrick!"—in extreme surprise.

"Why did you imply that I was selfish," she

continued, "because I said that my music seemed
to shut me out from everybody? I could not
forget your words, and for once I was conscious
of my environment. I saw you quite plainly,
Mr. Lorimer; you were at the end of the room,
and you had your arms crossed on the chair before
you, and you were looking as though you were
trying to understand something."

"By Jove!" muttered Reginald; then aloud, "I
must have been an awful nuisance, I am afraid;
but I cannot endorse your statement. You played
splendidly. I wished my sister could have heard
you."

Then Gloden flushed as though she were gratified.
"Do you know what your sister proposed?" she
said, looking at him in her quiet, serious way,
and there was something in her calm sedateness
that always attracted him. She had none of the
airs and graces of the ordinary young lady; he
had long ago discovered that she had no sense
of humour. Violet Winter was infinitely more
amusing, and could say far cleverer things. "Mrs.
Wyndham was anxious that I should go up to
town and study under Signor Boski. She was so
kind about it; she took so much trouble. It is
her opinion that a year or two under Boski would
enable me to play at concerts."

"Ah, no doubt," he returned coldly. "My sister is a clever woman, and never advances an opinion unless she is sure of her ground. Signor Boski is a great friend of hers."

"So she said; she seemed so sure, too, that he would reduce his terms at her recommendation. I cannot tell you how grateful I was for her kindness, and I hope she understood that. I am afraid she tempted me sorely."

"Do you mean that such a life would suit you?" he asked, and he had quite lost his genial manner. "I thought women did not care for publicity, and all that sort of thing. In my opinion, they are much safer and happier in their own homes."

"Do you not think that depends on their home, Mr. Lorimer?" she returned, and there was sadness in her tone. "I have lost the only home I could love. If my father had lived—ah, these *if*'s!—I could have lived all my life happily at Eltringham; but now——" She paused.

"Oh, you do not know what may turn up," he replied confidently; "you have not settled down yet. If I may venture to hazard an opinion, you will feel quite differently by-and-by, when you get more used to us." But Gloden shook her head.

"It is not the people or the place," she returned quietly. "I am making friends already, and Miss

Winter and Miss Logan are so good to me; but if
I could have my way I would leave Grantham
to-morrow, and put myself under Signor Boski.
It is work that I want—hard work, and guidance
and sympathy. If one has a vocation, Mr. Lorimer,
it is one's duty to follow it; but, as I told your
sister, I am not free."

Then he looked at her a little curiously. "You
mean that Harvey is the obstacle. Yes, I know;
Constance told me;" and then he added a little
obstinately, "and I am not sorry to hear it. I
don't believe the life would have suited you a bit;
they would have worked you to death between
them." And as she opened her eyes a little widely
at this contradiction, he continued somewhat decidedly, "I am not an ambitious sort of person;
I like to lead a peaceful existence under my own
fig tree. I think heated rooms and applause no
end of a nuisance, and if Harvey were a little
older he would agree with me."

"Do you know you are just a little damping,
Mr. Lorimer?"

"Am I? Well, I do not feel especially repen-
tant, but I suppose I have no right to be talking
to you in this paternal way. My sister is more of
your way of thinking, and Hamerton would be
too. You see, my domestic virtues have been

over-cultivated, and, as I said before, I hate publicity for women ; in my opinion they ought to
have something better. But we shall never agree,
shall we ? "—turning to her with a good-humoured
look.

But Gloden felt a momentary pang as he said
this. She had no idea that Mr. Lorimer held such
strong views, or she would never have mooted the
subject. These easy-natured men sometimes had
a fund of obstinacy underneath their smooth
manners ; but it was quite evident to her, from
Mr. Lorimer's remarks, that a womanly woman
was more to his taste, and he disliked excessively
the *rôle* of an artiste for any of his personal friends.
And, strange to say, Gloden felt some regret as she
admitted this fact to herself; and yet, after all,
what did Mr. Lorimer's opinion matter to her—a
country squire who refused to hold advanced views
on the subject of women, and whose ideas were
hardly up to date? Gloden, who was tenacious
by nature, longed to argue him out of his old-
fashioned notions, but she wisely refrained.

" I think we ought to go back," she said, rising
from her seat ; " I feel more rested now."

Then Reginald laughed outright. " Does an
argument rest you ? We were on the brink of a
disagreement just now. Come, I will make my

peace with you.   I will not cancel a word I said, and I wish Constance had never mentioned Boski's name, but I will own that it is hard lines for you under your present circumstances, and that I think you put a good face on things—to quote Harvey, 'you are awfully plucky.'"

"Thank you," she said, breaking into a smile ; and then they went back to the room, and Miss Wentworth, who had noticed their absence with much displeasure, pounced on Reginald as he entered, and Gloden did not see him again.

But on the following Thursday he was there, and again the week after, and each time he occupied the same place. Gloden, pausing in her playing for a moment, would glance towards his corner. He was always in the same attitude—his arms crossed on the chair before him, and his grave, intent look fixed on her. Sometimes she wished that he were absent ; the consciousness of his presence prevented her from losing herself ; the remembrance of his disapproval of her ambitious scheme haunted her with singular persistence. Why had he taken up that attitude of quiet resistance ? What was it to him that a stranger like herself should wish to be trained for a professional life ? And yet his hurt tone, his want of geniality, kept recurring to her memory, and she even once took Harvey into her confidence. It was one evening late in November, and she had just returned from the last "At Home" at the Gate House. She had walked home with Winifred Logan, and had heard from her that her cousin was expected for a few days shortly—a piece of intelligence that produced rather mixed feelings in Gloden's mind.

When she reached home she found that her Aunt Clemency had lighted a fire in the best room, and was on her knees tending it as she entered.

There was no change in the somewhat strained relations between them. Gloden was always perfectly civil, but she never abridged the distance that kept them apart; she never volunteered confidence, or expected any in return ; and she still regarded Clemency's maternal tenderness for Harvey with jealous suspicion, though, to do her justice, she tried to combat the feeling. With her uncle she was far more genial ; she treated him with marked respect and consideration. All her hauteur and reserve seemed kept for Clemency; but, true to her nature, Clemency never resented this, and, with a loyalty for which Gloden would not have given her credit, she always concealed her wounded feelings from her husband. "Reuben's getting fond of her, and I won't be setting him against her," she said to herself. "It is ill-doing, stirring up strife in a house. Gloden has got a cold manner, but she means no harm. I must just mother her, and bear with her;" and Clemency acted up to her word nobly.

"You and Gloden get on famously, Clem," Reuben once said to her, in his dense, masculine way.

But Clemency only smiled, and held her peace. It would not have helped her, or Gloden either, to have told him that there was no sympathy between them. "It is better to hold one's tongue than to make mischief," thought Clemency.

When Gloden, coming out of the November dampness and chillness, saw Clemency on her knees coaxing the fire, a feeling of compunction crossed her.

"How kind you are, Aunt Clemency!" she said, more pleasantly than usual. "It is so cold, and it is beginning to rain."

"There is nothing like a bit of fire for comfort," returned Clemency, adding another stick; "it will burn up in a moment, Gloden. Patty was busy; the Sedgewicks are coming in to supper, and she has some cooking to do."

Then Gloden's pleasant expression clouded over.

Mr. Sedgewick was the linendraper in Market-place—a warm, substantial man, as her uncle called him, who was certainly making his pile; and Mrs. Sedgewick was a comely, rosy creature who dropped her *h*'s rather freely, and called Gloden "Miss." But they were educating their children well, and would some day have the happiness of seeing them despise their parents, and set them aside after the manner of the youthful generation.

"The Sedgewicks!" she repeated blankly; "and of course you are lighting the fire for them" —in an injured tone, as though she repented of her former gratitude.

"No; they are only coming in late for a bit of supper and a smoke afterwards—at least, your uncle and Mr. Sedgewick will smoke, and Sophia and I will keep them company. I would send you up your bit of chicken, Gloden, only your uncle's feelings would be hurt, and he would not understand; and then there is Harvey."

"Of course I shall come down to supper, Aunt Clemency."

"Well, there is no call to come until it is ready," returned Clemency, good-humouredly.

She was anxious to smooth things all round, and perhaps she was shrewd enough to guess that Gloden's presence would hardly promote her

friends' cheerfulness. If she would have made herself pleasant, and volunteered to play to them,
things would have been easier. But it was not only
unselfish consideration for her niece's well-being
that had made her light the fire ; and it was after
Mrs. Carrick had gone downstairs that Harvey
joined her, and they sat on the big couch nestled
together, and in the firelight Gloden repeated the
substance of her conversation with Mr. Lorimer.

" I never thought he was that sort of man,"
she concluded. " Don't you think it was a little
foolish and old-fashioned of him, Harvey ? "

But Harvey stoutly contested this.

" Not a bit ; and you are awfully prudish yourself, Glow. We had a talk about it, he and I."

" About me ? " and Gloden looked intensely
surprised.

" Yes. He told me you had had a bit of a scrim-
mage at the Gate House, and that he was afraid he
had vexed you ; and then he asked me if I liked the
idea of Signor Boski. And I told him I thought
it would be awfully jolly for you to play at concerts, only I was afraid there would be no such
luck, as we had not got any money—hardly any,
I said, because, you know, there is that hundred
and fifty pounds that Uncle Reuben is keeping
for us."

"And what did Mr. Lorimer say, Harvey?"

"Well, he did not look pleased; and then he said I was too much of a child to understand. And then I fought him—he is teaching me to box, you know—and that finished the argument neatly; but he had his innings first, and said some sharp things. He said he hated to see women stuck up before a mixed audience; at least, women he knew, not other people. That if he had a sister he should look after her, and, though he did not care much about the shop, he thought it better than a London lodging; and he said he vexed himself about it rather, because his sister had put the idea into your head."

"Yes, I see."

"Oh, he was awfully nice about it. I tell you what, Glow—he thinks no end of you. He said you were too refined and sensitive to be knocked about in the world, and he wished I were a little older and could protect you. He said that after our wrestling-bout, as we were walking through the spinney, and I am sure from his manner that he meant every word."

Gloden was sure of it too, and she was much touched. It was evident that Mr. Lorimer took a great deal of friendly interest in her, and she was glad to know this.

CHAPTER X.

"YOU ARE NOT HAPPY HERE."

"Oh, how good it feels,
The hand of an old friend!"

LONGFELLOW.

ONE afternoon Gloden was returning from the Gate House, and walking briskly, as was her wont. The days were shorter and colder now, and as the road was a lonely one, Mrs. Winter had advised her daughter to take her lesson at an earlier hour, so that Miss Carrick might be set free by four. Violet willingly agreed to this, and, though Gloden smiled a little at this motherly precaution, and assured Violet that a dark road under wintry skies would not have daunted her in the least, she was obliged to submit to her friends' scruples.

On this occasion she and Violet had lingered so long over their leavetaking as they stood warming

themselves by the hall fire, that it was long after
five before she crossed the rustic bridge over the
moat and groped her way down the little lane.
But Gloden, who was country-bred, cared nothing
for the loneliness. She was cold, and walked
fast. She had no fear of losing her way; she
knew exactly where the cross-roads met—where
she had encountered Mr. Lorimer. She was thinking of him now, and of their conversation in
the chrysanthemum-house, as she struck into the
Grantham road. It was a curious fact that the
young squire of Silcote was often in her thoughts
just then.

She was almost sorry when she reached Market
Street. Exercise, even in the most inclement
weather, always exhilarated her. She would
willingly have walked half a dozen miles further,
but she knew that her Uncle Reuben disapproved
of these unconventional ways, so she controlled
her restlessness. She very seldom entered the
shop, but she remembered Patty had a faceache,
so she considerately spared her the trouble of
opening the door for her. There were seldom any
customers at this hour, and she was inwardly cha-
grined, therefore, to see a gentleman standing with
his back to her, so near the glass door that she
would have to pass quite close to him.

As she did so she paused involuntarily. Surely that long neck and those sloping shoulders were familiar to her. "Mr. Logan!" she exclaimed out loud, and Ewen Logan turned with a start, and a flush mounted to his forehead. Clemency, who was serving him, saw the flash of joy in his eyes.

"Miss Carrick!" and then he stood holding her hands and forgetting to let them go. "I was just asking about you. Your aunt told me you would be in soon, so I thought I would wait."

"Mr. Logan will be wanting a talk with you, Gloden," observed Clemency, in her mild way. "I am vexed, that I am, that that Patty has forgotten to light a bit of fire in the best room; but there, her face has been troubling her, and put things out of her head. But if you will step into the parlour, Mr. Logan, you will be kindly welcome."

"You are very good, Mrs. Carrick, and if you will put up those books for my cousin, I will take them when I leave. Shall I follow you, Miss Carrick?" and there was no mistaking the suppressed eagerness in his voice.

"He is glad enough to see her," thought Clemency, as she made up the parcel in her painstaking manner, for no pressing business ever hurried her quiet, deliberate movements. ("It is

waste of time to hurry," she would say ; "what is
the use of doing a thing badly, and having to do it
all over again?") "But I misdoubt if Gloden cares
as much to see him, though she was pretty hearty
in her greeting ; but it would be a blessing if some
good sensible man would persuade her to marry
him, for violin-playing is a poor set-off for a
husband and children."

Gloden's brow contracted with vexation when
she heard of Patty's forgetfulness. The little parlour, with its shining mahogany chiffonier and
horsehair-covered chairs, was abhorrent to her ;
but to Mr. Logan, hungering and thirsting for the
girl's presence, it was a shrine of heavenly comfort,
with its neatly swept hearth and Reuben's big
easy-chair, with its usual tenant, Jim, curled up
on it.

"I am so sorry Harvey is out," she began, as
she took off her hat and jacket and flung them
down carelessly on a chair, until Clemency should
spy them out and carry them away. Clemency
never remonstrated with her niece ; she would pull
out the fingers of the gloves and smooth them
tidily, while Gloden only tossed her head a little
disdainfully. She hated Aunt Clemency's primness
and old-maidish ways. "What does it matter?"
she asked once, when she was stung into momen-

tary irritation. "Uncle Reuben always leaves his pipes about, and you do not seem to object to that."

"A wife is bound to put up with her husband," returned Clemency, with unwonted dignity; "when you are married, Gloden, you will find that out for yourself. There's a deal of putting up, and bearing and forbearing, in matrimony. I often mind what an old aunt of mine, Aunt Peggy Winterbotham, used to say. She was never married herself, but she always talked as if she had had a dozen husbands. '"Honeymoon" they call it; I should give it another name. "Temper-test" would fit it far better, I should say.'"

"Harvey will be so sorry to miss you," went on Gloden, smoothing down her hair with both hands, an action strangely familiar to the curate. A look of tenderness came into his deep-set eyes, but Gloden only saw the gleaming of the glasses. "He is having tea with one of his schoolfellows, Bernard Trevor, and Griff is with him."

"I have seen Harvey," returned Ewen, absently. "Mrs. Trevor is a friend of ours; Winifred is very fond of her. Bernard brought him round to see us. He looks well, uncommonly well."

"Oh, he is much stronger; and did you notice, Mr. Logan, he is grown? He is quite tall for his age."

" Grantham seems to suit him.   But he grumbled
a bit; that is Harvey all over.   He says he hates
the grammar school."   And then his manner
changed, and he looked into the girl's eyes.   " We
will talk about Harvey by-and-by; I want to
hear about something else.   How are things with
you?   You look well, you are not quite so thin ;
perhaps you do not dislike Grantham as much as
you feared."

" Do you think," she said impulsively, and she
frowned as she spoke, " that this "—looking round
at the little firelit room—" is a good exchange for
the dear old room at Eltringham ?"

" Comparisons are odious," he replied gently,
for he had made up his mind to be gentle with
her; " it looks to me very comfortable, and you
know of old that I do not mind shabbiness.   You
have another room, Winifred tells me, where you
can practise and read to your heart's content."

" Yes," she returned ungraciously, " but I have
not grown to love it yet."

" Well, perhaps not "—in a good-humoured voice,
for he saw plainly she was in one of her perverse
moods.

Probably the sight of him had brought back
her home-sickness, and in this guess he was
right.   Gloden was answering him shortly, but the

tears were very near her eyes. His ungainly figure and sallow face were associated with her former life. She was almost surprised herself to feel how strongly she was drawn to him ; she had always respected and liked him, but she had never felt him so much to her. She was standing before him, with her hands hanging down among the folds of her dress. With a sudden uncontrollable impulse Ewen took the right hand gently in his, and for more than a minute she did not withdraw it ; in reality the action chimed in with her softened thoughts of him, but Ewen could hardly be blamed if he interpreted her compliance after his masculine fashion. Perhaps, after all, absence had done something for him.

Unfortunately, Patty entered with the tea-tray at this moment, and Gloden's hands were again fingering the folds of her dress. It was clearly necessary to choose some safe topic of conversation while the girl was clattering round the table with plates and knives, and eyeing them both with undisguised curiosity.

"You have seen a great deal of my cousin Winifred," he began. "I hope you have become good friends."

"Yes, indeed ; how is one to help liking her? She is so kind, so true, so perfectly unselfish."

"Winnie is all that," he returned, very much pleased. "She is a thoroughly genuine person; that is why people always get on with her."

"And Miss Winter is another friend of yours," he continued, after a moment's silence.

"Yes, indeed; and she is charming. She is very different from your cousin; she is so pretty and taking, and——"

"Oh, we all know that Winnie is no beauty," he observed in a vexed voice, as though he resented this speech.

Then Gloden felt she had expressed herself awkwardly.

"I was not thinking of Miss Logan's looks. What do they matter, after all? Your cousin is so good, so lovable, that one never stops to inquire whether she is plain or not; but when one is with Violet Winter it is quite different. She is good too, but one cannot help admiring her; she is so graceful, and her voice is so refined, and then she has such charming manners. She is quite the prettiest girl in Grantham."

"When she was younger people called her lovely, but she was never as handsome as Mrs. Wyndham."

"Perhaps not. I call Mrs. Wyndham beautiful; it is the only word that expresses her."

Then Mr. Logan smiled, as though he were amused.

" There are some nice people in Grantham, then ? " he asked mischievously.

And then Clemency entered the room.

" I have just made the tea, Mr. Logan," she said, pausing near the chair where Gloden had thrown down her hat and jacket, and, after her usual custom, straightening her niece's gloves. " My husband is coming in directly, and we shall be pleased and proud if you will take a cup with us, sir."

" You are really too good, Mrs. Carrick ; " and then he looked at Gloden, as though expecting her to endorse the invitation ; but she was staring at the fire, and took no notice.

" I shall be very glad of a cup of tea," he continued, after a moment's awkward hesitation. He felt sure, from Gloden's manner, that she wished him to decline ; but he could not resist the temptation of breaking bread with her again. He looked wistfully at her as she moved slowly and reluctantly to her place opposite to him. He could read her thoughts pretty accurately. It galled her inexpressibly that he should see her under her altered circumstances, and be a spectator of her aunt and uncle's homely ways, when he remembered

her under such different circumstances. How
often she had poured out tea for him in the dear
old study, or in the dim, sweetly scented drawing-
room, fragrant with roses and lemon verbena!
And then she thought of the melon-shaped silver
pot of which her mother had been so proud, and
the delicate Wedgewood china, and Aunt Clemency's staring red-and-blue teacups gave her a
real pang.

"Will you kindly ask a blessing, Mr. Logan?
My husband is just serving a customer, but he
will be in directly ; and you'll find those scones
very good, sir, if Gloden will hand them to you,"
she continued appealingly, presently glancing at
her niece.

And then Reuben came in, looking hearty
and pleased to see Mr. Logan. And the two
men began to discuss Grantham affairs, while
Gloden sat silently by, and Clemency only
interposed to press some more tea-cake on her
guest.

"And when do you leave Eltringham, sir?" was
the first thing that really roused Gloden from her
abstraction.

"Not until Easter. Mr. Snowden wishes me to
remain until then, and of course I am willing to
oblige him."

"And then?" asked Reuben, with kindly inquisitiveness.

"Well, Mr. Carrick, it is an open secret that the bishop means to offer me the living of Clacton-over-Fields."

And, as Gloden uttered a surprised exclamation, he bent forward as though he were answering her.

"It is not much of a living—my cure of souls will number about five hundred — and is only worth about two hundred a year, but there is a good house and garden, and my mother thinks I could take pupils."

"Oh yes," she returned quickly, "that is always what dear father advised ; and then you could have your mother and cousin to live with you——"

But here she stopped, warned by a peculiar expression in Mr. Logan's eyes that she was treading on dangerous ground. In her pleasure at hearing that such a piece of good fortune had accrued to her old friend, she had forgotten the last conversation they had held together, but Ewen's keen look suddenly recalled it. "If you could only bring yourself to care for me, and to overlook my defects of manner," he had said to her humbly, "I would do my best to work for you, and to shield you from adversity."

And the next moment this thought rushed into

her mind, " This is why he has come to Grantham, to tell me about Clacton-over-Fields, and to ask me to go there ; " and then she felt a little giddy and sick, and rose from the table with a muttered excuse. She had been so pleased to see him ; but if he came for this ? Oh, why was he so persistent, so obstinately bent on making her uncomfortable ? Why was he so cruel to her, and to himself too, when he must know how hopeless it was ?

Gloden remained away as long as she dared. When she returned to the parlour she found Mr. Logan was just taking his leave.

" I shall see you again," he said, as he shook hands with her. " Mrs. Carrick tells me that you are generally practising your violin in the morning. As my time is limited, perhaps I may look in to-morrow ; " and, without waiting for an answer, he turned away.

And again Gloden felt that he had been too much for her.

When she woke the next morning, she felt as though some dreadful ordeal lay before her. She had lain awake for hours, planning how she could escape an interview with Mr. Logan, and she determined at all hazards to avoid him. She would go out for the whole morning. It would be treating him badly, but it would be far kinder

in the end. He had no right to take it for granted
that she would remain in to see him. It would
be giving him encouragement; it would be better
to hurt his feelings than that. "He will take the
hint; he is obstinate, but he is not dense," she
said to herself, when she had arrived at this
conclusion.

"I have told Patty to make up a good fire in
the best room," observed Clemency, when they
had finished breakfast, and Harvey had caught up
his books and rushed out. " It is a raw sort of day
—your uncle thinks we shall have sleet presently;
and Mr. Logan talked about looking in."

"Yes, I know; but he was not certain—he only
said perhaps," returned Gloden, hurriedly. "Don't
trouble about a fire, Aunt Clemency; I think I
am going out."

Then Clemency looked at her niece incredulously; it was evident that she could not believe
her ears. Then she went on with the business
she had in hand, piling up the breakfast-cups on
a tray.

"I would not do that if I were you, Gloden," she
said quietly; "Mr. Logan told me before you
came down that he meant to come. 'I must
have a good long talk with your niece'—those
were his exact words; so it would be putting

a slight on him not to be here, when I told him
that you always stopped in in the morning."

"I am sorry you told him anything of the kind,"
replied Gloden, stiffly. "You will have to talk to
him yourself, Aunt Clemency, for I am certainly
going out."

Then a little flush mounted to Clemency's face
as she carried the tray away. She would not
argue the matter. If Gloden chose to be contrary,
and to put this affront on her old friend, it was
no business of hers. "Heaven help the man who
marries her!" she thought, as she called Patty to
bring her a bowl of water and a tea-cloth.

Gloden's feelings were not very enviable as she
went upstairs to get ready for her walk; it was
not a tempting morning for a stroll, and the best
room looked delightfully warm and snug as she
passed it. It was early yet; she could have an
hour's practice. But before half an hour had passed
she laid aside her bow. She remembered suddenly
that Mr. Logan was an unconventional person;
he might not think ten o'clock too early for his
visit. The idea alarmed her, and before ten minutes
were over she and Griff were on their way up the
town.

She had chosen the Silcote road, as she dare
not pass Chapel Street or the Market-place, for

fear of meeting Mr. Logan. When she had walked another mile, she meant to branch off in the direction of Donnington. She and Harvey had often planned to walk to Donnington, but all his half-holidays were now spent at Silcote, and, except on Sunday afternoons, they rarely went out together.

Gloden thought that she had managed very cleverly to avoid her old friend, but fate was too strong for her. She had only just left the town behind her, when she became aware of a black angular figure in the distance ; but before she could beat a retreat, Griff had rushed up to it with a delighted bark of recognition. Gloden grew hot and then cold, as Mr. Logan came eagerly to meet her.

"This is luck !" he said, in a pleased voice, as he joined her. "I was just prowling about until it was time for my call. Of course, you did not expect me for another hour." And then he looked at her, and something in her expression struck him. "You know I said I should call this morning."

"You only said 'perhaps,'" she returned faintly. "I was just taking Griff for a walk."

"And you meant to be back in time to see me?" and he looked at her a little searchingly.

But Gloden had no answer ready. She could

not tell him to his face that she had gone out to
avoid him, neither could she stoop to utter a
falsehood ; but her embarrassed look and silence
were sufficient answer.   Mr. Logan's face changed.

"You knew I was coming to talk to you, and
you went out to avoid me," he said, in a harsh,
strident voice.   "Was this kind, Miss Carrick ? "

"I did not mean to be unkind," she answered.

But her evident nervousness did not allay his
displeasure.   Last night she had been gentle and
gracious to him ; there had been a softness in her
mien that had given him hope, and now she had
put this insult on him.   Any other man would
have gone away and left her, but Mr. Logan was
not to be turned from his purpose by any amount
of silent opposition ; he had come to Grantham
to say a certain thing, and he meant to say it.
Nevertheless, the blackness of his brow did not
become a wooer.

"It was useless to try and avoid me.   I should
have followed you," he went on, in the same
offended voice.   "I have come to Grantham with
a purpose—a purpose that concerns you, and you
cannot prevent my saying what I have to say,
however difficult you make it for me to speak.
Shall I speak now, or will you come back with
me to Market Street ? "

Ewen's authoritative tone excited Gloden's resentment. No man had a right to speak to her in such a manner; she would not bear it for a moment.

"I am not going back," she said coldly. "Is it any use to tell you, Mr. Logan, that I should prefer to walk alone?"

"By heavens, no!" he returned angrily. "You are treating me as badly as possible; we have not met for months, and yet you tell me to my face that you do not wish for my society. I would not have believed that even you could be so cruelly hard."

Then, in spite of herself, she was touched by the pain in his voice. After all, he had a right to be angry with her.

"There is no need for us to quarrel," she said more gently. "If I make it evident that I do not desire your company, it is because your manner does not please me."

But he misunderstood her. "What does it matter about a man's manner," he retorted stormily, "if his heart be right? Could any man love a girl better than I have loved you? I have my faults, God knows, but I should not be ashamed for you to read my thoughts."

"Mr. Logan, will you let me say something?

I thought—I hoped that you would never speak
to me in this way again. I told you last time
that you were making a mistake. Why did you
not believe me?"

Then he stopped, and looked at her very
sorrowfully. "It is no mistake on my part. It
is as natural for me to love you as to breathe
the air; I think I have told you that before.
Such a love as mine is not to be despised or
thrown away."

Then she remained silent. She did not despise
him; in a way she loved him, for his honestness,
and his uprightness, and the gentleness of his
nature. He was a good man—she knew that, and
he had been very kind to her; but if she and he
were alone in the world, she could not have
brought herself to marry him. But how was she
to tell him so?

"Let me tell you more about myself," he went
on eagerly. "Things are different now. As the
vicar of Clacton-over-Fields, I shall have a better
position to offer you. The house is good—it is
nearly as good as Eltringham Vicarage, and the
garden far prettier. There is a little farm attached
that I think of taking into my own hands. You
once told me you would dearly love farming; and
in his holidays Harvey could live with us."

No answer. He looked wistfully at her, and went on. "You are not happy here; the shop does not suit you. I saw myself last night how you felt about things. If you would marry me, I think you would care for me in time. I would not ask much—only the right of being your husband, and protecting you; I have love enough for both. I know you trust me. In a way we are friends. I should not be afraid of waiting until you could love me in return."

"How good you are!" The words burst from Gloden in spite of herself. Oh, why could she not love this simple, kindly nature? What did it matter that he was awkward and brusque in his manner? Could she not overlook his insignificance, his want of attraction? He was offering her much—an assured position, a home almost as good as the one she had left, congenial work and protection for herself and Harvey, and last, but best of all, a love that would last her whole life. And he asked so little in return. He would be patient with her, until she had learned to care for him. And yet, why could she not bring herself to say yes? "How good you are! I am not worthy of such affection," she said, almost despairingly.

They were approaching the little village of Silcote, but Gloden, dazed and agitated had failed to recognize it. The next minute a young man in a dark tweed coat came out of a cottage they were just passing, with a beautiful black pointer at his heels ; and Gloden was startled to recognize the squire.

He raised his hat, and seemed as though he were going to speak ; then he glanced at her companion, and drew back with a muttered "Good morning." A denser person than Reginald Lorimer must have detected unusual traces of perturbation on Mr. Logan's face. He never even saw Mr. Lorimer, as he listened to that involuntary ex-clamation.

"You are worthy of far more than I can give you," he returned quickly ; and Reginald overheard him, and stood stock still in the road, looking after them.

"It is not difficult to understand that," he said to himself, as he walked on. "Now, I wonder who that fellow is ? I seem to know his face. By Jove ! I have it now. It is Logan ; he was a curate at Eltringham. Of course he has fallen in love with her there. He is not much to look at ; she is a cut above him, I should say. I wonder what sort of answer he will get ? She looked awfully flushed and uncomfortable when she recognized me. He is making love to her—I'd take my oath of that. Confound his impudence! But these clerics have cheek enough for anything;" and Reginald kicked a stone out of his path with decided irritation. "'You are worthy of far more than I can give you.' The deuce take it! the fellow must be a prig."

CHAPTER XI.

"IT IS NOT MY FAULT."

> " We, ignorant of ourselves,
> Beget often our own harms, which the wise powers
> Deny us for our good ; so find we profit
> By losing of our prayers."
>
> *Antony and Cleopatra.*

REGINALD LORIMER had just pulled himself together and walked on in the direction of Grantham, when Gloden turned quickly to Mr. Logan. There was a flush on her face, and a singular expression in her eyes.

"Do not say any more to me ; I cannot bear it. Why do you make me suffer so? I am not ungrateful, and I am not hard. It is not my fault if you have no power to touch my heart—it cannot be my fault." She spoke almost passionately, as though she wanted to clear herself from some inward accusation.

Mr. Logan's hopes died a natural death as he heard her. "You have no power to touch my heart." Could that indeed be the truth? Was it possible that his great love could fail to elicit any response? Had it come to this—that he must give it all up? Then for the moment there was despair in his heart, and, for all his courage, he could not answer her.

"If you had only believed me, and spared me this!" she went on. "If you knew how your kindness hurts me! It may be easy for some women to say no, but to me it is simple torture. A dozen years hence, if I live, I shall blame myself for this; I shall believe that it is somehow through my fault that this trouble has come upon you."

And then she shivered a little, as though the wind were suddenly cold. This roused him.

"You shall not blame yourself," he said harshly. "You have given me no encouragement. When you came out this morning to avoid me—well, a fool could have understood the meaning of that; but I would not listen to reason. I thought that if you were unhappy, you could be persuaded; that perhaps I should be able to touch you. But I give it up"—spreading his hands with a gesture of utter hopelessness. "You are right; you will never care for me."

"Not in that way." And then her voice choked, and no effort could keep the tears back. Oh, how wretched it all was! The bleak, wintry prospect; the wan, miserable face of the man beside her; the pitiless necessity that compelled her to give him pain; the inexorable laws of human life; its sadness and sorrowful complications. "If I could only help my own nature!" was her inward cry.

"And there is no other way that would satisfy me," was Ewen's answer; and then he stopped himself. "But there is no need for you to make yourself miserable about me; a man can always bear what he has to bear."

"And you will get over it?"

"Oh yes, I shall get over it. I have my work to do, and of course I do not mean to shirk that. The heart is taken out of me for the present. Clacton will be the abomination of desolation, at least for a while."

"But your mother will be with you."

"Yes; but even a mother cannot comfort a man under all circumstances, though she be the best of mothers."

"Mr. Logan, when you tell me this, you make me wish that I had never been born to bring this misery upon you."

Then he turned upon her with a stern rebuke. "You must not say that; it is wrong. How are you or I to know what is best for us? If I had borne my trouble better, you would never have said that to me; so the sin is mine."

"No—oh no!"

"But it is. I ought not to have shown you my unhappiness so plainly, but for the moment I was utterly overwhelmed; the iron had entered into my very soul. But I shall never be so contemptible in my weakness again."

"You are not contemptible, Mr. Logan. How can you talk so?"

"Well, I will not talk any more; we are near the town"—for they had turned unconsciously, and were retracing their steps. "Should you mind if I left you? I think it would be better for us both if I were to bid you good-bye."

"Oh no; do not leave me so;" and Gloden put her hand on his arm to detain him. "Do not leave me with bitterness in your heart; it may be long before we meet again. Tell me at least that you forgive me."

Then he took her hands, and held them firmly. "There is no bitterness in my heart against you; only a great sorrow, that I must learn to bear like a man. You have done me no wrong; you cannot help yourself. If I could only be different!" He looked at her moodily; then his glasses grew a little dim. "God bless you! I can at least without sin pray for your happiness." And then Gloden did let him go.

She stood still until he was almost out of sight, but he did not once turn. He walked doggedly on, his shoulders bent, his thin, ungainly figure lessening in the distance; and Gloden watched him with a dull ache at her heart.

There was a rude bench behind her, on which she sank wearily. Well, it was over; she had done her day's work, and she had done it thoroughly. She had robbed an honest man of his sweetest hope and purpose in life, and yet no sinner had been so innocent as she. She had done all in her power to like him; she had tabulated his virtues; she had told herself over and over again that no man was ever more deserving of a woman. "He has fewer faults than other men. What is a little brusquerie and a dictatorial manner, when he is really so kind-hearted and humble-minded?" she had told herself. "It is not necessary that a man should be handsome. If I loved him, I should get used to his little ways." And yet, in spite of these arguments, she had turned upon him almost fiercely. "It is not my

fault that you have no power to touch my heart."
That is what she had said to him.

Gloden could give no reason for the sudden
feeling of irritation that seized on her when she
met Mr. Lorimer's questioning glance. He was
about to speak to her, and then he had checked
himself. Had he suspected anything? But why
should he suspect anything? She had a perfect
right to be walking with a friend.

" Are you not a little imprudent, Miss Carrick ? "

And Gloden started in good earnest. She had
heard no footstep, and there was Mr. Lorimer
standing before her, while the pointer laid a cold
black nose on her lap.

"It is just beginning to sleet," he continued
carelessly. "I suppose you are tired, and that
Mr. Logan—the gentleman who was with you, I
mean—has gone back for an umbrella."

" Mr. Logan! Oh no ; he was obliged to go
back—to leave me. I was tired."

" So you seem "—sitting down beside her in a
friendly manner ; while Gloden, painfully conscious
of her red eyes, made much of Nan, and wished
Mr. Lorimer a hundred miles away. Why was he
always crossing her path now? There was some
fatality about it. When she least expected it, he
started up before her.

" I was awfully surprised to see you sitting here alone," went on the squire ; "and you were so deep in thought, too, that you never even looked up. Why, you quite jumped when I spoke to you."

"You startled me so."   Gloden took care not to look at him as she spoke.

But Reginald had sharp eyes, though he chose to appear unconscious.   His curiosity was fairly roused by this time.   He had met Mr. Logan striding moodily along in the direction of the town, and then he had come upon Miss Carrick sitting in a very despondent attitude, and he knew perfectly why Nan was absorbing all her attention.

"Don't you think we had better be walking on ?" was his next observation.   "You must not sit here any longer ; it would be a clear case of suicide ;" and he gave her his hand as though to help her to rise.

Evidently Gloden was to be allowed no choice in the matter ; anyhow, she yielded to Reginald's good-natured air of authority.

" But there is no need to take you out of your way," she observed, rather feebly.   "You were going home to luncheon, were you not ?"

"Oh, my luncheon is rather a movable feast, and I have no one to please but myself—at least, until Tottie is old enough to keep me company. When are you coming to see Tottie again, Miss Carrick? She is very faithful to your memory still. 'I love my Carricks;' I actually heard her say that the other day."

"What a darling she is! I should love to see her again."

"Your desire can easily be accomplished; Tottie is always on view in the afternoon. What does that reproving glance mean?" For Gloden, surprised by this into self-forgetfulness, had allowed him to have a glimpse of her swollen eyelids. "Am I putting my foot into it as usual — shocking the proprieties? I am afraid Tottie and I have no chaperone. Still, there is another way; Tottie can come and see you."

"Oh no—I mean you are very kind. Mr. Lorimer, please don't think me rude—I would not be that for the world—but I would rather not take you out of your way. I know it is your luncheon-time, and—and I am not good company to-day; I have been worried."

"I was thinking myself that you seemed a trifle low," he replied cheerfully. "I often have a fit of the blues; a big house all to myself—for, of course, Tottie does not count for much—is enough to make a man feel hipped."

"I think you bear your troubles wonderfully," she returned, with a sigh.

"Well, I don't know about that"—shaking his head. He had taken no notice of her hint that he should leave her. "I wish I had Aladdin's lamp at this moment, or that some genii would metamorphose this stick into an umbrella. This sleet is coming down rather unpleasantly ; I am afraid you will get awfully wet."

"It does not matter," she returned indifferently.

"You are anything but a fair-weather friend," continued Reginald, trying to jest. "I made your acquaintance in a thunderstorm. Now, if I were to believe in omens, I wonder what such a commencement would portend ?—that I am always to look out for squalls when I am in your vicinity ? "

But if he expected her to enter into the spirit of his joke, he was unpleasantly disappointed. It chimed in too ill with her strained and harassed mood.

"It means that you had better have nothing more to do with me," she broke out with sudden bitterness ; "that I am a source of trouble to myself and other people too."

Then he understood perfectly the cause of her present distress. "She has refused the fellow," he said to himself, and he thought that her tears

showed true womanliness. " She is not the ordinary
sort," he went on to himself. " She would not lead
on a man to propose to her out of sheer vanity and
love of conquest, and then turn him adrift without
a moment's scruple." And then he said in a kind
voice—

" One takes a morbid view of things when one
is a bit low; if the sun were shining now instead
of this confounded sleet, you would feel quite
different. Why, in the spring I felt fit to hang
myself; I could not stay in the house some evenings. I used to let the dogs loose, and take the
whole lot for a walk—they were company for
me, you see—and when I had had a five miles'
tramp I used to eat an enormous supper, and turn
in and sleep like a log. It was better than brooding over the fire, like an old woman with the
faceache."

" Or a young woman with the heartache "—
rather dryly. Reginald's manner was so droll, that
it was impossible to refrain from a smile.

" I am afraid young women's troubles have not
been much in my line," he returned, delighted with
this transient gleam of sunshine, though it was a
very poor specimen of a smile; "but I should
think the same sort of thing would suit them.
Take my advice, Miss Carrick; next time you are

in the doldrums, go across country as a crow flies—
stiles, five-barred gates, and all. Harvey will be
delighted to give you a lead, and in an hour's time
you will find yourself as hungry as a hunter.
Good lack, young gentleman, what is the meaning
of this?"—as a vigorous young arm was thrust into
his, and an affectionate push almost sent him in
the road.

"How fast you two walk!" grumbled Harvey;
"I am nearly out of breath catching you up.
What were you saying, Mr. Lorimer, about being
as hungry as a hunter? By Jove! if you only had
my appetite."

"Mine is Brobdingnagian." And as Harvey
looked rather perplexed, "My dear boy, have you
never heard of Swift's celebrated romance, 'Gul-
liver's Travels,' wherein the inhabitants are repre-
sented as giants about 'as tall as an ordinary
church steeple; everything else on the same pro-
digious scale,' so of course their appetites were
immense? But you have plenty to learn yet"—
shaking his head sadly.

"Oh, come, now, there is one thing you don't
know, does he, Glow? that Aunt Clemency has
made a steak-pudding for dinner. She makes
awfully good steak-puddings, Mr. Lorimer, with
kidneys and eggs and all sorts of things."

"Once in my life," observed Reginald, solemnly, "I partook of the dish you mentioned. It was at the house of a tenant. I was dead tired and wet through, and Farmer Denison was good enough to invite me to take a knife and fork; that was his mode of wording the invitation, I remember. 'Take a knife and fork with us, squire.' There were four of us," he continued, in a melancholy tone, "but I assure you I went for that pudding, and in a short time only the dish remained."

Harvey seemed to enjoy this anecdote. And as they were crossing the Market-place at that moment, more than one passer-by greeted the squire, and then stood and looked after the group rather curiously. Then a sudden inspiration came to Harvey. He chuckled, looked at his sister, then darted on in front, bolted into the shop, and returned breathless just as Mr. Lorimer was shaking hands with Gloden. Mr. Carrick followed him.

"Don't go, squire," he said politely. "My little chap here tells me that you are as hungry as a hunter, and that it is your luncheon-time, and that you have got a fancy for a steak-pudding. My wife and I will be fine and proud if you will take a snack with us."

Then a look of extreme delight came into Reginald's eyes. He hardly knew himself how famished he was until Harvey had begun to talk of the pudding. It is needless to say he accepted with alacrity.

Gloden, who was too much astonished at her uncle's audacity to make a remark, went off to her room to change her wet things; while Harvey allured Nan with a bone into the back yard; and Clemency, just a little bit flustered out of her usual calm, went in search of a clean napkin and to bid Patty take up the pudding carefully.

For one moment Gloden thought of sending down an excuse that her head ached, and that she did not need any dinner, but there was no bell in her room, and she was afraid that Harvey would make a fuss; so she hastily bathed her face and smoothed her hair, and then glided into the room, and into her place so quietly that Mr. Lorimer, who was speaking to Mrs. Carrick, did not notice her entrance, and started perceptibly when he saw her.

Clemency commiserated kindly with Gloden on her lack of appetite. "You have got a sort of chill with your wetting," she said. "I shall tell Patty to brew you an early cup of tea; there is nothing like a cup of tea for a headache."

"Mrs. Carrick, if you would only give my cook the receipt of this pudding, I shall be eternally obliged," observed Mr. Lorimer. "In my opinion it is a masterpiece of cookery."

Then it was evident that Clemency was very much pleased, and Reuben Carrick's eyes twinkled.

"My wife is a rare cook, squire. She has taught our girl a heap of things. In my opinion, every lass, high or low, should know how to cook. In our great-grandmothers' times the ladies were not above such work, but now every young chit of a girl thinks more about playing the piano and getting a smattering of French that would not be known for such by a native, than of beating up eggs for a cake or making a stew."

"Tottie shall be properly instructed in the art, Mr. Carrick," returned Reginald, easily. "She has already been detected making mud-pies in the spinney. We must not allow her talent to rust."

And again Harvey exploded. "That is the jolliest part about Mr. Lorimer," he observed confidentially to his sister afterwards; "he does make one laugh so. It is not so much what he says, as the droll way he says it, that is so killing. Was it not nice to see him sitting there talking so comfortably to Uncle Reuben? I tell you what, Gloden; he enjoyed himself awfully."

"Oh, do you think so?" asked Gloden, rather dubiously. But Harvey was right. Mr. Lorimer had thoroughly enjoyed himself.

In the first place, it was a new experience, and he loved new experiences when they were not too unpleasant, such as the extraction of a big double tooth, for example. It had never fallen to the lot of the young squire of Silcote to partake of early dinner in a small parlour behind a shop, with a pleasing view of a back yard. Then, though the viands were homely, they were excellent, and he had added the sauce of keen appetite. If any other ingredient entered into his enjoyment, he did not own it even to himself; only the sight of Gloden in her humble environment filled him with a sort of wonder. "Any one could see that she does not belong to the place," he said to himself. But he made no attempt to draw her into the conversation, and contented himself with chattering commonplaces to Clemency.

"I have got a half-holiday to-day, and I was just thinking what I could do with myself," observed Harvey, presently. "It is such a beastly sort of afternoon, you see; but now you have come"—nudging Reginald affectionately—"we shall find plenty to amuse us. Come along, and I will show you the Chinese room, where Gloden practises her fiddle."

Mr. Lorimer accepted this invitation with alacrity; but he stopped when he perceived that Gloden showed no intention of accompanying them.

"I hope that you intend to do the honours of the Chinese room, Miss Carrick," he observed, with languid politeness. "Harvey and I would only get into mischief alone."

"Perhaps you had better go up and have a look at the fire, Gloden," put in Clemency, rather anxiously. "Patty has been a little forgetful lately." Then Gloden felt herself obliged to go.

Reginald looked round with an air of satisfaction; the old-fashioned cosiness of the room pleased him. Patty had not forgotten her duty, and a bright fire welcomed them. Outside the prospect was sufficiently dreary; the sleet had turned to rain, and the wet street and heavy grey sky were not inviting.

"I am afraid I am weather-bound for the present, and must trespass on your hospitality," he said, with a hypocritical regret in his tones. And then he spied the violin-case, and his eyes brightened. "Now, if you would play to us!" he suggested, in a persuasive voice.

"Oh, bother the fiddle!" returned Harvey, discontentedly. "I thought we should have played

chess or backgammon. Gloden plays chess awfully
well, and I am first-rate at backgammon. We
could have tossed up, you know—chess heads,
and backgammon tails, or we might have played
by turns ; and there are some chestnuts I meant
to roast ; and——"

"Look here, Miss Carrick!" exclaimed Reginald,
in a tone of desperation, "if you are going to spoil
the boy in this way, I shall have to give him up ;
spoilt children are intolerable"—and here he took
Harvey gently by the ear. "Little boys should
be seen, not heard. Your sister is going to discourse sweet music to us, and if you do not shut
up and hold your tongue, I will bundle you down
the staircase, neck and crop."

But here Harvey broke away, and began dancing
round him in well-simulated rage.

Well, after a time peace was restored ; and
presently Harvey was seated on the rug in front
of the fire, with Griff beside him, watching the
chestnuts with absorbed attention, while Mr.
Lorimer, lounging at his ease in the roomy window-
seat, listened dreamily to the strains of the violin.

After all, the request had not been unpalatable
to Gloden. When anything agitated or excited her,
it was easier for her to play than talk ; music
always calmed and refreshed her, as the harp of

the young shepherd refreshed the tormented spirit of Saul.

Reginald, glancing from under his half-closed eyelids, saw the colour come to her pale cheek, and the light to her eyes. "Do not stop," he said more than once, and there was something urgent in his tone. The movement of the little thin hand seemed to fascinate him. When at last she laid aside her bow, and looked at him with an apologetic smile, his expression startled her.

"I forgot. Why did you let me go on playing?" she said, shocked at her own forgetfulness and absorption. "Harvey will be so tired, too. You ought to have stopped me, Mr. Lorimer."

"I could not bring myself to do that. I cannot thank you, Miss Carrick; no mere words could thank you." And then, as he stood aside to let her pass, there was a strange look in his eyes. But he was conscious of no actual thought—only a deep and subtle pleasure stirred him, as her dress brushed against him; and when he took her hand to bid her good-bye, a sort of thrill passed through him. "I shall come again; you will let me come again?" he said, in a voice so low that Harvey did not hear him.

Then Gloden's womanly instincts took alarm. "I think it would be better not," she said hurriedly ; but she dropped her eyes as she spoke. "You know what I mean, Mr. Lorimer ; " and her voice faltered a little.

"I shall not try to guess ; but if you will not give me permission, I am afraid I shall come all the same. I do not feel as though I can keep away ; " and before she could answer him, he had called Harvey and had left the room.

"What did he mean ? Why did he look at me like that ? I will never play to him again. He must not come here." But, though she told herself this, some unerring voice whispered that if he had a mind to come, it would be difficult to keep Reginald Lorimer away.

CHAPTER XII.

"WHAT IS WRONG WITH YOU, EWEN?"

> "Love that asketh love again,
> Finds the barter nought but pain ;
> Love that giveth in full store,
> Aye receives as much or more."
> DINAH MULOCH.

N O one would have changed places with Ewen Logan as he walked back to Grantham. Then, and ever afterwards, he told himself that it was the bitterest hour of his life. Never since he had attained manhood, had he been conscious of such bruised sensibility, of such mental aridity and lack of hope. The purpose and meaning of existence seemed utterly frustrated and set at nought. For more than four years he had nourished the secret hope that Gloden Carrick would be his wife, and had possessed his soul in patience.

"All comes to him who waits," he had often told himself. "In time she will realize the value of a love like mine. I will not lose heart. I will never give her up—never!"

But now for the first time despair had entered his soul. "It is not my fault if you have no power to touch my heart." Those were the words that had torn away the last shred of his hope—that showed him the truth in its bald and hideous verity. He would never win her; no amount of devotion or passionate insistence would ever make a responsive spark. She was not for him; and as he owned the humiliating fact, it seemed to him as though the winter of his life were come.

Poor Ewen! He was heavily handicapped. Was it any fault of his that nature had been so niggardly with her gifts? After all, what did his ungainly figure and short-sightedness matter in comparison with his good honest heart? The graces of manner may be much, but the virtues of uprightness and faithfulness are surely more. And to some women, even thin, sloping shoulders and clerical peremptoriness cannot obscure the inner beauty of true manliness and trustworthiness.

It was Ewen's loss that he had set himself to attain the impossible, while all the time the woman who should have been his helpmate dwelt beside him unrecognized and unrewarded. Had any one told him that he was the poetry of Winifred's life, he would have opened his eyes in amazement. He and Winifred were cousins, friends, chums; all his life he had looked upon her as a sister; he had told her all his troubles, he was sure of her sympathy; the tie of relationship made their bond a closer one than that which united Constance and Felix Hamerton.

Ewen took advantage of his position to lecture Winifred; he commented severely on any small failing or trifling dereliction of duty; and Winifred took his rebukes so meekly, with such sweetness of temper and cheerfulness, that he almost enjoyed his post of censor.

But, on the other hand, Winifred was not without her modest triumphs. She knew that she was necessary to Ewen—that he, as well as his mother, relied on her strong common sense and unfailing cheerfulness for most of their home comfort; and this knowledge was a continual spring of joy to her.

Winifred had no illusions about herself; she nourished no secret hopes that she would ever be more to Ewen. Her affections were never demonstrative, but deep down in her heart Ewen's image reigned supreme; his faults as well as his virtues were dear to her; his mannerisms were only beauties. Ewen was Ewen, and she had no fault to find with him.

Winifred had long tutored herself to look for Ewen's marriage; he would fall in love and marry like other men. When that day came, she meant to love his wife; she would take her into her heart and cherish her as a dear younger sister. Ewen's children should be as the very apple of her eye. "They shall love their Aunt Winnie," she would say to herself, in this shadowy day-dream of hers, as she trudged backward and forward to her work. She never dreamt about her own future; she was just "Aunt Winnie," and nothing else.

Many other women are as selfless and unexacting in their aims as Winifred Logan, and as ready to immolate themselves and their ideals on some shrine of domestic duty—who make no demands for themselves, and who find their happiness in the happiness of others, and pass twilight existences, growing grey before their time. "She hath done what she could;" may we not believe that such words will be said over many a one whose heart was often sore and wrung in this life by seeing others feasting in high bliss in upper rooms, while they are bidden to no such festivities? To some the bread of affliction and the water of

affliction are freely dealt—denied hopes, wasted
affections, famine of the heart's desires ; and yet
"she had done what she could," she had waited
and suffered patiently and without bitterness.   In
this life she had not received her good things ; they
are laid up for her in the divine treasury.

Ewen cared nothing for the sleet that drove
in his face and melted on his hat-brim ; nature
was sympathizing with him in his drear hour, and
not mocking him with sunshiny smiles.   He was
in no hurry to return to Chapel Street, where his
mother's anxious eyes would follow him about the
room.   He chafed at the idea of confinement to
four walls ; he walked on until he grew stiff and
tired with exertion before he set his face home-
wards.   Mrs. Logan uttered a cry of dismay when
she saw him.   He was wet through, and looked
utterly fagged ; a little river was running down
his shoulders on her neat oil-cloth.

"Oh, Ewen, where have you been?" she exclaimed, lifting up her hands.   "You must just
go upstairs and change your clothes.   Rebecca
is vexing herself because the dinner is nearly
spoilt ; but we must keep it waiting for all that.
Go, like a good lad, and I will just fetch a clean
cloth for the oil-cloth."

And Ewen, with some reluctance, followed his

mother's advice. But he could eat nothing, and very soon went off into the next room, on the pretext of writing his next Sunday's sermon ; but, as he sat there with the books before him, the thought of his crushed hopes and the cruel purposelessness of his life drove all but the text from his mind. How was he ever to preach a sermon again ? His tongue would cleave to his mouth with misery.

Winifred had had a hard day's work. The care of five high-spirited children, with all the insolence of youth and health, was certainly not a sinecure's part, and, dearly as she loved her pupils, and was beloved by them, there were occasional conflicts of wills.

The Parrys were famed for their hospitality, and the Red House was seldom free from guests, and the arrival of some favourite cousins had caused riot and insubordination in the schoolroom. Winifred, who had intended begging for a holiday on the score of Ewen's brief visit, discovered for herself that it would be cruel to ask for it, and that her presence for the next few days would be indispensable.

"It is rather hard," she said to herself with a sigh, as she closed the gate of the Red House behind her ; " Ewen will be obliged to go back to Eltringham on Saturday afternoon, and

what good will my half-holiday be to me? I shall
see so little of him—only in the evening, and then
I am tired. Ewen comes so seldom now, and
when he goes to Clacton—" But there she checked
herself; she could not trust herself to enter on that
subject. A dim fear that duty would detain her
at Grantham had more than once crossed her
mind.

As she let herself in with her latch-key, Mrs.
Logan stepped noiselessly out of the parlour.
Her face wore an anxious expression.

"I hope you are not wet, Winnie, my dear"—
feeling her tenderly over the arms and shoulders.

But Winifred only laughed. "Of course not. It
is quite fine, Aunt Janet. Where is Ewen?"

Then Mrs. Logan shook her head. "I will
come up with you a moment," she said mysteriously; "there is no need for me to make
the tea until you are ready. It has been a long
day, Winifred, and I have been wanting you more
than usual. Let me hang up your cloak; you
will be for changing your dress, of course; it
seems a pity to wear a good material like that
in the evening. I will give you out your old
black silk; with a lace bow, it will look as nice as
possible."

Winifred gave no heed to this economical remark. "What's wrong, Aunt Janet?" she asked, coming to the point as usual. "Why are you puckering up your forehead and talking under your breath, as though some one were ill?"

"Dear me, Winifred, how sharp you are!" returned Mrs. Logan, nervously; "there is no keeping anything from you. Why should you think anything is wrong? I am quite sure that Ewen hasn't spoken more than a dozen sentences since breakfast-time."

Then Winifred, with a trace of impatience in her manner, took the old silk dress from her aunt's hands.

"I wish you would sit down, Aunt Janet, and tell me everything straight out. Ewen was as cheerful as possible this morning. He was going to call on Miss Carrick, but he walked with me first to the Red House, and we were talking about Clacton all the time. How soon did he come back?"

"Oh, my dear, not until long past dinner-time— the joint was nearly spoilt; and then he came in wet through, and looking as fagged as though he had walked twenty miles. I made him change his things, but he could not eat more than two or three morsels—he said he was too tired; and then he went off to write his sermon, and he is writing it still for all I know."

Winifred remained silent—her eyes were fixed on the floor ; then she roused herself.

"Did he speak of Miss Carrick, Aunt Janet ? "

"Only a word or two. He said he had seen her, and that she was very well, but he did not enter into particulars. I think he must have been disappointed in his visit, he looked so glum and out of sorts. It is very strange, is it not, Winnie ? Ewen has such a sweet temper ; he is so seldom cross."

"Don't trouble about it, Aunt Janet ; we will just leave him alone—that is always the wisest way. He is a little over-excited about Clacton ; it is such a wonderful thing to him, you know. Why, he is only just thirty, and to have a living offered to him. It shows what a good opinion the bishop has of him."

"That was just what I was saying to myself, Winnie. Why, I could hardly sleep all night with thinking of it all. And how proud your uncle would have been ! But there, you will be wanting your tea, and the kettle will be boiling over. Come down to the fire as soon as ever you can, for you have got a starved look, Winnie."

And Mrs. Logan bustled away, drying her eyes as she went ; while Winifred, with a grave look on her face, finished her toilet. But she was very

cheerful when she came downstairs, and she took
no notice of Ewen's taciturnity. She would not
allow her aunt to question him about his progress
with the sermon. "Students never like to be
questioned," she observed smilingly, and she
covered his silence by talking herself on every
possible subject except one—she never mentioned
Clacton.

Ewen, numbed and frozen by hours of solitary
brooding, felt a little warmed and cheered by his
cousin's placid liveliness. He did not refuse food,
as he had at dinner, and he showed his need of it
by the avidity with which he swallowed it. When
Winifred quietly replenished his cup he took it
thankfully, and when he at last pushed aside his
plate there was more colour in his face. Neither
of the women offered any objection when he
announced his intention of going back to his
sermon. Mrs. Logan looked after him wistfully,
and her lips opened, but Winifred nudged her
significantly.

"Let him feel free to do as he likes," she
whispered, and as usual her good sense prevailed.

When prayers were over, Mrs. Logan gave her
son an appealing glance.

"You will not be sitting up, my boy," she said,
laying a thin hand on his shoulder, with the worn

wedding-ring very loose on it, and her voice was soft and coaxing.

"No, mother, I think not," he answered, with unusual gentleness; and then a touch of compunction made him add, "I will try to be more sociable to-morrow."

Winifred said nothing, except a brief good night as she left the room; but an hour later she opened her door gently and crept downstairs. She was still in the old black silk that looked so worn and shiny in the daylight, and a little grey woollen shawl was over her shoulders. Her pince-nez was dangling from her neck, and the large, short-sighted eyes looked a little pathetic. The little parlour was so dark that for a moment she could not distinguish anything. Ewen had turned out the gas, and had sat down to the fire as though to warm himself; his elbows were on his knees, and his chin propped on them. Winifred could see the gleaming of his spectacles as she came towards him.

He made no remark as she knelt down and roused the fire; but when a tiny blaze spurted up, she turned to him and said quietly, "What is wrong with you, Ewen?" Then he started in earnest.

"What do you mean?" he returned, and his

voice was rather gruff. "Why are you not in bed, Winnie? It is half-past eleven at least."

"It is more than that," she replied placidly. "I am not sleepy, so I thought I would keep you company. Tell me all about it, Ewen. I have guessed your trouble already; it flashed upon me in a moment. It is about Miss Carrick; you care for her"—Winifred could not bring herself to say "love;" the word stuck in her throat—"and she has disappointed you."

A dark flush sprang to Ewen's brow. "How could you know? I have never mentioned her name," he stammered. "Are you a witch, Winnie?" for there was something uncanny to him in the way she had surprised his carefully guarded secret.

"No," she said quietly; "but it is not easy to deceive me. You and Aunt Janet are all I have in the world, and your joys and sorrows are mine. You believe that, do you not, Ewen?"

She spoke without excitement. She was still kneeling before the fire, and her strong white hands were loosely folded before her. There was nothing in her expression or manner that conveyed the idea of suppressed emotion; it might have been his childish confidante Winnie begging to share his trouble.

For a moment he hesitated, but she had chosen her opportunity well; the quiet hour, the shadowy room, were all in her favour. After all, why should he keep his pain to himself? Winnie was reliable; she never chattered about other folk's business; she had a still tongue when she chose; she always knew the right thing to say, and when to say it. And so it was that Ewen opened his heart to her, and the story of his four years' love was made plain to her.

Winifred listened to it all in silence; she knew better than to interrupt him by a word. Now and then her eyes grew moist, and once she shivered slightly; but she had herself well in hand, and Ewen never noticed these signs of agitation.

"It is all over, Winnie," he finished; "she will never care for me—never!"

She seemed to take counsel with the fire before she answered him. If Ewen hoped that she would contradict him, he was disappointed. To Winifred's strong common sense, it would have been cruelty to fan the expiring hope.

"No," she said, very slowly and sadly, "she will never care for you; you are right to give it up, Ewen."

He winced at her plain speaking, as though she had touched a wound. In spite of his despair, was

there still a lingering spark of hope that Winifred
had quenched ?

"All these four years have been years wasted.
I have given her the best of my life!" he exclaimed
bitterly.

Then Winifred turned her face to him. "They
have not been wasted, Ewen," she said softly. "No
time or love that we give to one of our fellow-
creatures is ever or can be ever wasted ; it is blas-
phemy even to hint at such a thing."

"I do not understand you," he replied drearily.
"What has been the use of it all, either to her or
myself ? "

"Dear Ewen, that is more than I can say. No
man, or woman either, could ever properly answer
that question ; nevertheless, it is the truth I am
telling you. Your love for Gloden Carrick has not
been wasted, and never will be."

"I cannot follow you, Winifred."

"No, dear, perhaps not ; one must work out all
these problems for one's self. If I did not hold this
belief"—and here her voice trembled a little—"I
should not be the contented woman I am. You
must take this comfort to yourself—that the love
you have felt for Gloden all these years have
wrought some blessing for her, if not for yourself.
Ewen, you know more than I ; it is for you to

teach us. 'Through much tribulation——' How does that verse end?"

"Don't, Winnie; you make me ashamed of myself. What a selfish fellow I have been! But she has bowled me over utterly. How am I to live my life without her? Do you know, I hate the idea of Clacton."

"Never mind all that, Ewen." Then, as he looked at her in surprise, "Never mind how you feel about things; you must just go on living, and let the feelings take care of themselves. You are unhappy, my poor boy—yes, I know that—but all the same you will do your duty."

He shook his head. "Just now, before you came downstairs, I told myself that I should never be able to preach again."

"You will preach far better than you ever have done; this pain is part of your clerical education. I am not afraid either for you or your people." Then she stopped, and said persuasively, "You will let me tell Aunt Janet about this?"

"Is it necessary? Why should we make her unhappy?"

"It will not make her more unhappy; she already guesses that you are in trouble. I think we owe it to her, Ewen."

Then he made no further objection. "You must

tell her not to speak to me about it. Gloden's name must not be mentioned between us."

"I think you may trust Aunt Janet; and it is far better for her to know." She hesitated, cleared her voice, and then went on a little hurriedly, "When you and Aunt Janet are alone together at Clacton, it will never do to keep her in the dark about things."

"What on earth do you mean, Winnie? Why should mother and I be alone?"

"I had not meant to speak of this to-night, Ewen, and it is so late; but perhaps I had better say it. You will make a home for Aunt Janet, of course—it is what you and she have always wished; but it does not follow that you are to make one for your cousin;" but Winifred did not look at him as she spoke.

"What nonsense is this?" he exclaimed angrily. "Are you refusing to cast in your lot with us after all these years? You know as well as I do that you are necessary to my mother, and that neither of us can get on without you."

"You will soon learn to do without me," she replied, but, in spite of her efforts, she could not keep the tears out of her voice; "and Aunt Janet is stronger and better now. Indeed—indeed, you must try and see things from my point of view.

How could I live in dependence on a cousin?—not even a brother; and how do you suppose I could get my living in a place like Clacton-over-Fields? No, no; you and Aunt Janet will be as cosy as possible, and you must just leave me behind. Mrs. Parry will be too thankful to find room for me in the Red House, and if you choose to give me an invitation for the midsummer and Christmas holidays, why, I shall accept them thankfully."

"But, Winifred, this is absurd. As long as I have a roof over my head I shall expect you to make your home with us. You are my mother's adopted daughter, and—— "

"And Ewen Logan's adopted sister," she finished playfully, but her eyes were wet. "Thank you a thousand times for your generosity, my dear cousin, but my mind is made up. When Aunt Janet goes to Clacton Vicarage, I shall take up my quarters at the Red House as an independent working woman. Now I really must bid you good night, or rather good morning, for it will soon strike one, and I am positively growing sleepy;" and then she took his hand and smiled in his face, and Winifred's smile was very sweet.

CHAPTER XIII.

BROTHER DANIEL.

"Adapt thyself to the things with which thy lot has been cast; and the men among whom thou hast received thy portion, love them, but do it [sincerely]."—M. Aurelius Antoninus.

AS Reginald Lorimer walked home through the wintry twilight that evening, he told himself that not many days should elapse before he found some pretext for repeating his visit.

When he had said to Gloden that it would be impossible for him to keep away, he was acting under the influence of an overmastering impulse. He no longer disguised from himself that the girl attracted him strangely. She was unlike any one whom he had ever met. She reminded him of some rare flower hidden in a deserted garden. She had unfolded slowly and with reluctance, but it seemed to him now as though her pale bloom had a delicate beauty in it that exactly suited his taste.

But though this new friendship, as he termed it, was beginning to dominate his thoughts, he never called it by its right name; the idea that he was falling in love for the first time in his life, before Car had lain in her grave a twelvemonth, would have shocked him utterly.

But he was lonely and restless—this is how he put it to himself—and Gloden Carrick's music and her soft voice and quiet movements soothed and rested him. He was at his ease with her. She never seemed to expect him to pay her attention, and even when she was in one of her perverse moods, and kept him at a distance, she amused and interested him.

"She gives me very little encouragement," he said to himself, as he walked leisurely down the Silcote road; "she is always trying to put me in my right place. She is the proudest and the pluckiest girl I ever knew. But I like her all the better for her quiet insolence; it seems to draw a fellow on, and, though she told me just now that it would be better for me to stay away, there was a look in her eyes that contradicted her words. If she would only let herself go and forget all this nonsense about her uncle's shop, we should be good friends."

But though Reginald's will was good, he was unable to carry out his intentions. One of Lady Car's numerous cousins wrote to propose a visit to Silcote. The young squire, who was the soul of hospitality, gladly welcomed his guest ; and Sir Charles Egerton, who found his quarters comfortable, was easily induced to send for his wife and eldest daughter. After all, Reginald was to eat his Christmas dinner at his brother-in-law's house, for pressure of business detained Felix in town, and as Ninian had a bad feverish cold, Constance was unwilling to leave home.

And so it was that Mr. Lorimer found no opportunity of repeating his visit to Market Street, and was obliged to content himself with sending messages through Harvey when he spent his usual Saturday afternoons at Silcote Park.

Harvey had a great deal to say about Sir Charles Egerton, whom, he informed Gloden, was one of the biggest swells he had ever seen, but not a bad fellow on the whole. And about Lady Egerton, who was a flimsy, conceited piece of goods, in Harvey's estimation, with a fine lady's drawl, and a patronizing air that angered him excessively. And he had scant reverence for the slim, large-eyed Ursula, who was at that uncertain age of budding womanhood when youthful *gaucheries* blend with tremulous dignity. To Harvey this big, solemn young person was an anomaly.

"There is nothing she can do, and nothing she cares about, except reading; and Lady Egerton is always nagging at her for hunching her shoulders and spoiling her eyes," went on Harvey. "I pity her for having such a mother. I think Mr. Lorimer pities her too, for he is always trying to draw her out."

"I wonder you care to go there so much under the circumstances," was Gloden's rejoinder.

But Harvey flared up at this. What did it matter if a hundred disagreeable people were at Silcote, as long as he had his friend?

"He is jollier than ever, I can tell you that, Glow," he finished. "He is just like a great big brother to me." And thereupon Gloden held her peace.

But she was very grateful in her heart to Harvey's friend; and now and then the thought crossed her that, if only circumstances had been different, she might have been his friend too.

"He is always trying to be kind to me now," she said to herself. "I think it is his way to be kind; he likes to see people happy, and to be

happy himself. He has a sunshiny nature, one
can see that, in spite of his trouble. And he is
not selfish ; he would go out of his way to help
people."

Gloden told herself that she was glad, very
glad, that Mr. Lorimer had not come again. It
was far better for them both that there should
be no repetition of his visit. And yet when
Christmas had arrived, and the hall was empty,
she was conscious of a vague feeling of discomfort.

It was her Uncle Reuben who had returned
from the station, and had brought them the news
that he had seen the squire and his guests enter-
ing the London train.

"They had a mountain of luggage with them,"
he remarked ; "it took all the porters to wait on
them. The squire saw me, and wished me a
happy Christmas, and sent his kind regards to
the ladies. And where is Harvey ?"—interrupting himself. "There was a goodish-sized box,
and as heavy as lead, waiting for him at the
station, which I brought up with me. The
station-master told me it had just come from
London, and that he was going to send it on.
It is a present from the squire, I'll be bound.
He will spoil the lad. We shall never make an
honest tradesman of him, shall we, Clem ?" and

Reuben rubbed his hands gleefully, quite unaware
that his words had given Gloden a stab.

"Make a tradesman of you, my darling!" she
repeated indignantly to herself. "Never, if I
have to go on my knees to prevent it!" and the
next moment she heard Harvey calling to her
excitedly to come and inspect his treasure.

Uncle Reuben was right. It was the squire's
Christmas gift to his boy-friend. Harvey was
almost voiceless with delight. It was a set of
carpenter's tools in a handsome oak box—the
best and handsomest that could be got for
money; and Gloden felt a little pang at the
costliness of the gift, but she dare not give vent
to this feeling.

"How very, very kind!" she murmured, as she
pretended to inspect a chisel.

Harvey gave a scornful little laugh; his voice
wasn't quite under control.

"Kind!" he repeated. "Can't you find a bigger
word than that, Glow? He gets better and kinder
every day. He has got the heart of a king; he is
magnificently generous!" And here, in despair of
finding fitting words in which to express his feelings, Harvey brought the hammer in contact with
the table so sharply that Griff started from his
sleep and began to bark furiously.

"Hold your tongue, you duffer!" exclaimed his young master, brutally; "'for if dogs had nerves like humans, where were you?' Lie down, and leave your betters to talk. By-the-by, Glow, I have never given you the squire's message, and it was a pretty long one, I can tell you; I don't remember the half of it."

Gloden felt a little injured at this. When Harvey had so much, he might have taken the trouble to remember a message. But it was no good scolding him; boys were proverbially careless.

"I shall think of it directly," continued Harvey, pleasantly; he was ignorant of his sister's hurt feelings. "Won't I make a famous set of book-shelves for Uncle Reuben's birthday? He will be fine and pleased—ay, Glow? Don't you wish you were me, instead of being a girl, and then Mr. Lorimer could send you presents?"

"I would rather that you should have them," she replied gently. "Have you remembered any of the message yet, Harvey?"

"Well, I think I have it now. He sent his love, and——"

"He did nothing of the kind; you ought to be ashamed of yourself for inventing such things;" and Gloden coloured with annoyance.

Harvey looked up in placid astonishment.

"Why are you exciting yourself so? Well, perhaps he did not send love; it was kind regards,
or some such rubbish. You must not expect me
to remember all that. Now, don't interrupt me
again, or I shall forget everything. His kind
regards, and he was awfully sorry, and all that
kind of thing, that he had not been able to call
and say good-bye, but he wished you a happy
Christmas, and hoped you would be comfortable."

"And is that all?" It was a disappointing
message, but of course Harvey had forgotten half.

"Well, it is all I can remember," replied Harvey,
truthfully; "but he was a long time saying it.
I think, from his manner, he had been wanting
to come dreadfully, only those old Egertons prevented it. I know he said he was awfully sorry
two or three times over, and then he told me to
take care of you, and not let you tramp out all
weathers. 'Your sister is delicate, and you must
look after her.' I could not help laughing at that.
You are not delicate, are you, Glow?"

Gloden shook her head; she felt slightly
mollified. He had meant to bid them good-bye,
then, and it was not his fault that he had been
unable to do so; and he had begged Harvey to
take care of her. It was kind—it was very kind of
Mr. Lorimer to trouble himself about her. After

all, the message had not been so disappointing, and she forgave Harvey for his thoughtlessness.

Harvey's grand tool-box made him completely happy, and gave him and Bernard Trevor plenty of occupation. Uncle Reuben's bookshelves were measured, and a wood-box for Aunt Clemency designed, and during the daylight hours both lads were busy in a lower room that was turned into a workshop.

To Gloden Christmas could not be otherwise than dull. Violet Winter had gone to town, so there were no more visits to the Gate House for the present; and, in spite of efforts on hers and Winifred's part to appear as though nothing had happened, their relations were somewhat strained, and Gloden saw little of her friends in Chapel Street. But she fought her depression bravely. She practised her violin, and studied Italian sedulously, and was always ready when Harvey wanted her to walk or play chess with him.

It was evident, too, that Clemency had something on her mind, though, as usual, she kept it to herself; but the reason of the secret uneasiness that marred her enjoyment of Christmas was this: Clemency had one brother, to whom she was much attached. He was a draper at Stapleton, a town about eighteen miles distant, and it had always been a custom for Daniel Moore and his family to spend Twelfth-night with Clemency and her husband.

For the first time in her life Clemency looked forward to this evening with dread. Daniel was Daniel, and she could not pick holes in her own flesh and blood ; but whatever would Gloden say to Eliza, with her dressiness and loud voice? "Not that there is any harm in Eliza," thought Clemency with momentary compunction ; "for she is a good-hearted creature, and makes Daniel an excellent wife, and she has an eye for business that makes me ashamed of myself. But though Lavinia and Mary Anne are my own nieces, they are not to my taste. It is their upbringing, poor things ! Eliza was all for accomplishments and outward show, and so their manners have suffered. They are young and flighty ; maybe they will settle down when they get husbands of their own."

"I suppose you have been hearing from Daniel," observed Reuben, one evening when the young folks had retired, "and you have been ordering your goose as usual?" for hot goose was always the *pièce de résistance* on these occasions.

"I am afraid Dan and Eliza would be affronted if we passed them over this Christmas," returned Clemency, in a deprecatory tone.

Then Reuben laid down his pipe and stared at her in surprise. "Whatever has come to you, wife?" he asked mildly. "It is not like you to be setting aside old customs. Why, Daniel and Eliza have eaten their Twelfth-night supper with us ever since we were married. And there's Lavinia's sweetheart, too; he is a decent sort of young chap, they tell me, and she would be bringing him, of course."

"I am thinking of Gloden, Reuben," returned his wife, slowly. It is no want of good-will to my own belongings, but there is your niece to be considered. Gloden is stand-offish by nature, and she does not take to our friends, and Lavinia and Polly are not always as nice-mannered as I should wish them to be." And here Clemency broke off in much distress, for a most unusual frown was spreading over Reuben's forehead.

"You astonish me, Clem," he said rather severely. "Do you suppose your folk are to suffer because my brother's children have come under my roof? Nay, nay; there is no justice in that. Daniel shall eat his Twelfth-night supper here as usual. Your relations shall be as kindly welcome as mine. Gloden may be uppish, but she must put aside her pride for one evening, and help us entertain our guests. I am not one for spoiling

young people, and keeping them from doing their
duty. So you will set about writing at once to
Daniel, if you wish to please me; and you can tell
Lavinia, with my love, to bring her spark if
she likes—Hector Bradley; isn't that his name?
A heathenish sort of name, too, for a clerk in a
bank."

"Very well, Reuben," returned Clemency, duti-
fully; for she knew better than to argue with her
husband when he was in one of his high moods.
Any want of consideration to Clemency always
set his back up, as he phrased it.

"She is a cut above most women, and no one
shall look down on her," he would say in his
rough chivalry; for no knight ever fought more
bravely for his lady of delight than Reuben Carrick
for the rights of his homely little wife.

"My brother and his family always have supper
with us on Twelfth-night," observed Clemency, a
little timidly, when she found herself alone with
her niece the evening before the festivity.

Gloden looked up from her work in some
surprise. "I did not know you had a brother,
Aunt Clemency."

"Dear heart! to think of that, and Daniel the
only brother I ever had! but it is not often we
meet, for we are both of us busy people."

" I suppose he lives at a distance ? "

"Well, it is not what you call far. Stapleton
is about eighteen miles from here. He has the
draper's shop, and he and Eliza are most busy all
the year round ; but on Daniel's birthday and mine,
and on Twelfth-night, we generally sup together."

" That must be very pleasant for you," returned
Gloden, with chilly politeness.

An irritable sensation, as of multitudinous pins
and needles, began to torment her. The draper's
shop at Stapleton loomed largely in the background
of her consciousness.

Clemency, who was very sensitive on the subject
of her belongings, detected a certain irony in
Gloden's tone.

" We have always been good friends, Daniel
and me," she returned. " Eliza did not hit it off
with me at first. She was a smart woman, and
thought a deal of things about which I never
troubled my head. But there, it takes all kinds of
people to make up a world ; and she is thoroughly
good-hearted. As for Lavinia and Polly, they are
not your sort, I am afraid ; but it is their upbringing,
poor lassies. Eliza was always for spoiling the
girls."

" Are they—are they all coming to-morrow ? "
asked Gloden, faintly.

"Dear me! yes. Eliza never stirs anywhere without the girls; and they will bring a visitor with them too. Lavinia has a sweetheart; he is a very steady, promising young fellow. Daniel says his name is Hector Bradley, and he is in the Stapleton bank." Then, as she caught sight of her niece's face, she added hurriedly, "I hope you will put up with it, Gloden, if the company is not to your taste; for, as your Uncle Reuben says, it is ill work breaking with old customs."

"I hope I shall never interfere with any of your old customs, Aunt Clemency," returned Gloden, shortly, as she folded up her work.

She did not wish to appear ungracious, but there was no mistaking her manner; and poor Clemency went downstairs with a sigh, to see the batch of mince-pies that Patty had turned out of the oven.

Meanwhile, Gloden carried her grievance to Harvey; but if she had hoped for sympathy she was disappointed. Harvey first listened with deep interest to his sister's account, and then the sight of her disgusted face so aroused his risibility, that he flung himself face downward on the old chintz couch in convulsions of mirth.

Gloden gazed at him in affronted silence. "How can you be so absurd, Harvey?" she said at last.

"Absurd! you will kill me, Gloden, if you stand there looking like a tragedy queen. Why don't you see the fun of things, like me? Did you say the fellow's name was Hector? I wonder if he has a brother Achilles? And he is Lavinia's young man. Good lack, what names! Cheer up, Glow; it will be a regular lark. Perhaps they will play kiss-in-the-ring and hunt-the-slipper."

"It is no use talking to you, Harvey, when you are in one of your ridiculous moods."

And as he only buried his head in the sofa-cushions in another convulsive fit of merriment, Gloden left him; and Harvey jumped up and went in search of his aunt.

He found her making an apple-turnover for his supper; he had made the remark at dinner-time that apple-turnovers were first-rate. At the sight of his favourite delicacy, he gave her a rough hug, and then seated himself on the kitchen table.

"You are a first-rate hand at cooking, aren't you, Aunt Clem? Are all those tarts and pies for the supper to-morrow? What are you doing now?"— for Aunt Clemency had turned her attention to some eggs, that she was beating up with much energy.

"It is only the custard; but I want to give my mind to it."

But, disregarding this hint, Harvey propped his chin on his hands and watched the operation.

"Why did you not tell us you had a brother?" he began abruptly. "Is he like you, Aunt Clem? He must be a good sort if he is."

Then the soft colour came into Clemency's faded cheek. "He is better than I shall ever be, my dear; but your uncle says we should never be taken for brother and sister. He is a fine-looking man, is Daniel; and Eliza was an uncommonly handsome girl. They called her the belle of Stapleton when she was young. I think Lavvy features her mother; Polly has no good looks to boast of."

"And Achilles—I mean Hector—is he good-looking too?"

"He is nothing out of the common, Eliza says; but he has good principles, which is a sight better than good looks. I am afraid they are not your sort, Harvey, or Gloden's either. My folk are plain people, and do not pretend to hold up their heads like gentlefolks. They have not had your advantages; there's a deal in that."

"All right; I see what you mean. Well, I won't spoil your custard any longer, Aunt Clem;" and Harvey rushed off.

When Aunt Clem made these humble speeches, he never knew how to take them. "We must just put up with it, you know," he said, with unusual seriousness, when his sister came to wish him good night. "Don't mount your high horse, Glow; it is not worth it. We shall have to be civil for Aunt Clem's sake; and they may not be so bad. Just follow my example. I am going to enjoy the fun and the tuck-out;" and with this philosophical remark, the young follower of Epicurus turned over on his pillow and was soon asleep.

CHAPTER XIV.

AMONG THE PHILISTINES.

"Do what thou mightest, and come what come can."
Ancient Proverb.

"In one respect man is the nearest thing to me, so far as I must
do good to man, and endure them."—M. AURELIUS ANTONINUS.

GLODEN was somewhat rebuked by Harvey's philosophical cheerfulness, and certain pricks of conscience made themselves felt.

The next morning she asked her aunt quite pleasantly if she could not help Patty ; and, after a momentary hesitation, Clemency inquired if she would mind polishing the glass and china for the supper-table.

" The shop takes me off so much," she said apologetically, " and it is not as though I could give my mind to things ; and Patty is young, though she is willing. When my sister-in-law gives supper-parties, she has Lavinia and Polly to help her, and they are full of notions that they have got from their smart friends. They think a deal of smartness," she continued, with a glance at Gloden's black stuff, "and that is why your Uncle Reuben insists on my wearing my new black silk that he bought me last Christmas, and that has lain in lavender ever since, though it is far too good for the occasion."

"I cannot make myself smart, I am afraid, Aunt Clemency," returned Gloden, quickly, for this hint was not thrown away on her.

"The frock you wore at Dr. Parry's, when they had that children's party and you played for them, would do as well as possible, and it fits you to a nicety." For Clemency loved a quiet daintiness in dress, and Gloden's fine black cashmere, with soft ruffles at neck and wrists, was just to her taste, and in her opinion set off the slim, graceful figure remarkably well.

"I will wear it if you wish, Aunt Clemency," was Gloden's reply, for she had made up her mind to behave as well as she could. Harvey's words, "We must be civil for Aunt Clem's sake," had appealed to her sense of rightness. "I will try to make myself pleasant for this one evening," she said to herself; and she dressed herself in time to help Patty with the table.

"Dear me, Gloden, I call that beautiful!" exclaimed Mrs. Carrick, as she rustled into the room in her new black silk, a little breathless with her haste. "I wonder whatever Eliza and the girls will say to that?" For Gloden, who had an innate talent for decorations, had decked the table very prettily with holly-berries and evergreens, and had folded Aunt Clemency's fine napkins in some wonderful manner. "They look for all the world like white flowers," she admiringly continued.

"I am glad you are satisfied," returned Gloden, looking at her work with pardonable pride. "The fire is burning up beautifully in the best room, Aunt Clemency, and the tea-table is all laid out, and looks as nice as possible."

"That it does; and I am ever so much obliged to you, Gloden," returned Clemency, warmly. She would have liked to have given the girl a kiss in token of her gratitude, but she dared not venture on such a liberty; no kiss had yet passed between them. "I will not forget this in a hurry," she continued; "for, what with your Uncle Reuben wanting me so much in the shop, and fearing that things would never be ready, I got quite in a fidget. But now I am a lady at large, and can just sit with my hands before me."

"Gloden, there is a button off my wristband!"

exclaimed Harvey, bursting into the room. "Come and sew it on for me, there's a good girl ;" and Gloden immediately went in search of her workbox.

"Eliza won't get over those napkins," thought Clemency, as she moved away after them with a pleased smile; and the next moment the door-bell pealed through the house.

Harvey dragged Gloden with him to peep over the banisters.

"That is brother Daniel," he observed, in a loud whisper, as a big man came within view. "And do you see that stout party in purple satin? My word, isn't she a stunner !"

But Gloden would not listen to any more, though Harvey still insisted on leaning over, at the peril of his neck, for a good look at the girls.

"That Hector Bradley looks rather a cad," he remarked, in an injured voice, as he rejoined his sister. "He has red hair, and looks all collar. They are awfully smart, those girls; they are all colours of the rainbow. I hope they won't think you a dowd, Antelope ;" and then he relaxed into a chuckle. "I don't think much of Lavvy's young man."

"I suppose we must go down now," observed

Gloden, after a few minutes; and, as Harvey wanted his tea, he agreed to this with alacrity.

The sound of voices was almost deafening when they entered the room. The Moore family had excellent lungs, and it was a habit of theirs to talk all together, which was rather confusing to strangers, and especially as their good opinion of themselves prevented any shyness.

"I suppose this is the niece you have been telling me about, Clem?" observed Mrs. Moore, a high-coloured woman of goodly dimensions, dressed in questionable taste; and she shook Gloden's hand heartily. "I am glad to see you, miss; and, as we are amongst friends, I can tell you you are a lucky girl to have found such snug quarters. Reuben is a warm man, though he keeps it close;" and she shook a fore-finger at him playfully as she spoke.

"How do you do, Mrs. Moore?" remarked Harvey, easily. "I am very well, thank you, and so is Gloden. Why do you call Uncle Reuben a warm man, eh? I suppose it is some joke. You are a little warm yourself, are you not? Shall I fetch a fire-screen? or perhaps you will prefer a fan. It is not pleasant to feel hot, is it?"—with the utmost friendliness. "I never suffer from heat myself. I wonder"—confidentially—"which is

Miss Lavinia and which is Miss Polly? I suppose
it is Miss Lavinia in the pink frock, because that
gentleman is talking to her. He is engaged to
her, is he not?"

"Bless me, what a precocious young gentleman
you are!" returned Mrs. Moore, delightedly.
"Yes, that is Lavvy. Come here, Lavinia. Here
is some one wants to make your acquaintance."
And in another moment Harvey was in the
midst of a group; for not only Lavinia, but her
sister, Miss Polly, and the red-haired, large-collared
Hector joined the circle.

Harvey was quite equal to the occasion. He
leant against the mantelpiece, with one foot crossed
over the other in an easy attitude, and a lock of
hair tumbling over his forehead. "Why did they
call you Hector?" Gloden heard him say. "Was
it a family name, Mr. Bradley? I am not finding
fault with it," continued Harvey, with engaging
politeness, "but I have the misfortune to be
curious by nature. It is one of my besetting sins,
Miss Polly. You are Polly, aren't you?"

"Dear heart! they are all in love with him
already," thought Clemency, as she rinsed out the
orange-coloured cups that were the pride of her
heart; "and he is behaving like a prince, bless
him!"

"I hope—I hope they will not find out how he is chaffing them," thought Gloden, in an agony, as the tittering laugh waxed louder and louder. "He is in such high spirits to-night, and so brimful of mischief, that I am afraid that he will end by doing something dreadful, and it is no use my trying to keep him in order." But she quailed inwardly as scraps of conversation reached her ear.

Harvey was becoming audacious. He seemed to have taken a fancy to Polly—a plain, good-tempered-looking girl, with a loud voice and an outrageous style of hair. "Doesn't it hurt you to have all those pins running into you?" he observed by-and-by. "It must bother you awfully to get your hair into that frizzy pile. Oh, it is the fashion, is it?"—some remark to this effect having reached his ear. "Don't you wish you were queen, and could stop all these stupid fashions? If I were you I should comb it quite smooth; it would look ever so much nicer."

"You leave Polly's hair alone, and hand me another muffin," interrupted Mrs. Moore, in high good humour. She was charmed with the boy, and so was Polly, and so was Lavinia, only she did not dare to show it openly, as Hector was jealous by nature. "He is beginning early, is he not, Reuben, making love to my Polly like that?"

"Who could help falling in love with Miss Polly!" exclaimed Harvey, sentimentally; and then he caught an imploring glance from Gloden.

"It is all right, Glow," he whispered, as he handed her some cake; "we must do at Rome as the Romans do. Miss Polly likes it hot and spicy. She asked me if I admired hers and Lavvy's style of hair, and she wondered that you did not do yours more in the fashion; so what was I to say when she had turned her head into a pincushion?"

"But do be careful, Harvey. It is very nice of you to make yourself so pleasant to these people, but there is no occasion to carry it too far."

"Polly declares that she is a sort of cousin," went on Harvey. "I was obliged to tell her that there was no relationship between us. It was precious cool of her, wasn't it? I mean to try brother Daniel, for a change." And, to her horror, she saw him the next minute plant himself opposite Mr. Moore, with his thumbs in the armholes of his waistcoat, in exact and striking imitation of the portly draper, while he questioned him affably about trade.

"It is rather a good business, is it not?" he observed blandly. "Drapery is not in my line, but one never knows what may happen."

"You are right there, young sir; and it is as good

a business as a man need have, if he has a proper
knowledge of textures." Brother Daniel said this
with a twinkle in his eye. He was a heavy, loosely
built man, but he was acute enough not to be
bamboozled by a slip of a lad, who was poking
fun at him. "And what do they mean to make
of you, my boy? I suppose Reuben will be putting
you into the book trade."

" I was thinking of being a commercial traveller
myself," returned Harvey, mildly. "They have
rather a jolly life of it, and know how to make
themselves comfortable. Of course, one would
prefer being Archbishop of Canterbury, and if I
had only stayed at Repton, there is no knowing
what I might have done."

But here there was a sudden truce to Harvey's
nonsense, as Polly interrupted him by a querulous
complaint that they were all as dull as ditch-water,
and wouldn't his sister come out of her corner and
play them a tune ?

" We will get Hector to ask her," she continued,
as Harvey hesitated ; and Gloden was presently
accosted by the young man.

"The ladies hope that you will give us a tune
on the fiddle," stammered Mr. Bradley, a little
awkwardly. "We shall be truly obliged, miss, as
things are just a little flat, and there is nothing
so rousing as a good tune."

" I am very sorry, but I am afraid I cannot play to-night," returned Gloden, stiffly. There were limits to everything. How was she to stand up before all those vulgar, noisy people, and play to them ? The thing was impossible.

" Oh, come, now ! I hope you won't be so disobliging," went on the fascinating Hector, with an affable smile ; "we are all in the family, so to speak." But Polly, who had been listening, broke in a little petulantly—

"You need not be so persuasive, Hector. If Miss Carrick does not wish to amuse us, let us play post ; we shall get far more fun out of that. I have got a pencil and paper in my pocket, so I will put myself down as Petersham ; and what will you be, Lavvy ?"

Gloden did not stop to hear any more ; she would take refuge in her own room until supper-time. No one would miss her, and Aunt Clemency was below, looking after Patty and the goose. She gained the door unperceived, opened it, and came face to face with Reginald Lorimer. Her surprise was so great and so undisguised that Mr. Lorimer could not refrain from a smile.

" You look as though you were interviewing a ghost," he said, shaking hands with her. " Your looks are wonderfully eloquent, Miss Carrick ; I will allow that my presence is unexpected, but I trust I am not unwelcome."

"We are pleased to see you, of course"—in a flurried tone, "but there is nowhere to ask you to sit down. They are playing games in there, and the supper is laid in the parlour."

"Come down to the shop a moment; the noise those lively young people are making won't let us hear our own voices. I want to tell you why I am here." And, to her own astonishment, Gloden meekly allowed herself to be conducted downstairs.

The shop was still lighted up, though the outer door was closed. Mr. Lorimer gravely handed her a chair, and leaned easily against the counter.

"I like this old shop," he remarked, glancing round him approvingly; "it is so quaint and old-fashioned, and all those books have such a friendly look. I should not mind being in the bookselling trade myself; it is perfectly respectable."

"Mr. Lorimer, please tell me why you are here."

"Called to order," murmured Reginald. "You are a terribly practical person, Miss Carrick. The fact is, some papers that my lawyers require have been left by mistake at the Hall, and there was nothing for it but to fetch them myself; so I have come down for one night. I go up to town again to-morrow by the 11.30 train."

"And you called here on your way to Silcote?"

"Precisely so. It came into my head suddenly that I would look you and Harvey up, and ask him to breakfast with me. I suppose Mrs. Norton will have something for us to eat, though I am not sure; he must take that on faith. I had no idea that you had a party, and my spirits sank at the sight of the supper-table. Mrs. Carrick was good enough to ask me to stay," he continued, looking at her as though to judge the effect of his words.

She flushed up at once. "Mr. Lorimer, please do not. You have no idea how dreadful it is. You have heard the noise, and I am afraid it will get worse and worse. Harvey is enjoying it, because he is only a child, and sees the fun of everything, and just for once he does not mind; but I came away because I could not bear it. I have never been accustomed to such things;" and there were tears in her eyes.

Reginald looked away quickly; her emotion made him feel uncomfortable. He did not like to tell her how sorry he was for her.

"Yes, I know; it must be an awful bore." But his tone said more than his words.

"They are Aunt Clemency's relations, but of course they are nothing to us," went on Gloden.

"And they are so ill-bred and familiar. Harvey is making fun of them all, and I am so afraid they will find it out before the evening is over. If you only saw them, you would understand. Aunt Clemency is a hundred times better than they are."

"I have a great respect for Mrs. Carrick," he replied quietly, and Gloden felt somehow as though she were reproved. "It is hard lines for you, and Harvey too; for I expect the young monkey sees things as clearly as you do. Won't it make it better for you if I stop?" and his voice grew persuasive. "It won't hurt me, and no one will be the wiser; and I should rather like it myself."

"I would not have you stay for the world," returned Gloden, vehemently; "it would make things worse for me."

But what other argument she would have used was never known, for at that moment Polly of the frizzy hair flew down the staircase shouting loudly, with Harvey after her, the game having degenerated into a romp.

"Give it up; it is not fair! You have cheated, Polly!" exclaimed Harvey. But his boisterousness died away at the sight of the squire; the lad's face grew crimson as he met his friend's eye.

"What's the game, Harvey?" asked Reginald,

with a droll look. "I thought the house was coming about our ears."

And Harvey, who looked rather ashamed of himself, became slightly cross. "Gloden would not play the fiddle to them, so we had games ; and they said they liked noisy ones ;" for Polly, giggling and abashed at the sight of a strange young man, had fled to her sister.

"Suppose you play your fiddle now," observed Mr. Lorimer, looking kindly at the girl; "you will have one appreciative auditor, and it will keep the barbarians quiet."

"Do you mean that you are coming too?" asked Harvey, incredulously; and his brief sulkiness vanished. "I would not have believed even you could be such a brick. Isn't he a brick, Glow?"

"Oh, you must not expect your sister to endorse such a flattering statement," returned Mr. Lorimer, with a laugh. "But we understand each other, don't we, old fellow?"—pulling his ear in an affectionate manner. "Miss Carrick, I have made up my mind. I am going to see you through this, and no amount of argument will stop me. Now, will you take my advice about the fiddle?" And as he evidently meant what he said, Gloden wisely held her tongue.

There was an astonished silence as the trio

entered, and Mr. Lorimer said quietly, "Your niece is going to play to us, Mr. Carrick." And Gloden in silence took out her violin from its case.

Why was it possible for her to play now? But Gloden was too prudent to ask herself that question. But as she played, Polly's giggles and Hector Bradley's loud whispers died away.

When Gloden raised her eyes, they rested on Reginald's rapt face, as he and Harvey sat together in the window-seat. Aunt Clemency, re-entering the room, seated herself behind her husband and listened with moist eyes and a happy heart.

"Music hath charms to soothe the savage breast," wrote the poet; and even an honest draper might feel his soul uplifted by those sweet, searching strains. Daniel, looking across at Clemency's placid features, thought of the old days when he and the little lass went blackberrying together in the deep, fragrant lanes.

"I can call to mind how she looked then," he thought, "in her pink sun-bonnet, and her lip black with the juice." "I must pick my posy for mother, Dan," he could hear her say that; and the way she looked at him, with the curls tumbling out of the sun-bonnet, and her eyes dancing with eagerness. "A bit thing," as their father always called her, when she nestled up to him on Sunday evening.

"Well, I never!" ejaculated Mrs. Moore, in awestruck tones, when Gloden had finished. "I am thinking, Clemency, that your niece must be fit for the stage. I have heard fiddle-playing in my time. Bob Rogers used to play at our place when he was courting Penelope, but this beats Bob."

"Come and have a bit of supper, Eliza," was Clemency's answer. "The squire has promised to take a knife and fork with us;" and Clemency's voice was full of modest pride as she spoke.

"Law, now, you don't say so!" ejaculated Eliza; but her voice hardly expressed pleasure. The presence of the distinguished stranger was a decided incubus to the good woman; and, in spite of Mr. Lorimer's affability and his excellent appetite, there was a certain restraint on the general hilarity.

Hector indeed whispered soft nothings in Lavinia's ear, but Polly had become very prim and silent. Harvey was too busy enjoying his own supper to pay her any attention, and all his remarks were addressed to Reginald.

As for Gloden, she was thankful to sit silent. She felt Mr. Lorimer's presence was a sufficient protection. She did not want him to talk to her, and he had the tact to leave her alone.

"I knew I should make things easier for you," he said, when he took his leave. "I should have despised myself if I had left you unprotected in that bear-garden. We kept the cubs in order, didn't we, Harvey?"

"You have been very, very kind, and I am not ungrateful," returned Gloden. "I know that you only stayed on my account."

"You are very clever to have found that out," he returned lightly; but her look haunted him all the way home. "The life is killing her by inches," he said to himself. "She cannot stand it much longer. Her pride suffers, and her feelings suffer, and, upon my soul, I don't believe I can stand seeing her there much longer either." But at this point Reginald checked himself suddenly, and began whistling "Young Lochinvar" at the top of his voice, until Lassie heard him and commenced barking excitedly, and then all the other dogs about the place began barking too.

CHAPTER XV.

"BOYS WILL BE BOYS."

"There is one thing of which I am afraid, and that is fear."—
MACKENZIE.

WHEN Gloden woke the next morning, she
was conscious of some pleasurable sensa-
tions which were at first difficult to trace to any
special cause, and it was some time before she
acknowledged to herself that she had been much
gratified and touched by Mr. Lorimer's kindness
of the previous night.

"It was good of him to stay when he must have
hated it so," she said to herself; "but of course
he knew that his presence would be a restraint.
How few young men would have acted so un-
selfishly!"

But it was doubtful if Reginald would have

endorsed this. A mild taste of Bohemianism was
a novelty to the young squire; the genus Moore
was unknown to him. As he ate his supper he
was smiling to himself at the idea. How shocked
Constance would have been if she had guessed
how he was disporting himself!

But the next minute Gloden's thoughts veered
round to Harvey. "Poor boy, how disappointed
he will be!" she thought; for the snow was falling
fast, and the driving particles quite darkened the
room. "Uncle Reuben was right; he said there
would be a heavy fall to-day, though Harvey
laughed at him; and now it will be impossible for
him to go to Silcote. I wish Mr. Lorimer had
not asked him; he will be so restless all day."

Gloden's sympathy was thrown away, for at
the very moment that she was cogitating so ruefully over the boy's disappointment, Harvey was
making his way as fast as he could down the
Silcote road. Harvey, in spite of an adoring
sister and aunt, was no more perfect than other
boys of his age. He was self-willed and head-
strong, and was capable at times of a vast amount
of naughtiness. He knew, when he looked out of
his window, that Gloden would not hear of his
going to the Hall.

"But she always forgets that I am not a girl,

to mind weather. Mr. Lorimer says boys ought
to be tough. Why, he called me a molly-coddle
one day when it rained, and I was afraid of getting
wet. He shan't call me a molly-coddle to-day."

So Harvey dressed himself with guilty haste,
and, taking his boots in his hand, crept down in
what Clemency would have called "his stocking
feet." Patty stared at him when she saw him
lacing his boots, and with the collar of his coat
drawn up to his ears.

"You are never going out, Master Harvey," she
protested. "Why, the milkman says there is a
rare snowstorm brewing. He looked pretty nearly
frozen. You couldn't find your way out of the
town, I'll be bound."

"Hold your tongue, Patty," returned Harvey,
good-humouredly. "Griff and I know what we
are about ; don't we, old boy? We aren't made of
sugar and salt. We are going to have a lark this
morning." And while Patty was still shaking her
head, he slipped out of the shop door.

"Poor little chap, how disappointed he will be !"
thought Reginald, as he sat down to his solitary
breakfast. Tottie was not beaming at him from
the opposite side of the table as usual, "making
daddie's bexfast," as she termed it. She was in
the nursery at Hyde Park Gates, tyrannizing in

her babyish fashion over Rex and Ninian, and being petted and spoiled by her aunt Constance.

Reginald was not in the best of humours. The snowstorm was an awful nuisance. He wanted to get back to town. Hamerton expected him to dinner, and he had half promised to drop in to afternoon tea with the Greshams, with whom Violet Winter was staying. He was seeing a good deal of Violet just now, and the Greshams were of opinion that he was only waiting for the first anniversary of his wife's death to pass before he first proposed to Violet; and Constance and Miss Wentworth were of the same opinion.

" They will be engaged before Easter, you may depend on that, Amy," Miss Wentworth said more than once. And this belief made Mrs. Winter very happy.

Reginald hated the idea of being boxed up in his big lonely house, with nothing especial to do except to turn over his papers and knock about the balls in the billiard-room ; but it would be madness to attempt the journey. Constance would not expect him. The documents could be sent on to his lawyer when the snow fell less heavily. The groom must make his way somehow to Grantham and send a couple of telegrams, and he must kill time as best he could ; and he proceeded to do

this by sauntering through the rooms with his
hands in his pockets and Lassie at his heels,
thinking rather irritably about the events of last
night.

When Gloden found Harvey was not in his
room, she questioned Patty a little anxiously, and
her distress was so great when she found out that
he was really gone, that Clemency found it difficult
to soothe her.

Gloden had gone in search of her aunt at once.

"Oh, Aunt Clemency!" she exclaimed, almost
in despair, "Harvey has set out for Silcote; but
he will never get there. No one could find their
way in such a snowstorm; the postman said he
could hardly see a yard before him."

Clemency looked aghast when she heard this;
then she put her hand kindly on her niece's
shoulder.

"He is a very naughty boy," she said seriously;
"but you must not lose heart like this, my dear.
Harvey is a shrewd lad, and has a head on his
shoulders; he will not be losing his way, I'll be
bound."

"But he will be wet through, and he is so
delicate," returned Gloden; the poor girl's lips
were trembling as she spoke. "He has more spirit
than strength, Aunt Clemency; and if he should

take cold—and the doctor always told us to be so
·careful."

"Nay, nay, dearie; the weakly ones often fare
best, and he has gained flesh wonderfully since he
has been with us. It is downright naughty and
perverse of him to have 'given us the slip like this,
but I doubt we are spoiling him amongst us;" and
Clemency shook her head seriously as she pondered
over the lad's delinquency.

"Couldn't Uncle Reuben send some one to see
if he is safe?" implored Gloden. And Clemency
carried this request to her husband.

"Your uncle declares he has no one to send,"
she said reluctantly, when she came back to the
parlour, "and he will have it we are troubling
ourselves unnecessarily. He thinks Harvey is far
too sharp to miss his way; besides, the snow was
not so thick an hour ago. He says he is eating his
breakfast, for sure, at this moment, and that we
had better get ours."

But Gloden was not to be consoled in this easy
fashion.

"I would go myself if I thought I could possibly
find my way," she said disconsolately; but Reuben
only scolded her in his good-natured manner for
making such a poor breakfast.

"You and Clem are fashing yourselves for

nought," he went on ; " the young rascal is making a hearty meal at this moment, and laughing at us all in his sleeves. He deserves a thrashing, that he does, though he is not likely to get it. ' Spare the rod and spoil the child,' eh, Clem ? "

"You never laid a finger on Davie," returned Clemency, tenderly. "Do you mind that day of the hard frost, Reuben, when Davie gave us the slip, most as Harvey has done, and went off to skate on the big pond ? You said then that he deserved a caning, but he had two helps of apple-tart at supper, all the same, in spite of all that I could say."

Then Reuben gave one of his low laughs of amusement. Gloden listened to them vaguely. Those endless reminiscences of the boy David that were so sweet to the bereaved parents, could not divert her thoughts from the young truant; a strange heaviness and presentiment of evil affected her nerves. The noiselessness of the falling snow, the semi-darkness and the dreary look-out on the back yard, gave her a feeling of suffocation. She thought of the wide ditches on the Silcote road, and the white desolation of the park. How was any lad, however sharp, to keep to the footpath that led to the avenue? At this very moment he might be wandering round and round the

Hall, unable to find the right turning. And at this point her eyes looked so wide and strained, that Clemency asked her husband rather hurriedly if it were not time for him to be in the shop. But Reuben, manlike, refused to take the hint.

"There is no hurry, wife," he said, unfolding his papers; "customers will be scarce this morning."

Then Gloden in desperation rose from the table. The best room overlooked the street; it would be better to endure the cold there than the sight of those black walls.

Clemency followed her, and knelt down to kindle the fire that Patty had just laid. The room was still in disorder from last night's festivity, but Gloden took no notice of the fact; she made her way to the window-seat, where Mr. Lorimer had sat the previous evening, and tried to pierce through the white density.

"It grows worse," she murmured; "I cannot see across the street."

Then Clemency, giving another finishing touch to the fire, rose and joined her.

"You are troubling over-much, my dear," she said kindly; "we must not forget Providence is watching over the little lad. There is not a sparrow falls unseen; we must mind that, Gloden. A half-hearted faith is worth nothing."

"I know that, Aunt Clemency"—with a sigh of impatience; "and yet accidents happen every day. People are drowned and run over, in spite of their faith. I often puzzle over that."

Clemency was silent. The only answer that occurred to her would have been cruel at such a moment; that they had met the doom foreordained for them, would hardly be a comforting reflection to Gloden at the present time. "We cannot rightly understand things," she said at last, softly; "there is a terrible mystery in life. One man is called to lie down in his bed and suffer, and another is taken by some sudden judgment. There are paths that wind and paths that are just short cuts, but they all lead to the same end. One need not mind drowning if it is God's way of fetching us home."

"Aunt Clemency"—in a troubled voice—"you may be right, but I cannot bear it. If harm should happen to Harvey, I could not think it for the best; it would seem to me terrible—terrible. Think if he were to be lost! He may be wandering about in Silcote Park now. Oh"—quickly rising from her place in uncontrollable agitation—"I must go after him! What does it matter what happens to me? I cannot endure this any longer."

Then Mrs. Carrick put her arms firmly round the

girl. "Nay, nay, my dear, you are excited. Do you suppose your Uncle Reuben and I would suffer you to run into danger? and what good will it do Harvey? The storm was not near so thick two hours ago, though it means mischief now. Take heart, child; your uncle is probably right, and Harvey, bless him! is just eating his breakfast, and laughing at us all."

And Gloden, after a long struggle, tried to take this reasonable view of the case.

Clemency was relieved when she saw her straightening the room and dusting the china as usual. She even offered to wash up the glass, and put away the old-fashioned silver that Clemency only used on state occasions—those thin, worn old teaspoons that had belonged to her grandmother were treasures not to be lightly used—and Clemency was only thankful to see her occupied.

It was some hours before the storm lessened, and it was nearly three o'clock before Reginald could send off his groom with the telegrams and a note for Gloden. The poor girl's anxiety by this time had taken the form of a racking sick headache, and Clemency had just tucked her up carefully on the big couch with some warm rugs and shawls, and a hot bottle to her feet, when Patty brought up the note.

Gloden tore it open. "Oh, he is all right, Aunt Clemency!" she exclaimed with a sob, sinking back on the couch; and Mrs. Carrick read the note for herself.

"DEAR MISS CARRICK " (it began),

"I feel sure you will be anxious about Harvey. The young rascal tells me that he gave you the slip this morning, so I am sending off Evans to assure you of his safety. You may imagine my astonishment at seeing him. I am afraid my welcome took the form of a lecture on his idiocy; but, as you have often said to me, 'boys will be boys.' He did not turn up until long after breakfast-time, and as he had had a good soaking, we had his things dried, and wrapped him up by the fire. He looks rather like a mummy at present. I shall keep him with me to-night, as I think he has had enough fatigue; but I will bring him over on my way to the train to-morrow morning.

"Trusting that you have not been very uneasy, and with kind regards to Mrs. Carrick,

"Yours sincerely,

"REGINALD LORIMER."

"There, my dear, what did I tell you?" observed Clemency, tearfully; and in the fulness of her joy she kissed the girl's cheek. "Providence has been good to us, and we might have spared ourselves all our worrying."

"I am not unthankful, Aunt Clemency," returned Gloden, gently; "but if you knew what I suffered!"

Then Clemency smoothed her hair. "I know all about it, dearie, and my heart was just aching

for you ; but you must try and get a sleep now,
and I will bring you up some hot tea presently."
And Gloden promised faintly to do her best.

"She will just sleep like a worn-out baby," she
said to Reuben, when she acquainted him with
the contents of Mr. Lorimer's note. " It went to
my heart to see the pitiful look in her eyes all the
morning. But there, I should have felt the same
if it had been Davie. It seems strange to me at
times to think we shall never know anxiety about
Davie again. Those who mother lads have a deal
to go through in this world."

"You are mothering Gloden to-day, aren't
you, Clem ?" observed her husband, slyly.

And Clemency's quiet smile lighted up her face.
It was true that the barrier had broken down a
little between her and Gloden.

Reginald had made the best of things in his
letter. He did not tell Gloden that Harvey had
never reached the hall until nearly one o'clock,
after five hours of wandering. He and Griff were
utterly exhausted when at last they found their
way to the back door.

Reginald broke into an angry remonstrance
when he first saw him. "Why, you young idiot,
what folly is this ? " he began ; and then his wrath
died away at the boy's miserable condition. Harvey

was sobbing with cold and exhaustion; and Griff looked a draggled and disreputable object as he dragged himself to his young master, and with a dog's unselfish devotion began licking his hand.

Reginald rang up his housekeeper furiously, and begged to know what was to be done with the young lunatic; and then he put his arm round Harvey and petted him, and told him not to be a duffer, and he would soon feel all right again.

"You had better give him some hot wine and water, sir," advised Mrs. Norton; "and then a hot bath, and put him to bed, while we get his things dried."

But Harvey, becoming restive with warmth and petting, refused to go to bed, so Reginald wrapped him up in his wadded dressing-gown; and as soon as Harvey had appeased his appetite, and had related his forlorn tale, he was so far recovered that he challenged his host to a game of chess.

"I suppose you will let Glow know if you keep me all night," he remarked, as he languidly set the pieces. And then Mr. Lorimer wrote his note.

"You deserve a jolly good licking for giving your sister all this anxiety," observed Reginald, sternly, as he returned to his seat.

And then Harvey grinned defiance. In reality

he was as penitent as heart could wish, but nothing
could long subdue Harvey.

"I don't believe I should be here now if it had
not been for Griff," he observed lazily, as he took
a pawn. "He stood still and whined when I was
turning off from the road. We had been beating
about the park for hours, and I was so tired out
that I thought I must give it up; but when the old
fellow whined, I made up my mind that he should
be leader, and he brought me straight to the back
door. You should have seen Norton's face when
he looked out and saw us."

Harvey became weary of chess presently, and
entreated for a game of billiards.

"I will go on wearing the dressing-gown if my
things are not dry yet," he went on.

And Reginald agreed with his usual easy good-
nature.

Griff followed them stiffly. The fire in the
billiard-room had been recently lighted, and the
room was only half warmed. Griff infinitely pre-
ferred the soft rug in Mr. Lorimer's dressing-room,
and he coiled himself up on the divan with a low
whine of disgust.

"You must not get cold, Harvey," observed
Reginald. "There is not much of a fire."

But Harvey was too much engrossed with his

stroke to heed this. "That was a jolly fluke," he returned, as the ball rolled into the pocket. "You need not give me thirty again. I shall be ahead of you in no time if I fluke like that;" and he broke into a crowing laugh. It was a regular lark, he thought, as he stumped round the table in the gorgeous dressing-gown. A *tête-à-tête* dinner, and "beggar my neighbour" afterwards. Could any boy ask more?

CHAPTER XVI.

"I LOVED HIM TOO MUCH."

> "Of comfort no man speak :
> Let's talk of graves, of worms, and epitaphs."
> *Richard II.*

THE following morning, as Gloden was about to leave her room, there was a quick tap at the door, and the next moment Patty entered with a note.

"A man on horseback brought it, Miss Gloden," she remarked. "He didn't wait for any answer; he said he had a message for the Red House."

"For Dr. Parry?" and Gloden turned very pale as she opened the note ; a quick prevision of evil made her divine the contents.

"DEAR MISS CARRICK" (wrote Reginald),
      "I am sorry to tell you that Harvey is very unwell,
and I am sending for Dr. Parry." ("No good beating about the

bush," thought Reginald, as he wrote this.) "He was all right when I wrote to you yesterday, but in the evening he seemed very cold and shivering, and I persuaded him to go to bed, and Mrs. Norton gave him a warm drink. I looked in at him before I retired myself, and he was sleeping fairly comfortably; but when Mrs. Norton went to him early this morning, he seemed so feverish and complained of such pain and difficulty of breathing, that we thought it only right to send off at once for Dr. Parry. As I know you will be uneasy about him, I shall send the carriage for you at nine o'clock. Harvey begged that you would come to him at once.

> "In great haste,
> > "Yours sincerely,
> > > "R. LORIMER."

Mrs. Carrick was making the coffee when Gloden entered the room a few minutes later, in her hat and jacket.

"What's to do, my dear?" she asked anxiously, startled by the girl's set white face.

"He is ill—Harvey is ill; read that for yourself, Aunt Clemency," returned Gloden, hoarsely, throwing down the note on the table.

And Clemency's fingers trembled a little as she took it up. "If it is the truth, God help us all," she thought; and then, with her usual unselfishness, she set herself to comfort Gloden.

"It is his chest, no doubt; nice hot linseed poultices, that's what he will be needing. Don't you fash yourself, Gloden, my dear. I have perfect confidence in Dr. Parry; if any one would have saved my Davie, it would have been Parry.

Reuben "—as her husband came in from the shop—
"Gloden is in a bit of trouble. Mr. Lorimer has
written to say Harvey is but poorly; he has got
a feverish cold, I doubt, and it has flown to the
chest. The carriage is coming for her in half an
hour, and I mean to get on my things and go
with her, if you and Patty can do without me for
an hour or two."

"Dear me, dear me!" returned Reuben, tremu-
lously; and he put on his spectacles to read the
note, and then took them off again to wipe them.
"Oh, we will get along all right, the lass and I.
Don't you moither yourself, Clem; you will be a
deal of help to Gloden."

"Indeed, Uncle Reuben, I do not need Aunt
Clemency," began Gloden, her youthful selfishness
disliking the idea of any interference.

But Reuben shook his head solemnly. "Sit
down and eat your breakfast, like a good lassie,"
he said in his kind way. "You will need your
strength if there's nursing to do. Your aunt has
had a deal of experience; there is not a better
hand at nursing, though I say it, and you will be
glad enough of her help. It will be pleasant for you
to have a woman at hand, for, with all the good-
will in the world, young men are not the best of
sick-nurses."

Then Gloden held her peace; the thought of
Mr. Lorimer had not even occurred to her.

Clemency was quite aware of Gloden's reluctance, but her good heart took no offence; she even
made allowances as she went off to put on her
bonnet, and give Patty her orders. "It is natural
that she should want to nurse him all herself," she
thought; "I remember it went sorely against me
when Reuben would sit up with David; I was
jealous even of my boy's father, so I have no call
to be hard on Gloden. It has not entered her
heart that Mr. Lorimer is as good as unmarried,
and a young man still, and that it might be
awkward for them both; but I am bound to think
of these things for her, and I know that Reuben
wants me to go."

There was little talk between the two during
the drive to Silcote. Now and then Clemency
made an observation, but Gloden only answered in
monosyllables. She was pondering gloomily over
what Dr. Tritton had said about Harvey's delicacy
of constitution, and never even noticed when one
of the horses slipped on some frozen snow, though
Clemency's heart went into her mouth, as she told
Reuben afterwards.

Dr. Parry's carriage was still at the door when
they reached the Hall; he and Mr. Lorimer had

just left Harvey's room, and were coming downstairs. Reginald had a bothered look on his face,
but Dr. Parry uttered a cheery exclamation at the
sight of Mrs. Carrick.

"Come, our patient is in luck's way," he said;
"there is not a nurse in Grantham to beat Mrs.
Carrick."

But before Clemency could answer, Gloden
pressed forward.

"I intend to nurse my brother, Dr. Parry," she
said decidedly, hardly looking at Reginald, as he
shook hands with her. "I know Aunt Clemency
will kindly help me, but you must give your orders
to me as well."

"Settle that between yourselves, ladies," returned
the doctor, in an offhand manner; "but my
directions must be strictly followed."

And then Mr. Lorimer left them for a few
minutes. When he returned Dr. Parry had gone.
Gloden, who looked much distressed, came forward
to meet him.

"Which is Harvey's room, Mr. Lorimer?" she
asked; "I must go up at once."

But he put his hand on her arm. "You shall
go in a moment, but I must speak to you first.
There is no hurry; Mrs. Norton is with him.
Indeed"—as she looked at him impatiently—"you

must give me a minute. If Harvey be ill, I shall never forgive myself."

"But he is ill," she interrupted; "Dr. Parry could not disguise the fact. It is pneumonia—that is another word, is it not, for inflammation of the lungs?—his temperature is very high." Then, as she noticed his expression, "But it is not your fault. How could you guess, when you gave the invitation, that Harvey would be so mad as to go through that snowstorm?"

"No, I was not to blame there," returned Reginald; "but let me make a clean breast of it. It was my fault that Harvey was all those hours in the billiard-room. I was a fool to allow it. The fire had not been long lighted, and Dr. Parry thinks that a good deal of the mischief is due to that; so you may imagine my feelings."

"Oh, you did not know," she said hurriedly. "Perhaps Dr. Parry was wrong in putting it down to that; he was wet through and worn out"—and here her voice choked. "Do please take me to him, Mr. Lorimer;" and then Reginald led the way upstairs.

"We put him in the south room, because it had been recently used," he observed; "and I am glad now that we did so. Parry says it is the best room we could have chosen."

And then, on hearing voices, Mrs. Norton
opened the door. She was a pleasant-looking
woman, and had been housekeeper at the hall as
long as Reginald could remember; she and her
husband were the oldest servants there.

"The young gentleman is very feverish, ma'am,.
so you will be pleased to be careful and not let
him talk," she said in a low voice; and then she
caught sight of Mrs. Carrick, and nodded to her
in a friendly way.

The good housekeeper had often had a chat
with Clemency over the counter. But here the
sound of a hard, dry cough reached Gloden's ear,.
and she pushed past her.

Harvey was at the further end of the room; he
was propped up with pillows, and looked flushed
and feverish. As Gloden threw her arms round
him, he pushed her gently away.

"Don't, Glow. I don't deserve it; it serves me
right. It was real mean of me to play you that
trick." But here the painful cough checked his
penitent confession.

"My darling, hush! Dr. Parry says you must
not talk."

"It is a regular cropper," panted Harvey. "Of
course I have got a bad cold, only I wish it did
not hurt so;" and he put his hand to his breast.

"There!"—his face twitching with the pain—"it almost took my breath away. Why, there's Aunt Clem"—with a ghost of a smile. "Aunt Clem, I know I was very naughty."

"There's a brave lad; but you will be good now, Harvey, and mind what your sister says. There is to be no talking, the doctor says."

"But you are going to stop," pleaded Harvey; "you will let them stop, won't you, Mr. Lorimer? I couldn't part with Glow; and it is nice to have Aunt Clem. You'll be fine and glad to stay, won't you, Aunt Clem?"

"They will stay if you obey orders, and hold your tongue," returned Reginald, trying to be stern.

And then he turned to Gloden, and asked her softly if there were anything he could do for her; but she shook her head without looking at him. She wanted nothing but to be left alone with Harvey. But as he left the room, a sudden thought struck her, and she went after him. He was walking slowly down the corridor, but he turned back when he heard her footsteps. "You have thought of something," he said eagerly.

"No; there has been no time to think. I only want to be certain that you meant what you said just now to Harvey, that we may stay. Are you sure that we shall not be a trouble? But I could not leave him. If only he had not been taken ill here, in this house!"

"I am quite sure you do not mean to be unkind," replied Reginald, gravely; "but you would not like any one to make such a speech to you. Oh, I forgive you"—as she looked disturbed at this. "You are too much bothered to know what you are saying; but I am only too glad that the little chap should be here. If you care to please me, you will just make yourself at home, and ask for everything you want. My servants have literally nothing to do, and it will be a charity to employ them. Will you tell Mrs. Carrick this?"

"You are very kind;" and then she looked up in his face rather pitifully. "He is very ill, Mr. Lorimer; I have never seen Harvey look quite so ill as that, and it is so sudden."

"Oh, these sort of things are always sudden." But Reginald did not add that Dr. Parry had told him that he had just lost a patient with inflammation of the lungs in two days. "Parry is coming again this afternoon."

But Gloden made no answer to this; she had said all she wanted to say, so she went back to the room.

Clemency had already divested herself of her bonnet and cloak, and was sitting, knitting in hand, beside the bed; but she left her place as Gloden entered.

Harvey beckoned to her to come closer. "I don't want Aunt Clem to hear," he whispered; "but I am glad to be ill here; it is better than David's room and the back yard, eh, Glow?" and as Gloden looked round her, she endorsed Harvey's opinion.

The south room was always appreciated by Reginald's guests. In reality it was Constance's old room, and the furniture had been left intact. It had a large bay window overlooking the park. Some of Constance's books had been left in the bookcase, and her writing-table and easy-chair still stood in the bay. A couch, covered with blue cretonne, was drawn to one side of the fireplace, and blue cretonne curtains shaded the small brass bedstead. When Violet Winter had slept at the Hall, she had begged for Constance's old room, and since then it had been used by Ursula Egerton.

"Isn't it a jolly room?" continued Harvey; and then another of the cruel stitches made him finish with a groan.

Before many hours were over Gloden was thankful for her aunt's company, for that night and the next day Harvey grew rapidly worse.

Clemency was a good nurse, as Dr. Parry had once said, and had all the instincts of one. Her touch was at once light and firm, and her eye and nerve never failed her. As the temperature of the patient grew higher, and the pulse became more frequent and full, and the difficulty of breathing grew more marked, Clemency did not lose her courage or her quiet cheerfulness, and she never failed to give the right word to Gloden when the poor girl appealed to her in her trouble.

"Oh, Aunt Clem, I cannot bear it! I will ask Mr. Lorimer to send for Dr. Parry back!" she exclaimed once; for the doctor had paid his second visit. His directions had all been given to Clemency, but Gloden had ceased to resent this. All selfishness had been swallowed up in her intense anxiety; she was certain that Dr. Parry had looked grave, though he had reserved his opinion.

"There's no need to trouble Mr. Lorimer," returned Clemency, quietly. "Dr. Parry will be here before night."

Then Gloden uttered a low moan. There needed nothing else to prove to her her darling's danger : Harvey had become light-headed, and was rambling to himself in an aimless way of the old Repton days.

"It was a beastly fluke of Jones minor," he muttered.

"Aunt Clemency, he is worse—I am sure he is worse. Look at his eyes! he does not seem conscious of our presence."

"Ay, the fever is high, my dearie, but it is only what we are bound to expect. You must keep up your heart, Gloden ; there's not many girls of your age that has such a notion of nursing, and the doctor will soon find that out for himself, though, being older and having had children of my own, and us being such old friends, he gives me all the directions."

But Gloden was too full of misery to take heed to this delicate compliment, and when the door opened and Reuben Carrick stepped in on tiptoe, with the air of a man well used to sickness, she slipped past him and went out. She wanted to get away from the sound of that hoarse voice, and the dry, suffocating cough.

Reginald, prowling restlessly about the house, came upon her crouched on one of the old-fashioned window-seats in the corridor, looking out drearily over the whiteness of the park. He hurried up to her with a remonstrance.

"This is very wrong, Miss Carrick; you will take cold in this draughty passage, after being in that warm room so long."

"I wanted a breath of air," she returned, in the strained high voice that betrayed jarring nerves; "the room seemed to suffocate me, and there was nothing I could do. Aunt Clemency does everything far better than I. When will Dr. Parry be here, Mr. Lorimer?"

"I am expecting him every minute; he said he would come as late as possible to-night, and it is ten now."

"If he would only come! It is so cruel to see my darling suffer. He is worse—I know he is worse"—and now she was cold, and shaking all over—"and he is all I have in the world."

"I don't like to hear you talk in that way."

"In what other way can I talk when I know the danger he is in?" she returned, almost harshly.

And Reginald was silent out of sheer pity. How was he to contradict her when Dr. Parry had refused to hazard an opinion? The boy was in a bad way; it was impossible to deny that. He was a delicate little fellow, and those hours of exposure and fatigue had been too much for him. And then his cursed carelessness about the billiard-room; the room had been like a vault. Some one had told him that it was a bad sign when delirium came on in the early stages of inflammation of the lungs, and he wondered what Dr. Parry would say to that. He would have given much to be able to speak a cheering word to the girl. His heart was full of pity for her, and anxiety for his favourite; he would almost have consented to have taken the boy's place if he could have spared her this pain.

"It is all my fault," he sighed at last; and Gloden roused up at this.

"It is strange, but I don't feel as though I could blame you," she returned, in a softer tone than she had used before. "You meant kindly, and it was only a mistake. It was the dear boy himself who was to blame; and it was my fault too, because I had spoiled him, and that made him self-willed. Mr. Lorimer, if he does not get over this illness— and he will not; I feel he will not," she added hysterically—"it is because I loved him too much, and God is punishing me for it."

"No, no; you must not be so hard on yourself." He had not a notion how to comfort her, but as he spoke he put his hands over hers and held them firmly. "You could not love him too much," he said vehemently; "he is a dear little chap, and I love him myself. I never took to a boy in my life before as I have taken to Harvey."

"Yes; and he was so fond of you," she murmured. She made no effort to free herself from the kind hands that held hers; indeed, she was hardly conscious of the pressure.

"And I would not lose heart if I were you," he continued. "We will have down another opinion if you like, but I have great faith in Parry; I would trust Tottie to him if she were ever so ill. Now you will go back to Harvey, will you not, and hope for the best?"

"Yes, I will go back to him," she returned meekly.

She could not have recalled a word of their conversation, and yet she felt insensibly soothed by Reginald's sympathy. As he released her hands, he put his arm round her as though to assist her to rise.

"When Parry comes I will send him up," was all he said as he left her at the door; but Gloden's "Good night, and thank you" were spoken almost gratefully.

CHAPTER XVII.

CLEMENCY'S REWARD.

" Misfortune may make us proud, suffering makes us humble."
Thoughts of a Queen.

DR. PARRY remained at the Hall all that night. Mr. Lorimer proposed it; he told the doctor that it would be a relief to him personally to have him at hand, and Dr. Parry consented very willingly.

"If there is not some slight change for the better before morning, I will not answer for the consequences," he said very plainly to Reginald. "I was just thinking that it would be as well if I could be on the spot; it is one of those cases that will be short and sharp. His temperature must not go any higher."

Gloden felt a glimmer of hope when she heard

Dr. Parry would sleep there, but Reuben Carrick, who was going back in the doctor's brougham, carried a heavy heart with him.

"I wish we did not set such store by the lad," he said to Clemency, when she accompanied him to the head of the stairs. "It will go hard with us to part with him."

But Aunt Clemency, in her simple faith, would not hear of this. "We will not weaken ourselves by troubling about the future, Reuben. When sorrow comes the strength comes with it. I must just give my mind to following the doctor's orders. 'When the child was yet alive;' I always think of David's words." And then she bade Reuben put up the collar of his coat, to keep him from the cold, and went back to Harvey.

It was a trying night for every one; even Reginald found it impossible to sleep, and more than once put on his dressing-gown to listen at the door of the sick-room. But to Gloden it was a night of anguish. Clemency, moving about the room in her quiet way, would glance at the girl pityingly from time to time. Gloden was always ready to assist her, to see what was wanted, but the moment she was free again she returned to her place beside Harvey. Clemency could never have guessed at the thoughts that were passing through Gloden's mind. When she said to herself, in her pious way, that the dear Lord was giving the child one of His hardest lessons, she was very near the truth.

During those weary hours, strange, self-accusing thoughts mingled with her anxious ones for Harvey. At one moment she could think of nothing but of him ; the next, she was regarding her past conduct to her uncle and aunt with feelings of remorse and abhorrence. In that solemn watch with Clemency, the truth without any disguise seemed to start up before her and upbraid her with her want of tenderness.

When she saw Clemency's pale face bending over the boy—who was not Davie, not her own flesh and blood—and remembered all her goodness to them both, she hated herself for the jealous pride that would have separated her from the boy. How she had wronged the gentle and kindly soul, who had never given her a reproachful word! How patient she had been with her !

"Why did I never see it before? Why have I taken all and given nothing?" thought the girl. "It is for this I deserve punishment, not because of the love I gave my darling. It cannot be a sin to love those who are given to us ; it is only our want of love for which we shall be judged."

There are some natures whose latent nobility
is only roused by painful circumstance—who need
more than others the purification of suffering.   An
atmosphere of unfailing sunshine would only
enervate them ; they require a more bracing discipline.   In tropical countries vegetation becomes
rank ; so in a life of ease Gloden's faults would
have increased.   Her pride needed humbling, her
strong will had to learn how to bend to others ;
her self-love must be eradicated ; she must see
herself in the mirror of perfect truth, before she
could experience that salutary shame that brings
redemption.

"Lie down a bit, Gloden," urged Clemency
once towards morning ; "it is only a tough body
like me that can put up with watching and loss of
sleep. It makes me feel bad to see your white face,
my dear."

"Oh, Aunt Clemency, I cannot rest!   I do not
deserve to rest."

And as the thin little hand with its worn wedding-
ring rested on her shoulder, Gloden, with a sudden
impulse, touched it with her lips.

"You are so good, so forgiving !" she murmured.

Clemency flushed up with surprise ; the caress
was so utterly unexpected.   Then her good heart
seemed to grasp the meaning, and the next moment

she put her arms round the girl and laid her head on her shoulder, holding it there with her hand.

"There—there, you poor child," she said tenderly. "I would bear it all for you if I could; but the dear Lord knows best, and we can trust Him. It is borne in upon me that this sickness is not for death; I have been thinking so all the night;" and as Gloden hid her face in her neck in a sudden passion of tears, she rocked her gently to and fro, as though she were a baby.

"It is only a mother's love that knows how to look on at suffering," thought Clemency, when she again stooped over Harvey. "It is the sword-piercing that many a woman feels in a small measure, though there was only one that could have borne to stand beside a Son's cross. I always had a more kindly feeling for St. John," she went on, in her simple manner, "than for any of the others, for the way he took her along with him to his own home. If Reuben's father had not been David, I should have called our little lad John."

A few minutes later, Gloden, who had at last consented to lie down on the couch for half an hour, heard her call her softly.

"Gloden," she said quietly, "I think Harvey is breathing a bit easier, and his skin is not so dry;

he has not been rambling so much during the last half-hour."

But Gloden, worn out with the long watching, was in no state to mark the improvement. "You must not give me hope," she said, in a faint, exhausted voice that made Clemency look at her sharply.

"Gloden, my dear," she said, with unusual decision, "you will just put yourself back on that couch, and shut your eyes like a good child, or I shall have more than one patient on my hands. You may trust me to call you if there is any change."

And Gloden, who felt herself unable to stand, threw herself down, and fell into a heavy sleep.

"Young eyes are not used to watching," thought Clemency, as she sat down by the bed. She was tired, and her head throbbed with weariness, but her heart was full of peaceful happiness. Old prophetical words seemed to echo in her ears: "Then shall thou say in thy heart, Who hath begotten me these, seeing I have been bereaved of my children, and am solitary?" And again, "For more are the children of the desolate than the children of the married wife, saith the Lord."

"Ay, it is true," she said to herself, as she

glanced at the sleeping girl; "there is a power of truth in those words. The Lord be thanked for His goodness. We have children in heaven, and children on earth; for Harvey will live, please God, to be a son to Reuben; and now Gloden has opened her heart to me, I feel as though I have nought left to pray for."

When morning came, Dr. Parry endorsed Mrs. Carrick's favourable opinion of the patient.

"He has taken a turn for the better," he said to Mr. Lorimer, as they sat down to breakfast together. "I begin to hope that we shall pull him through after all, though last night I would not have said as much; but we must not halloa until we are through the wood." And then he began eulogizing Harvey's nurse. "Mrs. Carrick is a trump," he said enthusiastically. "I wish I could get her for our matron at the hospital. If I were at death's door, I would rather have that woman to nurse me than any of our trained nurses. She has a genius for it; she has a cool head, never gets flurried, and never forgets an order."

"Miss Carrick seems to me a good nurse too," observed Reginald, who had been much struck by Gloden's devotion the last two days.

"Humph—yes; she has a head on her shoulders;

but she has not Mrs. Carrick's staying powers. But she has done very well on the whole, poor thing; she seems wrapped up in the lad. Nice boy—very."

"Oh, Harvey is more than that—he is a fine fellow; and if you pull him through, doctor, we shall all be your debtors for life;" and Reginald's voice was slightly husky. He was surprised himself to find how much he cared for the boy. "I think I had better adopt him," he said to himself, with an attempt at a smile.

When Dr. Parry had left, he sent up a message, begging that one of the nurses would speak to him, and, as he hoped, Gloden came down to him. She looked very pale in spite of her long sleep, and Reginald pushed a chair near the fire, and told her to sit down and rest a moment.

"Oh, I cannot stay," she said hurriedly; "Aunt Clemency is going to lie down for a couple of hours, while I take care of Harvey." And then she looked up at Reginald, as he was leaning against the mantelpiece watching her. "Do you know that Dr. Parry thinks that Harvey is a little better?—'less bad,' were his words, and he says that the improvement is owing to Aunt Clemency's nursing."

"Yes; he said as much to me."

" Oh, she is so good, so kind ! "—in a choked voice.
" If my dear boy recovers, I shall never be able
to do enough for her. I have not been good to her,
Mr. Lorimer."

"Oh, I would not be troubling my head about
that now," remarked Reginald, in his easy-going
philosophy. "You have got to take care of yourself, and look after Harvey—that is your whole duty
of woman at present; you may make as much as
you like of Mrs. Carrick when you have got her
home again."

" You always say kind things," returned Gloden,
with a faint smile ; "but you don't know how I
have treated Aunt Clemency. ' I thought myself
better than she, and I cannot hold a candle to her.
Harvey has not been ill more than three days,
but I feel as though I have been living through
a lifetime of repentance."

"Anxiety and fatigue have made you morbid,"
observed Reginald, treating this confession in an
offhand way. "That is just how I went on about
Car," he thought—"I made myself out an utter
brute ; but I think differently of things now." And
then he smiled pleasantly as she looked at him
with wide, anxious eyes. "It is an awful mistake,
thinking about one's self at such times ; there's
no good to be got out of it at all. Take my

advice, Miss Carrick, chuck all those morbid thoughts overboard, and start afresh; it will be much better for everybody."

"Yes, you are right," she said, so humbly that Reginald felt quite uncomfortable. "You make allowances for every one, Mr. Lorimer, even for me, though you know how proud and disagreeable I have been to every one."

But here he checked her. "I am not going to let you talk in that way," he said, with brusque kindness. "Disagreeable! Why, you are the pluckiest girl I know; the most patient of saints would have turned rusty in your place. Come, now, if you call yourself names, I shall just tell you plainly how much I respect and admire you."

But here Gloden stopped him. "Please don't talk so, Mr. Lorimer"—blushing a little. "But, of course, it is my fault for troubling you with my stupid thoughts; but somehow you always seem to do me good. I think you have a healthy way of looking at things. Now I must really go back to my post." And he reluctantly let her go.

"Do her good," he remarked to himself, as he sat down in the seat she had just vacated, and took Lassie's head between his knees. "I felt an awful duffer talking to her just now. I wish

I had Hamerton's knack of putting things; she will find me uncommonly stupid when she comes to know me better. I know Car did—poor dear Car!" and here he sighed. He always sighed in this oppressed manner when he thought of his wife. His eyes were gradually opening to the fact that his marriage had not brought him all he had expected. "If Car had lived, I know we should not have hit it off exactly," he had said to himself once. "I was always sure to kick over the traces, and Car couldn't bear running out of her groove." And there was a good deal of truth in this. "I never noticed before what wonderful eyes she has got," he went on; "they seem to darken and change their colour with every word she speaks. I dare say she has not treated Mrs. Carrick very well, but she has a hard life of it, poor girl!" And here Reginald fell into a brown study, as he twirled his moustache and stared at the fire.

There was still cause for great anxiety about Harvey. When Dr. Parry came the next day, he looked a little grave and spoke vaguely of the danger of a relapse. "If he gets through, it will be by the skin of his teeth," he muttered, as he put on his great-coat in the hall. Later in the day he told Mr. Lorimer that Mrs. Carrick was not to be allowed to sit up.

"I can't have my best nurse knock herself up," he continued, "and she has been up for three nights; so Mrs. Norton and Miss Carrick must do it between them. I had Carrick round at the Red House last evening, begging me to see that his wife had her proper rest. 'She will just go on until she drops, doctor,' he said. 'She will never give in—that's her way;' so I have kept my promise by ordering her off to bed."

"Mrs. Norton is a capital nurse; there is no need for Miss Carrick to sit up," returned Mr. Lorimer.

"So I told her, but she chooses to be obstinate about it; that young lady has a will of her own, and no mistake. Well, we shall have her breaking down one of these days." And Dr. Parry, who had daughters of his own, went off grumbling.

"Suppose I have a try," thought Reginald, as he closed the door upon the doctor; and then he went upstairs and begged Gloden in a low voice to come outside for a moment.

She followed him reluctantly. "Do you want me particularly, Mr. Lorimer? Aunt Clemency is going to bed, and I am very busy."

"You are not too busy to give me five minutes, I hope. Mrs. Norton will look after Harvey all right;" and he coolly drew her to the window-seat, and placed himself beside her.

"Miss Carrick, I want you to do me a great favour;" then, as she looked at him apprehensively, "I want you to go to bed, and allow me to share Mrs. Norton's watch to-night."

"You!"—very much surprised at this request. "I don't think Dr. Parry would approve of a fresh nurse for Harvey."

"You are wrong; he is quite willing for me to do it, though he said at the same time that Mrs. Norton would do quite well alone. But I know you would be happier if I keep an eye on him."

"But I could not leave Harvey," she replied, quickly; for the determined look on Reginald's face alarmed her. "I know Mrs. Norton is a careful woman, but while he is so ill I could not keep out of the room, and you must not ask me to do so."

"But if I do ask it"—very persuasively—"don't you think you could trust Harvey to me?"

"Yes, of course; and I know how good you would be to him. But indeed—indeed I could not leave him to-night. If anything were to happen! Dr. Parry does not seem quite satisfied about him, and if he should have a relapse."

"You are conjuring up fears; Harvey is not any worse to-night. Miss Carrick, I am in earnest. I cannot let you lose your rest in this way. There is no one to look after you, and you will not take care of yourself; you will be utterly worn out."

"What will that matter?" she returned recklessly, amazed by this pertinacity on Mr. Lorimer's part. "I cannot and I will not leave Harvey to-night."

Then there was a hurt look on the young man's face. "Very well, then, there is nothing more to be said;" and Reginald stood up and prepared to leave her. "I may as well wish you good night."

"Why do you speak as though you were offended with me?" she asked, troubled by his manner. Since the first time they had met, he had never spoken to her coldly or indifferently before.

"I have no right to be offended," he returned stiffly; "but I must confess that I am hurt. I had hoped that you would have trusted me; but no matter. I see I expected too much."

Gloden turned to him quickly. "You have no right to make it such a personal matter. It is no want of trust on my part. How can I help trusting you when you have been so good to my darling?" Then her voice trembled, and her eyes were full of tears. "You shall not say that again; I cannot bear it; it seems to make everything so much worse. You shall stay with him if you like."

"Do you really mean it?" and Reginald's face grew radiant; "and you will try to sleep?"

"I don't know about that; but I will at least absent myself until morning."

Then there was a look of triumph in Reginald's eyes; after all, he had prevailed with her. He felt as happy as a king as he went off to Harvey's room. She had not shunted him after all; his will had been stronger. But Gloden, tired and unnerved as she was, wept long and bitterly in her little room.

"Why was I so weak?" she said to herself again and again. "Dr. Parry and Aunt Clemency both tried to persuade me, but I was firm with them; but when he looked so dreadfully hurt, I could not bear to pain him." But though Gloden chafed and fretted over her ready submission, and would have given worlds to have taken back her word, she kept her compact with Mr. Lorimer religiously, and he had the satisfaction of seeing her the next morning looking all the better for her enforced rest; but when he told her so, Gloden blushed and made no response.

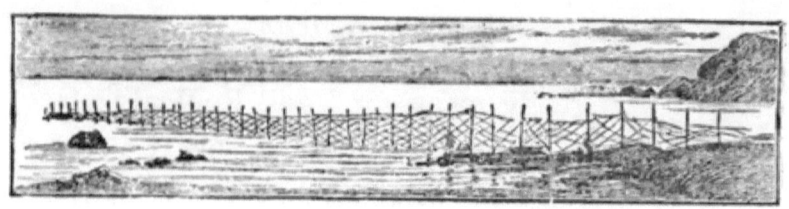

CHAPTER XVIII.

REGINALD KNOWS HIS OWN MIND.

"The pleasure of love is in loving. We are happier in the passion we feel than in what we inspire."—ROCHEFOUCAULD.

ROM that night Gloden was conscious of a subtle change in Mr. Lorimer's manner. It was as though her acquiescence in his request had given her a new claim on him. The unaffected cordiality that had always been so winning had deepened into something quieter and stronger; each day she was conscious of an added gentleness and deference; when he looked at her, there was a new meaning in his eyes.

Neither was the change solely on Reginald's side. Even while Gloden had wept hot tears of indignation over her own inexplicable weakness, she was conscious of some secret unacknowledged pleasure in the thought that Mr. Lorimer was watching over her young brother.

The next morning, when she entered the sick-room and saw him leaning back in the chair she always used, with his fair hair rumpled, and his eyes heavy with want of sleep, her heart felt suddenly drawn to him, and her hand trembled with some unwonted feeling as he took it in his.

"You are better," he said in a low eager voice, that brought the colour to her face. "I can see for myself that you are more rested;" and as she turned away without answering, he followed her closely.

"Harvey is better too. Mrs. Norton is sure of it."

"Do you think so? Oh, my darling, are you really and truly better?" and Gloden sank down on her knees beside the bed and laid her cheek against Harvey's hand.

Reginald looked at her for one moment—at the coils of brown hair and the white shapely throat, and then at the soft cheek resting against the little rough, boyish hand; a sudden strange glow came into his eyes, and he turned abruptly away. At that moment he knew the truth—that he loved Gloden Carrick as he had never loved before, and that henceforth life would have no meaning to him unless she would consent to be his wife.

The thought was overwhelming, and he felt a little dizzy as he walked from the room. He dare not trust himself in her presence, lest she should read his secret in his eyes.

"It is too soon," he said to himself, as later on he sat down in his chair before the library fire, with Lassie stretched on the rug at his feet. "It is very soon;" and as he spoke half aloud he raised his eyes to his wife's picture. In the soft firelight, her fair face seemed to look down on him with a smile. At the same instant some words came back to his memory, and the weak tones of her voice as she said them. He had been sitting by her bedside one evening, not speaking much, but stroking her hot hand with that pitying tenderness that one would use to a sick child, when she had suddenly clasped his hand a little feverishly.

"Reginald," she had said in a faint inward voice, "I want to say one thing to you. When the right time comes you will marry again; I should not wish it otherwise;" and again, "Dying people ought not to be selfish, and I have always taken such care of you and Tottie."

"Car always meant what she said," he thought,

and again the dull throb made itself felt as he recalled his old married life. "She always liked to see me happy; but it is far too soon. I will not speak to her until February is over, and then——" His eyes brightened, but he did not finish his sentence. He rose from his chair, and walked to and fro, pushing away the furniture that was in his way; then, as though the library were too narrow for his restlessness, he went into the great empty music-room, while Lassie, faithful as ever, followed him step by step with shivering and reluctant devotion. The ways of men were wonderful to Lassie, casting furtive glances of longing to the warm bearskin she had left.

He was craving to see Gloden again, but he would not seek her. More than once he stole up to Harvey's room, but he dare not trust himself to enter; he felt that she would read his thoughts. He would stand and listen to the sound of her light footstep, and then go back again to his solitude.

But the longing to see her increased towards evening, and he found it hard to keep his resolution. Perhaps she would come down to him to wish him good night, or to give him a report of the day. He would wait a little, and then—— But at that moment the light sprang to his eyes—he had heard her speaking to Lassie in the hall; she was on her way to him, and Reginald got up from his seat and walked to the fireplace.

Gloden hesitated for a moment on the threshold; she was sensible of an unaccountable timidity. Mr. Lorimer did not come forward to meet her as usual. "Aunt Clemency wished me to come and tell you that Harvey is so much better to-night," she said a little hurriedly; "he is quite himself, and has spoken to me."

"And you have come down to share your good news with me; that is very kind, Miss Carrick." He had offered her a chair, but she had motioned it away, and now he had gone back to the rug, with his arm resting on the mantelpiece. Gloden thought he was shielding his face from the blaze; she had no idea how keenly she was watched. "It was very good of you to come to me. I was getting dreadfully tired of my solitude." Reginald tried to speak in his usual easy fashion, but something in his voice made Gloden look at him.

"I am sorry you are dull," she said gently. "I am afraid you miss Tottie, and it is all our fault keeping you here. These rooms"—looking round her—"must seem very large and empty sometimes."

"I am not dull in the way you mean," he returned quickly. "I have had pleasant thoughts to keep me company. Tottie is not much of a companion to me yet; our conversation is limited. You may make your mind easy about me, Miss Carrick; I am staying here for my own pleasure."

"I wish I could be sure of that"—rather wistfully. "Dr. Parry says it will be a long time before Harvey gets strong, it has been such a severe attack; you will not get rid of us yet, Mr. Lorimer."

"I never want to get rid of you again," rushed to Reginald's lips, but he restrained himself. "You know by this time that I am glad to have you and Harvey," he said quietly. "Please do not get it into your head that you are any trouble to me. I know what a scrupulous person you are."

"It is impossible to thank you properly," she returned seriously. "I have never even thanked you for all you did last night. I have not given you Aunt Clemency's message yet, Mr. Lorimer. She hopes that you will not sit up late, as Mrs. Norton tells us that you never closed your eyes at all last night."

"Mrs. Norton has no right to tell tales, and I never felt better in my life. I think nursing must be my vocation. Now tell me, what arrangements have you made for to-night?"

"Oh, I am going to take the first part of the

night, and then Aunt Clemency will relieve me.
She will come to me at one o'clock."

" Honour bright ? "

" Oh yes, of course."

" I don't know whether you are to be trusted.
You want a lot of looking after, Miss Carrick,
and I begin to think it is my business to look
after you."

He checked himself, as Gloden put out her
hand a little timidly and wished him good night.
He did not venture to detain her, but as he
walked beside her down the hall, he told himself
again that he could not trust himself to be much
with her. At the foot of the staircase he bade
her good night again ; but on the landing she
turned round and saw he was still watching her.
As she waved her hand he smiled back at her,
and then walked slowly away.

Gloden's heart beat a little quickly as she re-
entered the sick-room ; in her whole life she had
never seen a smile like that. Ewen Logan,
though he loved her with the whole strength of
his nature, had always looked at her with some
solemnity in his eyes ; but the peculiar tenderness
of Reginald's smile was a revelation. It was the
smile with which a man looks on his nearest and
dearest.

"I must never go and wish him good night again," she said to herself, with quick sensitive alarm. "Of course he understood that Aunt Clemency sent me ; but, though he was very kind, he did not seem quite like himself."

But Gloden never guessed how strong had been Reginald's impulse to call her back as she moved slowly away from him up the broad staircase, and to take her in his arms and pray her never to leave him again.

After all there was no relapse. Harvey's progress, though slow, was satisfactory, and Reuben Carrick's face grew brighter after every visit.

"He will do now, Clem," he would say as he stood looking down on the boy. "Of course he is pulled down, poor lad ; but we will make a man of him yet, please God ;" and Clemency's low-toned "Ay, Reuben" always came like an echo.

"It is the first time we have been parted," he said somewhat ruefully one evening, "and the days and nights seem to double themselves. I feel lost without you, wife, and that's the truth. But there, I am a selfish old fellow to be thinking of my own lass, while you are mothering Nat's children."

Then Clemency looked at him with her tranquil

smile. "Reuben, my lad," she said, using the phrase that had often come to her lips in the old courting day, when she was a trim, bright-eyed lass, and Reuben was her sweetheart—" Reuben, my lad, it has been in my mind to tell you something that will give you pleasure. Nat's girl is my girl now."

"Now, what might you be meaning by that, Clem?" observed Reuben, in a puzzled drawl; but Clemency laughed joyously at his bewilderment. How was he to know without telling that her loving motherly heart was no longer a-hungered?

"Gloden and me, we understand each other," she said in her gentle way, that gave a charm even to her homely language. "Her heart, poor lassie, is no longer closed to me; Harvey's illness has broken down the hardness in her. Ay, but God's ways are wonderful and past finding out. Who would have thought of you and me having a daughter to cheer us in our old age?"

"I am fine and glad that the girl has come round." But though Reuben said no more, that slow brightening of his eyes was eloquent to Clemency.

"Clem is rarely happy," he said to himself, as he trudged patiently along the snowy roads; for

Griff, as usual, had declined to accompany him, but spent his days and nights on the rug in Harvey's room, only retiring under the bed when the doctor made his appearance. "Well, she has had a heap of patience with her—I could see that for myself—and now she is reaping her reward. I always knew there was grit in the girl, though, like all young lassies, she had her whimsies and fads ; but I am finely glad that things have come right between her and Clem."

Reuben always walked over to Silcote every evening when the shop was closed. No weather, however rough, would have kept him from wishing Clemency good night, for the sturdy, quiet man had the heart of a lover for the homely little wife who was the sunshine of his life.

Clemency's eyes used to shine as she saw him creeping noiselessly into Harvey's room night after night ; she would put down her knitting and slip her hand into his, as they stood together by the bed.

Reuben never stayed long, and they were never alone except for those few minutes when she followed him outside into the dim landing to bid him good night. Now and then she would beg him to be easy in his mind and stay at home. "Harvey is doing nicely now," she would say,

" and there is no cause for you to be braving the weather like this, and you no longer a young man, Reuben ; " but his answer was always the same.

" Ay, the lad is doing finely, thank God ; but it is yourself I come to see. It would be against nature not to set eyes on my wife's face once in twenty-four hours. So good night to you, lass ; " and Reuben would shake hands with her gravely, his huge hand nearly swallowing up her little palm. He knew well that Clem would be too shy to offer one of her wifely kisses out of her own house, though he missed them keenly.

Clemency would watch him until he was out of sight, and then go back to her work with the love-light still in her eyes—that strange, mysterious radiance, God-given and divine in its origin, and which is as lovely in aged eyes as in the eyes of youth.

Reginald's quick ardent love was only a flickering torch as yet, compared to the steady lamp lighted in Clemency's quiet eyes. It takes a lifetime of proving and bearing before the full mellow glow can be reached, that light that comes from God, and burns to all eternity.

To the student of human nature, there is a solemn beauty in the love-idylls of the world. The aged couple tottering downhill together, with

their old hands still clasped, and leaning on each
other in their feebleness, touches us as nearly as
the young lover and his lass. The old widow
who has followed her young husband to the grave
a lifetime ago, and is still faithful to his memory,
lays herself down contentedly to die, knowing
that in eternal youth she shall clasp him again.
" I shall go to him." Is not that the longing cry
of every bereaved heart, be it old or young ?
" To him, to her ; " those dear ones within the veil.

When the long strain of anxiety was over, and
Harvey was slowly but surely recovering strength
day by day, and was beginning to tyrannize over
his nurses, Gloden felt happier than she had done
since she lost her father. The secret springs of
her youth overflowed as they had in the days of
old ; and Clemency smiled to herself when she
saw the brightness of the girl's eyes, and noticed
how often she sang, out of pure joyousness, as she
sat over her work.

In spite of Gloden's many faults, there was
nothing small or mean in her character. Half
measures were abhorrent to her. From the hour
of her reconciliation with Clemency there had
been no return of her proud reserve. Harvey,
lying hollow-eyed on his pillows, his face shrunken
to half its size, felt a faint surprise as he heard

her altered tones. "She is the same jolly old Glow as ever," muttered the lad, as he closed his eyes out of sheer weakness.

One night when she was about to leave him, and Clemency had gone out of the room for a moment, he put out his hand to detain her.

"What is it, darling?" she asked, sitting down beside him. And then she looked sadly at the little hand that had clutched hers. Alas! it was no longer rough and brown; its blue-veined whiteness for once put hers to shame. She kissed it with sudden passionate tenderness. "Oh, Harvey, do—do get well soon!" she exclaimed.

"Dr. Parry says I am getting on like a house on fire. What an old goose you are, Glow!" but Harvey's voice was a trifle unsteady. "Look here"—putting his arm round her neck as she stooped over him—"I want to ask you something. What made you kiss Aunt Clem just now?"

Then a deep blush came to Gloden's cheek.

"Are you getting fond of her?" persisted Harvey, trying to see her face.

To his delight, a whispered "Yes" reached his ear.

"Really and truly, Gloden?"

"Yes, dear, really and truly. Oh, Harvey"—

remorsefully—" I wish I had been more like you.
You took to her from the first."

"Well, I don't know about that," returned
Harvey, with a restless movement under the bed-
clothes that made Griff, who was curled up on his
feet as usual, supremely uncomfortable. " She
was rather frumpy at first, don't you know. When
she came through that glass door I thought she
was the cook—cooks have pleasant faces sometimes—but when she tucked me up that night I
found out she was a good sort, and so I stuck to
her."

"Yes, my darling ; you were always so sweet and
loving to her, so no wonder she is so fond of you.
But, Harvey dear, I am so grateful to her. Dr.
Parry says you would never have pulled through
without her care and nursing, so I feel she has
given you back to me."

"I would not talk to him any more if I were
you, Gloden," observed Aunt Clemency, as she
came in at that moment. " Harvey gets a little
feverish when people talk to him at night."

"I am not a bit hot, and we are having a
jolly talk," grumbled Harvey ; but Gloden rose at
once and kissed him.

"You are quite right, Aunt Clemency, and I
ought to have remembered," she said gently.

"You must go to sleep now, Harvey ; our talk will keep till to-morrow."

Clemency and Gloden slept by turns on a little bed in Harvey's room, and as Clemency moved about the room, putting things straight for the night, she saw Harvey was lying with his eyes wide open, watching her.

"Is there anything you want, my dear?" she asked, a little anxiously.

"No, Aunt Clem ; I am quite comfy, as Tottie says. I was only thinking how jolly it is that Glow and you are such good friends."

"Ah, that it is, Harvey ; " and Clemency paused to give emphasis to her words. "'He maketh men to be of one mind in a house'—that is what I am always saying to myself."

"Is that a text, Aunt Clem? It sounds like one. What a lot of texts you do know! Well, you and I have always been friends, haven't we? But I wanted Glow to find out for herself how good you are, and all that, because when Glow once likes a person she never changes." Then he lay and looked at her a moment. "Are you going to like her as much as you do me, Aunt Clem?"

"I am going to love her as though she were my own girl," returned Clemency, quietly; but

Harvey was clever enough to read this answer truly.

"Oh, you may like me best," he returned in a sleepy tone, "because we have been friends for so long, and I remind you of your boy. Glow never minds if people like me best."

As soon as Harvey had had strength enough to know his own wishes, he had begged for Mr. Lorimer's company. It was quite an understood thing that Reginald should come and see him once or twice a day; and as he grew stronger these visits were lengthened, until Reginald spent every afternoon in Harvey's room.

To Gloden as well as to Harvey these hours were the pleasanter part of the day; those quiet firelight talks, while Harvey played with Lassie, and Aunt Clemency sat by and knitted or dozed in her snug corner, were almost as delightful to her as they were to Reginald. Harvey, who was still languid and indisposed to much exertion, was quite content to see his friend, and showed no impatience if he and Gloden talked about books or music. Reginald was always lending her books now, and by his orders the room was kept gay with hothouse flowers.

"Harvey and I are getting quite spoiled," she said one day, when Clemency had gone down to

speak to Mrs. Norton, and Reginald had brought
up a portfolio of rare engravings to amuse her.
She spoke with unusual 'seriousness, and there
was a momentary sadness in her clear grey eyes.
" How do you suppose Market Street will look to
us after this ? "

" I hate to think of you in Market Street," was
Reginald's impetuous reply. " When I see you
there you remind me of a disguised princess ;
the place is not fit for you—— " But here the
deep flush on Gloden's face checked him.

" I do not like it myself," she said in a low voice,
" and Harvey does not like it either ; but I have
made up my mind that I will try to be as contented as I can. Uncle Reuben and Aunt
Clemency are so good ; they make me ashamed of
all my pride."

" Oh, you are not proud now, not a bit," returned Reginald, in a cheery voice. " I used to be
terribly afraid of you. I thought you never meant
to have anything to do with me."

" I am afraid I was very disagreeable."

But Reginald only shook his head and smiled,
and then he took another engraving out of the
portfolio. He must not allow himself to touch on
personalities. When he was near her he was so
keenly alive to his own feelings that he was

obliged to keep himself well in hand. These visits to Harvey's room, these fireside talks, were perilously sweet, and each day he found it harder to restrain himself. "If it were not so soon ; if I might only speak to her now!" was Reginald's inward cry ; but he was strong enough to keep firm to his resolution. "In six weeks, perhaps less," he said to himself, "I will go down to Market Street and ask her to be my wife."

END OF VOL. II.

PRINTED BY WILLIAM CLOWES AND SONS, LIMITED, LONDON AND BECCLES. *G., C. & Co.*

www.ingramcontent.com/pod-product-compliance
Lightning Source LLC
Chambersburg PA
CBHW030923050726
47498CB00003BA/882